DEAD
GIRL
WALKING

BOOKS BY ROBERTA GATELY

Lipstick in Afghanistan
The Bracelet
Footprints in the Dust

DEAD GIRL WALKING

ROBERTA GATELY

bookouture

Published by Bookouture in 2020

An imprint of Storyfire Ltd.
Carmelite House
50 Victoria Embankment
London EC4Y 0DZ

www.bookouture.com

ISBN: 978-1-80019-027-6
eBook ISBN: 978-1-80019-026-9

In loving memory of my cherished brother Jim Gately, an adored husband, father, brother, uncle and friend. Gone too soon. Forever Missed. Forever Loved. ♥

AUTHOR'S NOTE

I worked in the Boston City Hospital Emergency Room for many years (now the Boston Medical Center) just as Jessie Novak does in this series, but this book is a work of fiction. Any resemblance to actual events or people is purely coincidental.

PROLOGUE

"Nine-one-one. This call is being recorded. What's your emergency?"

Silence, except for a distant smattering of sound, impossible to discern, and other than that—nothing but a chilling kind of quiet.

"Nine-one-one. What's your emergency?" the dispatcher repeated, an unmistakable hint of tension in her voice.

"I… I need help."

"We'll get help to you right away, sir, but first, what is your emergency?"

There was a pause, for minutes it seemed, though it was only eight seconds.

"Sir? Are you there?"

"Help me," the caller cried again.

"Where are you, sir? What's your emergency?"

"I… I've been shot. My wife, too. I think she might be dying. We were robbed. He had a gun."

"Can you tell me where you are?"

"I don't know for sure. It's so dark. But we've been shot. Both of us."

"Is the person who shot you still there?"

"No, no. I don't think so."

"What's your location?" This time there was a crispness to her voice, a practiced, almost calming response.

"I… I don't know. Just come. Please." The caller's words were punctuated by rapid breathing.

"We will. We're here to help. What's your name?" This time her voice was low and soothing.

"Umm… my name's Rob."

"Rob, can you tell me what happened, where you are?"

"We were out… celebrating… and I don't know. A man came up behind us. Just get here. Please. There's so much blood."

"Rob, I need your location. I can send help as soon as you help me."

"We're in an alley. The one by the theater on Warrenton Street, I think. I'm not sure. A man just robbed us and then he shot us. Both of us…"

"We have a hit on your location now. Help is on the way, but stay with me. Where is the bleeding?"

"My side. He shot me in the side." He let out a short whimper.

"And your wife?" There was an urgency to the dispatcher's voice.

"Her head," he answered in a strong, impatient voice. "She's not speaking. She hasn't answered me. Ann?" he called. "I don't think she's breathing either."

"Rob, I have units on the way. Can you check your wife for a pulse?"

No answer. Just silence. Maybe he was doing that, checking for a pulse. The tension was palpable.

"Rob? Are you there? I'll stay on the line with you. The ambulance will be there in just a minute or two."

There was only silence, as though a mute button had been hit. Suddenly, in the distance came the familiar drone of approaching sirens. "Rob? I can hear the sirens now. Are you strong enough to get to the street so they'll see you?"

And then there was a click, and the drone of a dial tone.

CHAPTER ONE

The ER's C-Med radio crackled to life, the static almost blocking the transmission.

"Paramedic one-thirty-two calling base. Are you there? Pick up."

"Oh, no," Jessie mumbled to herself as she ran for the radio. Her ER shift was over, she'd been busy clearing out a couple of patients who'd been waiting for beds, but a paramedic call could keep her over into the night shift and it was already well past midnight. She'd promised to stay until the understaffed night shift was settled and then she'd planned to head to Foley's. It was the late-night bar of choice for ER nurses and the policemen who patrolled Boston's streets, though her favorites of those were the undercover guys who always had great stories. That was probably a lost cause tonight. She sighed and lifted the receiver. "Boston City Hospital here. What do you have? Over."

"We're en route with two gunshots. The first is a male with a gunshot wound to his right flank. The other is a woman with a gunshot to the head. Male is stable. Female had ineffective, agonal respirations, intubated at the scene, pulse forty, no blood pressure. We are three minutes out. Copy?"

"Trauma rooms One and Two. We'll be ready." *Forget fun tonight*, she thought, pressing the intercom. "Two, yes two, GSWs en route. ETA of three minutes, more like two now. Trauma teams to Trauma One and Two please." Jessie swept her shiny chestnut-colored, shoulder-length curls up hoping to restrain them with a clip. She'd only just let her hair down and run her fingers through it in preparation for going out. At least she hadn't done eyeliner yet. She'd get grief for that in the trauma room though they'd never mention her ever-present lipstick. "What's the difference between a Pitbull and a triage nurse?" She'd often posed the question to the newest EMTs, those emergency medical technicians who looked as though they might faint. They invariably stood there, not sure what to say. "Lipstick," she'd answer with a laugh. "Now, tell me about your patient."

No time for fresh lipstick tonight, she thought as she raced to the trauma hallway calling out to Neil Doherty, the surgeon on duty. "I'll take the woman into Trauma One with you. As long as the male's stable, the team can get lines in and get him X-rayed. Okay?"

Neil nodded as he pulled on a pair of sterile gloves and hurried along the hallway. Jessie turned and headed to the ambulance bay, the sudden screech of sirens announcing the arrival of at least one ambulance and an assortment of police vehicles. She stepped through the doors, the biting wind, or perhaps the blackness of the night, sending a shiver through her spine. A policeman, sweat beading along his forehead despite the chill, reached her first. He seemed familiar but she couldn't quite place him.

"There's press just behind us. You should probably close the entrance off. Okay?"

"Close the entrance? The whole ambulance bay? Who was shot?"

"An aide to the mayor. Some wunderkind, a Harvard guy, and the mayor's chief of staff."

And suddenly, she recognized the impish grin, the steady blue eyes that could stare you down or make you melt, all in the same glance. "Ahh, Nick," she said, remembering one very late night at Foley's.

"One and only. I know I still owe you a beer."

"More than that if my memory serves me."

The backup beep of the ambulance interrupted their conversation, and before the vehicle came to a full stop, the doors flew open and a medic jumped out. "Give me a hand, will you?" he shouted to Nick.

"Which one is this?" Jessie asked.

"Male, age thirty-two, gunshot wound to the right flank," the medic said.

Jessie had a quick look. The patient looked stable enough: good color, awake, eyes open wide. "Trauma Two," she said pointing to the long hallway. The medic and Nick set off at a jog, the stretcher between them. Jessie turned back as a stream of flashes and people filled the ambulance bay. The second ambulance had pulled in and the medics were trying to move their patient into the ER but a crowd of reporters and television cameras surrounded them, the few cops trying in vain to push them back. She elbowed her way through the pack and got hold of one end of the stretcher, pulling it behind her. "Trauma One," she shouted over the din as she raced through the entrance, the noise of the crowd dimming as the automatic doors closed behind her. "Lock those doors down, will you?" she directed the security guard on duty. "And check all IDs at the walk-in entrance. No reporters, got it?" The guard nodded.

As they approached Trauma One, Jessie got a look at her patient—young, pretty, thick brown hair tumbling around her face, rose petals tangled in the loose strands, her appearance so like Jessie's she might have been her twin. But this poor woman was intubated—the tube snaking through her lips into her trachea; a medic was pumping oxygen into her lungs through a football-shaped bag, an ambu bag. They worked quickly to move the patient to the ER stretcher as the medic began his report.

"Gunshot wound to the back of the head, no exit wound," he said. "We don't have much more than that. It happened downtown. A robbery, dispatch said. Anyway, her husband said she's twenty-eight years old, no significant medical history, healthy until tonight. She's unresponsive, pulse is forty-two, blood pressure back after

IV fluids, now she's eighty over zero. Name is Ann Hart. That's it? Questions?"

The medics pulled off their gloves and began to tap away at their iPads. A medical aide hooked the patient to the ER's wall monitors while a respiratory tech checked the placement of the breathing tube and connected the woman to a ventilator. The remaining staff, another nurse and an intern, began to cut away the patient's clothes—a pink wool jacket and matching dress, a pearl necklace, a Tiffany bracelet—all cut away leaving Ann Hart naked under the glaring lights. Jessie threw a sheet over her patient and slipped off the woman's diamond ring and wedding band, her fingers as cool and lifeless as though she was dying from her fingertips on up. Jessie squeezed her hand, a rose petal inexplicably clutched there as well. She brushed it to the floor. "Ann," she said softly, "you're safe now. You're in the emergency room. If you can hear me, squeeze back or wiggle your fingers." There was nothing, no response, not that Jessie had really expected one, but it always paid to hope. Sometimes, you could be pleasantly surprised, and this was one of those times she prayed for just that.

She busied herself once again with trying to save this woman. She wrapped a tourniquet on her limp arm. She was going to need more fluids, maybe blood. She snaked an IV catheter through the best vein, drew the necessary vials of blood and hooked her patient up to a bag of fluid. "Call Radiology. Tell them we're going to need a stat CT scan," she shouted to no one in particular, but someone would do it. That's the way the ER worked. What seemed chaotic to an outside observer was actually a well-oiled machine. The team worked quickly on the woman who lay on the stretcher, her skin as pale as the sheet, the only evidence of her gunshot wound the gauze bandage that covered her head.

"How long ago did this happen?" the surgeon asked as he waved a flashlight in front of the woman's eyes.

The medic looked up. "Not long ago. Don't have an exact time. The husband was pretty upset. He didn't have a good grip on the timeline, but it wasn't long ago. Once the assailant left the scene, the poor guy waited to make sure it was safe before he even moved. The shooter took his phone, so he had to go through her stuff," he said, pointing to the patient as though she was already dead. "So, I don't know, maybe thirty minutes. We were a while at the scene. The press was all over the place. It's like they have radar for the bad stuff. Anyway, that's all I have. Heard the mayor's on his way in, so we're outta here."

"Fixed and dilated," Neil announced referring to Mrs. Hart's eyes' reaction to the flashlight, a sure sign of brain injury. He stood up, rubbing his back. "We'll need a head CT, an EEG to check brain activity, and a word with the family. Did someone page Neurosurgery?" he asked.

"On the way," Carol, the second nurse, answered, pushing her eyeglasses up on her nose. "Chief's on his way too." There was a low murmur in the room. Tim Merrick, the Chief of Surgery, could be a real pain; he could be arrogant, insulting and rude, though never to nurses. He was a darn good surgeon and when he was on call, people seemed to have a better chance of surviving their injuries. He'd served in Afghanistan after nine-eleven, and Iraq after that. He knew gunshots like nobody else, which was why he could get away with sometimes being such an insufferable windbag.

"Glasgow Coma Scale is three," Carol said, shaking her head. The Glasgow Coma Scale was a fifteen-point scale designed to estimate and categorize the extent of brain injury and likely outcome for a patient. A score of three, they all knew, likely meant a dire outcome. "She's so young."

Jessie leaned in closer and snipped away the gauze bandage that the medics had wound around the woman's head. The woman's mascara and eyeliner had run, tracking black streaks along her face. Maybe she'd cried when they were being robbed, maybe she'd begged for her life, and the makeup she'd applied for a happy night on the town had smudged with her tears, the flowers she'd clutched breaking apart as she fell. Jessie bit back the lump in her throat and snipped the last bits of gauze away.

Neil continued his exam, gently rotating Ann Hart's body to have a look at the back of her head, the area of the wound where another cluster of rose petals was tangled in her hair. Jessie brushed them away. "Can you shave that area?" he asked as he poked and prodded the woman's lower back looking for any wounds the medics might have missed. A razor appeared and Jessie carefully shaved along the back of the woman's scalp until they spotted the entry wound—a small oval-shaped indentation, hair and bits of tissue stuck to the wound. There was little blood and what there was, was already drying.

"At least there are no other injuries, but that bullet likely ricocheted around her brain," Neil said with a sigh. "Just wrap her head back up and we might as well start a Mannitol drip and maybe diminish the swelling a bit. We'll let Neurosurgery deal with the rest of this." Jessie grabbed a new gauze roll and wrapped it round her patient's head as Carol connected the Mannitol to the patient's IV fluids.

"CT scan is ready," the secretary said, popping her head into the room. The team disconnected the monitors and lines and hooked everything to portable machines. The respiratory tech unhooked the ventilator and began pumping oxygen into the patient with the ambu bag once again. Jessie checked the wall clock. They'd been in this room only fifteen minutes.

"I'll go," Carol said. "You should try to go home. This is going to be a long night."

"Which is exactly why I'm stuck here," Jessie answered. "I'm going to check on her husband. Let me know if you need help."

Carol nodded and the team guided the stretcher and their equipment along the hallway to CT scan.

Jessie turned and looked at the room, the gloves and remnants of their work scattered on the floor, and then she saw it—the woman's jacket and dress, the pearls and bracelet and rings laid gently on top of the EKG machine. She picked them up, the woman's perfume—a sweet lavender scent—wafted to her nose, and she felt a sudden and unexpected sadness. She'd always managed to distance herself from the misery that happened here; that was how she'd managed to survive and even thrive as a nurse in this busy inner-city ER. But this woman wasn't much older than she was. At twenty-eight, Ann Hart was only a year older than Jessie's twenty-seven, though tonight, she felt older, much older. Maybe she'd seen too much already. Too much of what she did see in the ER was life at its worst, the unfairness of it all rarely getting to her. Until tonight. But there was something about Ann Hart, or maybe it was just that Jessie saw herself when she looked at Ann, the dark hair tumbling out, the clear skin, the pert nose, all of it so much like her own. And the flowers, was she celebrating something? Jessie's shoulders sagged as she gently folded the clothes and ran her fingers along the pearls, their glossy smoothness somehow soothing. She sighed and dropped the jewelry—the rings and pearls and bracelet—into a small manila envelope, sealing it and recording the contents before slipping it, along with the clothes, into a plastic patient belonging bag. There was still work to be done. Jessie peeled off her gloves and hit the intercom button.

"Housekeeping to Trauma One, please."

CHAPTER TWO

Jessie opened the door to the Trauma hallway and stopped. She couldn't go any further. The small space was packed with police and men in suits, all talking in hushed tones, but together the hush became a din that blocked out all other sound. What the hell. "Hey!" Jessie shouted. But they never heard her above the noise. She tried to elbow her way through to no avail. They'd taken over. She lifted her fingers to her lips and blew hard, and suddenly there was silence. All eyes were trained on her.

"You can't stay here. You're in the way." She began to push through the crowd.

"And you are?" A tall man stepped forward, a cell phone in his hand.

"I'm the nurse in charge. Who are you?"

"Sorry. I'm Sam Dallas, detective in charge." A gold shield was clipped to his belt, his tie undone, his suit coat draped over his arm, his full attention focused on Jessie. "I know you're busy working on them, but we have a job to do, too. We need to get working on this, get that shooter off the streets. How is she?" He nodded toward the trauma room.

"She's in CT scan, and then Neurosurgery will have a look, and then we'll know more."

Sam ran his fingers through a shock of thick brown hair speckled with streaks of gray. "How's it look? Will she make it?"

"I can't say, not yet at least."

"And him?" The detective turned back towards Trauma Two.

"That's where I'm headed. If you guys will just move from the hallway, I'll keep you posted."

"We have to keep a few uniforms here, just in case. Understand?" He moved closer and she caught the faint but unmistakable odor of stale cigarettes on his breath. Poor guy—he'd probably already finished his shift, inhaled a quick smoke, and had been called back.

"I do. I know this is a tragedy, no matter how it turns out, and I want to help you. I really do, but just give us a chance to save them first." She adjusted the stethoscope that was draped around her neck.

"We will. We'll be quiet, and we'll be nearby to watch over everyone."

There was something so comforting in that phrase—*watch over everyone*, and despite herself, she smiled. Sam reached out and pushed a stray tendril of her hair back in place, a very unexpected thrill running through her. "Okay, I've got to get in there." The rows of men parted and she moved easily through, turning just as she pushed on the trauma room door. Sam's gaze was on her, and even across the hall, she could see the sparkle in his gray eyes and the firm, reassuring set of his jaw. She flashed him a half-smile before she caught herself. *Geez. What the hell is wrong with me?* She pushed open the door.

A crowd of nurses and doctors hovered over the man on the stretcher. He was crying, and she moved in to see that his clothes, too, had been cut and then thrown haphazardly into a corner of the room. She could see a catheter draining bloody urine, and the sheet that covered him was spotted with blood. Two IVs drained fluid into his veins. The overhead monitor recorded a stable pulse and blood pressure.

"Please," the man was saying. "Don't let me die." The surgeon leaned close. "You're not going to die. We're taking care of you to prevent that. Understand?" The man grimaced and closed his eyes.

"What's going on?" Jessie asked Elena, the nurse assigned to this room.

"He's stable, good blood pressure, normal sinus rhythm, hematocrit of forty, but…" She pointed to the urine bag. "You can see—he's bleeding pretty badly. We're waiting for Urology and CT and then he's off to the OR."

The trauma room door burst open and, as if an apparition had appeared, Tim Merrick stood there, already in scrubs. "Someone fill me in." He motioned to the surgical resident who seemed to wilt under the pressure.

"Single gunshot, Dr. Merrick. Entry in the right flank, no exit wound. Blood counts stable, no other injuries, but draining blood from his catheter. We're waiting for GU and CT scan. X-ray showed the bullet in his pelvis." The resident lifted the sheet, turned the patient gently and pointed out the gunshot wound on his right flank. The wound was small, the blood seeping around it a bright red.

Tim leaned in and had a close look before slapping on gloves and probing the small entry wound in Hart's right flank, just below his waist. "Hmm," he mumbled as if considering the precise damage the bullet might have inflicted. "OR ready? Typed and crossed?" he said. The resident nodded. Tim lifted the urine bag for a closer inspection. The fluid was bright red and opaque. There wasn't much urine in there, if any. It was all blood.

"Okay," Tim said brusquely as he leaned over the patient, palpating his abdomen as he spoke. "I'm the surgeon in charge. We're gonna take you to the OR and clean this all up. Understand?"

"Yes," Rob Hart whispered, his voice so faint Tim had to lean in to hear. He patted the man's shoulder as if to comfort him, but to anyone who knew Tim Merrick, this was simply an absent-minded gesture which had no special meaning, certainly not one of comfort. Tim was usually abrasive to everyone—well, except for nurses. Rumor was, his first wife, or maybe his second, was a nurse. For everyone else, often including patients, he had little time for sympathy or niceties and his surgical outcomes were so good, no one had the nerve to question him. He turned to the resident. "Make sure to get a signed consent, and once he's had his CT, I'll see you in the OR."

He turned and motioned to Jessie. "A word?" he asked, pointing to the hallway.

Jessie followed him out. A few policemen, including the detective, still hovered in the hallway and they seemed to come to attention when they saw Tim. His air of authority was apparently universal.

"I heard the story. Where's the wife?"

"Hopefully in the ICU with Neurosurgery. She has a single gunshot wound to the back of her head—no exit wound. Glasgow Coma Scale of three, intubated, bradycardic. Looks pretty bad, but you never know."

He patted her shoulder just as he had Rob Hart's. "Nice work, Jessie. Want to come to the OR with us? See where the real work is done?"

She shook her head. "Too busy, but thanks for the offer. No one will ever believe that you really asked."

He forced a laugh as the detective stepped forward. "A few questions, sir? I'm Sam Dallas, Boston Police Department." He held up his badge.

"I don't have anything for you right now. Talk to her." He pointed to Jessie.

"Can I have a few minutes with the patient?" Sam asked, slipping a mint into his mouth.

"He can have five minutes, not a second more," Tim said, looking at Jessie, and not at Sam.

"That's fine. We'll take it. Thank you."

Tim strode off, heading for the OR.

"That one's a charmer, huh?"

Jessie smiled. "In his defense, he's a great surgeon. Not much personality, but good enough at what he does that it doesn't matter." She turned to the door. "Remind me again who you are."

"Aah, how quickly they forget," he said with a wink. "Sam Dallas, Homicide."

Jessie stopped. "Homicide? No one's dead yet. Aren't you jumping the gun?"

He shook his head in reply. "We know how dire the situation is. From what I heard at the scene, the wife is likely to die. I suppose he might too, and in that case, we need to speak to him before he goes to the OR. He's our only witness right now. We have to jump on this while everything's fresh in his mind. That'll give us a better chance of keeping the dirtbag who did this off the street."

"Alright. Let me tell them you're coming…"

"Jessie," the secretary called as she handed her a piece of paper. "The results were just called back. You might want to call the ICU."

"Thanks," Jessie said, scanning the results until she reached the last one. "Oh, wow," she muttered.

"What is it?" Sam asked.

"The wife's pregnant, maybe eight to ten weeks or so by these numbers. Not that it matters, but that would explain her alcohol level of zero, too. She wasn't drinking tonight." She sighed. "I'm just gonna call these to the ICU, and then I'll take you in there." She pointed to the trauma room but headed to an office off the hallway. "Give me a minute," she called over her shoulder.

"As long as it doesn't count against my five."

It seemed only seconds when she slipped back to the trauma room to speak to the patient. "Mr. Hart," she said softly. "The police would like to ask you a few questions. That okay? You feel strong enough?"

He hesitated before finally nodding his head. "I don't know what I can tell them, but yes. It's okay."

Sam stepped inside the trauma room, and moved slowly amid the blood and debris that littered the floor. "Rob," he said "I'm Sam Dallas, a detective. Just a few questions before they take you up to the OR. That okay? You up to it?" He held a pen poised over a small notebook.

A tangle of creases sprouted on his forehead. "I don't know how I can help. I didn't see anything, but I had the feeling that he was a big guy, he seemed to loom over us. I mean, we were walking to our car and suddenly, too late I guess, I heard footsteps. Before I could even think what to do, I felt a gun in my back. *'Just do what I say and I won't hurt you,'* the man said."

"Anything special about the voice? Accent? Words?" Sam asked, his pen flying across the page.

"He had a heavy Spanish accent, almost like he was new here."

Elena rolled her eyes. "Why do they always have to be Spanish, huh?" She muttered something in Spanish and turned her back to the scene as Hart continued.

"But he... he knew enough to order us to look straight ahead and to force us into the alley. Then he told me to empty my pockets and pass everything back to him. I did that, I passed him my wallet, my iPhone, and some loose cash. I figured he'd just run, but he didn't. He shot me. He shot me." He sounded as though he couldn't quite believe it himself. He paused then, exhaling noisily as if to gather his strength so that he could continue.

"I... I fell to the ground, and then I heard another gunshot, and then another, and then Ann fell right next to me. It all happened so fast. I just froze and pretended I was dead. I heard his footsteps as he ran, but I didn't move, I didn't open my mouth for fear he was coming back. I don't know how long I waited, but..."

And he began to cry, soft whimpering sounds. He covered his face and spoke haltingly. "It all happened so fast. I waited, and when I thought it was safe, I fished through Ann's bag for her phone, and that's when I called for help. I just don't know anything else."

"Sorry to put you through this," Sam said as the trauma room staff listened with rapt attention. "Where were you coming from?"

"A bar downtown. I don't remember the name."

"And you were on Warrenton Street headed where?"

"To the car. We'd had dinner and then walked through the Public Garden and around the Common. I bought her flowers from one of those street vendors."

Ahh, the rose petals, Jessie thought.

"We went to a bar after, and…"

The door snapped open. "CT's ready, and Dr. Merrick called. He said time's up." And suddenly everyone was moving again, disconnecting monitors and lines and printing out labs. The surgical resident grabbed the end of the stretcher. "We ready?" he asked as he pulled the stretcher toward towards the door.

"Someone call Dr. Merrick. Tell him we're in CT and then we'll be up."

CHAPTER THREE

The procession to CT scan moved briskly leaving just Jessie, Elena, the nurse who'd helped run this case, and Sam behind. "Hey," Elena whispered to Jessie so that Sam wouldn't hear "How's the wife?"

"She's in pretty bad shape. Does he know?"

Elena shook her head. "No. He was more worried about himself. Never mentioned her. I guess he was just still in shock."

"Hmm, yeah, I guess you never know how people will react. Seems strange to me, but…" She shrugged.

"Can I ask some questions?" Sam asked as Elena peeled off her gloves and threw them to the floor.

"Not of me," she answered. "Too busy." She pressed the intercom. "Housekeeping to Trauma Two," she said before she slipped away.

Sam took in the debris scattered over the floor, his eyes resting on the patient's clothes. "I'm going to need those," he said. "And the wife's. You got those?"

Jessie nodded and donned a pair of gloves to collect the clothing and any other belongings. She folded the jacket and pants and slid them into a plastic bag, before folding the remainder—the shirt and tie and underwear. Underneath it all, a flash of silver sparkled beneath the room's bright lights. She leaned closer. It was a wristwatch, a fancy one by the looks of it. The band was dotted with blood.

"I'll get that," Sam said, reaching around her with one gloved hand and scooping the watch into a small plastic bag. "Guess the robber missed that."

"He missed all the wife's jewelry, too—pearls, diamond ring, wedding band, Tiffany bracelet. She didn't have a purse though. Maybe the shooter got that?"

Sam shook his head. "We have that. Took possession at the scene. She had some money, lipstick, and a credit card. He missed that, too. Not the brightest thief. Maybe that'll make him easier to catch."

"But if he was out to rob them, why shoot them? You heard the victim, he never even got a good look, so why shoot a woman in the head and him in the back? It doesn't make sense to me."

"I hate to tell you this, but criminals never do make sense to the rest of us. With any luck, he's made a mistake that will help us find him. This one hits home for all of us. We're going to work this all night." He lifted the bag of clothing and slipped the watch inside. "Got her stuff for me?"

He followed Jessie into Trauma One. It had already been scrubbed clean, the floors shiny, a gleaming new stretcher in the center of the room, ready and waiting for the next victim. The housekeeper had placed Mrs. Hart's belongings bag on the counter, the scent of lavender faint but still noticeable. "Here you go," Jessie said, pulling out a drawer in the corner and handing a pen and slip of paper to the detective. "You just have to sign there." She pointed to the bottom of the form. "Just says you took all of their possessions, including jewelry."

He pulled off his gloves and signed the form with his left hand, no wedding band in sight, but that didn't necessarily mean anything. He pulled out a business card. "Call me if you think of anything, or even if you don't and just want to have a drink, okay?" His eyes, which had seemed to sparkle earlier, now looked drawn and heavy, which was exactly how she felt. Too tired to even speak, she nodded and slipped the card into the pocket of her scrubs.

Jessie checked with the supervisor—both gunshots were in the OR; nothing left for her to do except go home and crawl into bed with a bottle of wine. She slipped into her jacket, fished out her keys and headed for the door.

"Hey, hold on, Jessie. I've been waiting for you."

She turned to see Nick, a smile on his lips, his brown hair ruffled, his uniform showing off the work he did at the gym, his biceps evident through the deep blue fabric. She couldn't help herself and she smiled in return. "I thought you'd be long gone by now."

"I'm off duty, thought I'd see if you want to collect that beer. I know it's been a rough night."

"You're right. It's been pretty awful, probably for you guys too, huh?"

"Yeah. We're more used to the usual troublemakers, bumbling robbers, domestic calls and stupid kids. A young couple targeted hits home for all of us."

He moved in closer, and she could smell the clean, fresh scent of him, and something else—a flowery scent—maybe that's what it was, and she realized he'd had a tough night too, being at what must have been a horrific scene. She considered his offer, but only for a millisecond. Every inch of her ached, and she only wanted to go home and crawl into bed.

"So, what do you say?" he asked. "The after-hours club is open."

She remembered it well. The Boston Police had a private club tucked away on the second floor of a nondescript building in an industrial area not far from the hospital. If the usual bars were closed, the club was next on everyone's list, the perfect way to end a night. It was tempting. She looked at her watch—already after two a.m. She heaved a long sigh. "Any other night, I'd love to, but tonight, I'm beat. Raincheck?"

"You got it. I'll call you." He planted a quick kiss on her cheek and squeezed her shoulder, reminding her that this nice guy was just the type of man she should fall for. Time to change her track record—she'd always chosen the hard-to-get ones who never failed to disappoint her in the end. "I've been meaning to call," he added. "This time, I promise I'll do it."

They'd met months before at Foley's and had connected right away, but though he'd stopped in to see her a few times in the ER, he'd never called. "I'd like that," she said, kissing him full on the lips before she turned and walked through the ambulance bay to her car, the closeness of him lingering on her mouth. Jessie pulled up the collar of her jacket against the heavy, early-November fog.

A crowd of reporters and the bright lights of their cameras sliced through the hazy air lighting up the night. She stopped to have a look. It was the mayor and his aides, and the police commissioner over by the walk-in entrance. Half a dozen microphones were pushed up close to their faces. She couldn't tell what they were asking, or what he was saying, but it was easy enough to read the anguish on their faces and in their hurried words. She felt it too, and as she turned to go, one eagle-eyed reporter chased after her. "Miss?" she said, a microphone in her hand. "You were in the ER tonight?" The woman never waited for an answer, instead she rushed on. "Any information you can share on tonight's shooting?" She held a microphone up.

Jessie kept her head down, ignoring the question, and hurried through the darkness to her car, a too-old Toyota that was going to die one of these days, and tonight, hastily parked on the street. It was only there, in the quiet of the driver's seat, that she pulled out her phone. It lit up with missed calls and texts—all from the same person. She shook her head angrily before turning it off.

She slipped her key into the ignition, a satisfied smile on her lips when the engine purred into life. She latched her seatbelt and froze. Someone was watching her; she was sure of it. She locked her doors and checked her rearview mirror. A sudden flash of movement caught her eye but it was gone almost as quickly as it had appeared. In the distance, she could still see the glare of camera flashes and the small crowd of reporters. She sighed and pulled out of her spot. No one was watching her, she decided; it was probably a reporter or a strobe of light from one of their cameras. A sure sign that she needed sleep, or wine. More likely both.

She navigated the back roads and narrow streets of Southie, the nickname for this neighborhood of Boston, where the houses and buildings were packed together tight as teeth. At last she reached K Street, nestled in between L Street and East Broadway boasting sturdy, brick row houses alongside colorful three-story homes painted in fading reds and greens and yellows. In Summer, trees perched at the edges of sidewalks offered greenery and shade but now they were bare, spindly skeletons reaching for the sky. The only bits of green that had survived November's first frost poked out from the almost hidden gardens squeezed into the tiny spaces between buildings. A few window-boxes were filled with wilting greenery, but in the Spring, they'd burst with new flowers and welcome color. Jessie belonged here. She'd felt that the moment she'd seen the neighborhood, all noise and crowds to an outsider but a place of security to Jessie, one where she could slip in unnoticed, as though she'd always been here.

Home was a tiny, one-bedroom walk-up that had likely once been a part of a lovely old single-family house, until it had been broken up into smaller apartments. A handcrafted wooden bannister was the only evidence of the house's once grand past. Her place included a living room, galley kitchen, one tiny closet and a postage-stamp-sized bedroom. She let herself in, peeled off her light blue scrubs, and stepped into the shower, the heat and steam rising around her, almost, but not quite, erasing the uneasy feeling she had.

She wasn't even sure why she'd carried that feeling home with her, or why she'd thought someone was watching her. She'd been involved in countless traumas with equally tragic stories—the little boy who'd been shot on Christmas Eve when his drug dealer father had used him as a shield in a gunfight; the student nurse who'd been stabbed to death as she studied for finals; the woman who'd survived a house fire only to lose her husband and children in the blaze. There were so many others, too numerous to count, so why had tonight's tragedy affected her so? She supposed it was bound to happen sooner or later—one of these awful stories would simply stick to her and she'd be unable to shake it off.

She stood in front of her mirror and wiped away the last bits of eye makeup and lipstick that had somehow survived her shower. She leaned in close, her hazel eyes, which Nick, or maybe it was someone else, had described as *mood eyes*, like those rings of the eighties, seeming to reflect her mood. Tonight, they were a dull light brown; when she was happy, they really did sparkle a hazy green, and when she was serious, they were the soft gray of a Winter's day. She swiped off the last of her mascara and piled her hair, a deep, almost black shade of brown, into a ponytail, the curls spilling out around her face.

She picked up her toothbrush, peered at her reflection, and froze. It was Ann Hart who stared back. Jessie opened her eyes wide and moved closer to the mirror. The resemblance was striking. She looked away, blinking to erase the image.

CHAPTER FOUR

The sounds of the neighborhood—the rumble of trucks, the screech of sirens, the blare of car horns and shouts from the street—seeped through her windows, rousing her from sleep. Jessie nudged herself awake, closing her eyes quickly to the harsh sunlight trickling in through the half-opened blinds. She sat up, massaged the knot in her neck, retrieved the bottle of wine and lone glass from the floor and headed to her minuscule kitchen. To open her fridge to replace the wine or to retrieve anything, she had to stand to the side and nudge the door gently to avoid banging into the stove. She rinsed her glass, brewed a cup of coffee and padded back to the couch, turning to the morning news.

"Breaking news," the reporter almost shouted into the camera, almost giddy as she recounted last night's shooting. "The police have little to go on. The shooter was said to have a heavy Spanish accent and was taller than Rob Hart, who stands just over six feet. Though that description could fit thousands of local men, the police are asking you to call their hotline if you have any information at all. They remind us that no tip is too small." She paused while the camera panned out to frame the ambulance bay in the shot. "The life-saving work goes on here, but for Rob and Ann Hart, it all hangs in the balance. Mayor Reilly is putting together a reward for any information leading to the arrest of the shooter. We'll pass that on as soon as we have it. Reporting from Boston City Hospital, back to you in the studio."

The gray-haired anchor nodded sadly, a smiling photo of the Harts just behind him, Ann Hart looking so like, and yet so unlike, the lifeless woman on the stretcher just hours ago. Jessie clicked to the next channel, and then the next, until she'd about exhausted her channel lineup. The shooting was the top story, apparently the only one, and one reporter after another shared the same meager facts, and what they didn't know, they seemed to be making up. One after another described the couple as young urban hipsters, childless by choice, both on the same trajectory upward. "Congress?" one reporter asked peering into the camera. "The sky was the limit, friends say, for this popular and politically connected young man. Now, we can only pray for his and his wife's recovery as the police track down the vicious criminal responsible for this heinous crime." A picture of a smiling Rob Hart with the mayor, and another of him alone, working the polls on election day, flashed across the screen. His wife seemed forgotten already. "The victims, we've been informed, are still in the OR. More news as it comes in."

Jessie looked at her watch—nine-thirty. They couldn't possibly still be in the OR, could they? It seemed unlikely, but maybe the hospital had decided to cut off the release of all information. She sipped her coffee and picked up her phone. Maybe she'd just call the ER to see what was going on. She switched it back on. The screen lit up once more—calls, texts, most now from the ER. *Call ASAP*, one message directed her. *Darn it!* She wasn't even scheduled to work today, and they surely weren't calling to update her on last night's shooting victims. What the hell did they want? She punched in the number and sat back. She could at least ask them if there was any news. The phone rang only once.

"Jessie?" Donna Serra, the day-shift charge nurse asked, her voice almost a whisper. "Is that you?"

"Yes, what is it? And before you ask, no, I don't want overtime today."

"Don't answer yet."

"I can barely hear you." She muted the television. "Why are you whispering?"

"Because there's not one empty space here. We're overrun with the mayor's staff, Boston police, state police, reporters, you name it—they're here, or on their way."

Jessie couldn't hold back her laughter. "Sounds like last night, but that doesn't explain why you called me."

"Overtime. Please don't say no. I need you."

What part of no didn't she understand? "I'll think about it," she said to placate her and change the subject. "How are they, by the way? Still in the OR?"

"No, out hours ago, but we're not releasing any information. I'll fill you in when you get here."

And there it was—the hook. She knew how to reel Jessie in. "Give me an hour or so," she said, exhaling noisily so Donna would understand that she owed, *really owed*, Jessie. Next time she needed a day off, she better just get it. She pulled on a clean pair of scrubs, a comfortable sweater, and her favorite work clogs, broken in enough to be comfortable but not so much that they looked too worn. She tugged at her curls, coaxing them into a loose braid and swiped a splash of color on her lips. Retrieving her backpack, she grabbed her phone just as it began to ring.

She groaned. She'd have to deal with this guy sooner or later, but later looked better right now. She hit the *decline call* button, and headed out. She'd had to park a block away from her apartment the night before. Parking in this crowded neighborhood was at a premium and apartments that included parking were not just coveted, but well out of her reach, making every day a parking spot puzzle.

The morning was sunny, last night's Fall chill replaced by an Indian Summer day, but it was trash day and much of it had been spilled, allowing the sour scents of the city—of rotting food and decaying dreams—to hover over the streets, the stench as sharp, on this warm day, as old cheese. The final remnants of Halloween—plastic pumpkins, candy bags long emptied, and torn fabric ghosts—skittered along the streets with the last of the season's leaves. She tugged off her sweater, wishing she'd checked the weather forecast, but this was New England and the temperature would likely drop within the hour.

She popped into the local corner store for another coffee and came to a stop. The headline on every newspaper shouted about last night's shooting. She picked up the *Globe* and had a quick look, the Harts' wedding photo on full display underneath the bold words—*Tragedy Strikes Mayor's Inner Circle*. The *Herald* took a more dramatic approach with a color photo of the bloody crime scene, a spray of roses scattered about, and the headline—*Search for Hispanic Shooter Intensifies: Mayor Demands Answers*. She picked up both copies, stuffing them into her backpack. "Morning, Patrick. The usual, plus two newspapers." Patrick, whose thick Irish brogue sounded as if he'd arrived only yesterday, though he'd been here twenty-odd years, wrapped her cinnamon muffin in tissue and passed it to her along with a large black coffee. Armed for the ER, she set out for her car, sipping coffee along the way.

At the hospital, she pulled into the garage and headed to the main floor. The hospital, a series of old buildings over a full city block, was connected by a string of often neglected tunnels. But this morning, the tunnels and hallways were a flurry of activity, housekeepers mopping the tiled floors, lab runners rushing specimens to the lab and men in suits talking in hushed tones, all of which could only mean a surprise inspection from the Department of Public Health or another accrediting agency. *Darn!* That was probably why they'd roped her in to coming in today. She considered turning for home, but what the hell, she'd come this far, and she needed the money. Might as well just keep going.

She cut through the waiting room on her way in only to spy Eddie Wilson, an old alcoholic she'd long ago befriended, curled up in a chair loudly resisting the security guard's attempts to evict him. Though disheveled and sporting a graying beard that was likely a nest for a bevy of small creatures, he was harmless, a sweet old guy with no family, no friends and nowhere to go. He'd long given up on finding work or a home, but had found safety and solace here in the waiting room where staff fed, clothed and took care of him. The ER was the sanctuary for the city's grittiest secrets—secret lives, secret dreams, secret crimes—they all found their way here sooner or later, and most found what they were looking for—methadone for their misery or sympathy for their woes. Eddie was one of the latter.

"Hey, Eddie," Jessie called. "I got your breakfast." She fished the muffin from her bag, and turned to the guard. "Morning," she said, flashing a smile for the guard as she passed the muffin to Eddie who chomped hungrily, crumbs disappearing into the tangled web of his beard. "Sorry about the confusion. I told Eddie to meet me here. We're going to see him in the ER today." Some days, it just paid to outright lie. Today was one of those days.

"Sorry, Jess, the boss says everyone has to go unless they're signed in to be seen."

"I'll sign him in, but why? What's up?"

He pointed through the front window where a bank of microphones, cameras and lights were set up, ready for a press conference or an announcement, it seemed. "You can see for yourself. It's last night's shootings. Everyone who's anyone has shown up. Live television shots, reporters, detectives, the whole nine yards. Administration says we can't look like a homeless shelter. Gotta clear the place out."

Jessie winced and suddenly noticed how clean the waiting area was—no urine or bloodstains on the floor, and no scent of vomit in the air. The floor was polished and someone had scrubbed the worn fabric on the chairs till the padding underneath poked through. "What the…?"

The guard put his hands up. "Don't shoot the messenger." He smiled. "Sorry, poor choice of words."

"No problem, but I'll take care of Eddie. See you later." She grabbed one of the registration clerks. "Will you sign Eddie in? He's got a cold." The clerk, already overworked, barely acknowledged her but began to type Eddie's information into her computer. Convinced that Eddie was safe, Jessie swiped her ID against the locked ER entryway and, as if by magic, it swung open.

She hurried along the hallway, expecting the usual crowd of stretchers waiting for beds or X-rays or a final diagnosis, but instead, the hallway was empty of stretchers, the place almost eerily quiet. The rooms that ringed the perimeter of the hall were only sparsely occupied, the residents and interns almost leisurely discussing patients. Susan Peters, a day-shift nurse, was just hanging up the desk phone. "Hey, what's going on? Why so quiet?"

"Last night's shooting. Put us in the spotlight, I guess, and Administration wants us to look good instead of being overwhelmed by patients and work, the way we usually are. Go figure." She shrugged and stuck her pen behind her ear. "Just another day in paradise."

"Where's Donna? She called me in for overtime. It doesn't even look busy."

Susan pointed along the hallway and Jessie rounded the corner, bumping into Donna on the way. Jessie stepped back. "Why am I here? It's quiet as a Sunday morning over there." She pointed back along the hallway to the non-acute side.

Donna pulled herself to her full five feet five, two inches taller than Jessie, smoothed her auburn-colored bun, and offered a weak smile. "That's because I've had three sick calls, and on top of that, the director has been inundated with television requests. He wants to keep the walk-ins and regular homeless to the barest minimum, but the ambulances are coming fast and furious. Seems like everyone wants to have a peek or learn something about last night. We're suddenly the epicenter of trauma care. Can you take the patient in Trauma Two once you're settled?"

"Sure. Give me a minute."

"Thanks, Jess. I owe you."

"And don't think I'll forget."

Jessie made her way to her locker where she collected her stethoscope and her pens before moving on to Trauma Two where Elena, her co-worker from last night, was drawing up meds. "You're still here?" Jessie whispered. "You must be exhausted."

"You have no idea. Check this dose for me, will ya? I can barely read the numbers." Jessie confirmed the dose and read Elena's note.

"You all set? Any questions?" Elena asked.

"Just one. Any word on last night's patients?"

"Only a matter of time for the wife. CT showed damage and blood in all hemispheres, a midline shift and her EEG was almost flat. Waiting for her family from out of town. It doesn't look good for her at all."

"That's too bad," she said, remembering the scent of lavender that had lingered on her clothes. "And the husband?"

"Fine, I heard. Had only a minor renal injury, didn't need even a partial nephrectomy, just a repair. He's a lucky guy." She seemed to catch herself. "That sounded awful, but you know what I mean."

She nodded, though it did seem as though Rob Hart had all the luck last night. "Alright, get out of here, Elena. Get home and get some sleep." Jessie turned back to the work at hand. The stretcher held an almost lifeless old man, a few staff huddled over him, discussing the best options for his brain bleed.

"Not a candidate for TPA," the neurologist said, scratching his head. "No way to know how long he was down. Let's just admit him to the ICU and watch him."

"I'll get his papers in and call report," she said, already forgetting last night's victims.

CHAPTER FIVE

"The medical ICU has no beds. He's got to go to the surgical ICU. I called and told them you'd be up to give report. Okay?" Donna flashed an easy grin. "And I can let you go home at two. I have more staff coming in."

This time, it was Jessie who smiled. "Bed ready? Can we go up now?"

Donna nodded. "Transporter's on his way."

Jessie gathered the paperwork, disconnected the patient's wires and tubes and reconnected them to the portable monitors and pumps, and within minutes, they were all in an elevator heading to the fifth floor and the ICU. When the doors slid open, a uniformed police officer appeared. "This floor's closed," he said.

Jessie moved in front of the gurney. "Not to me it isn't, and not to my patient. What's going on?"

"Sorry. I've been told to keep everyone out. I wasn't even looking. Reporters tried to sneak in earlier." He moved to the side. "Go on."

"This is crazy," she muttered to herself as she and her little band moved towards the ICU. Another policeman stood guard at the entrance to the ICU. She showed him her ID and moved aside so he could see her patient. "We're going in there." She pointed to the closed door and swiped her badge across the blinking light. The door swung open and she stepped inside, the familiar hum of monitors, ventilators and beeping infusion pumps filling the small space.

"Room eight," the clerk said, nodding her head to a room at the end of the nursing station. A nurse appeared. "I'm taking him. Transport and the aide can get him set up. Want to give me report and have some coffee? We have donuts, too, courtesy of the mayor's office."

"God, I'd love some. I'm starving." And though she didn't say it, she knew what every nurse knew—that there wasn't too much that was better than free coffee and donuts on a busy morning. She followed behind to the nursing station and into the small office. Several boxes of donuts and muffins were piled alongside a tall chrome pot that exuded the scent of fresh coffee. Jessie poured herself a cup and plucked a chocolate-frosted donut from the box on top. "I had to pass two policemen to get in. Are the Harts both still here?"

"Yes," she answered with a sigh. "I know it's sad, but I long for the routine of a regular day without all the interruptions and calls—from the mayor, reporters, you name it. I'd even give up the donuts." She smiled and picked one out, taking a bite. "Well, maybe not the donuts."

Jessie gave her report on her patient and followed the nurse out to the corridor, where all the rooms were surrounded by glass so staff could watch their critically ill patients even from the desk. But the first room, right across from the nursing station, held Rob Hart, who was sitting in a chair, a newspaper on his lap, a smiling intern by his side. It was a bizarre scene considering his wife's condition. "He's a jerk," the nurse said, catching Jess's glance. "He doesn't need the ICU. Should have gone from Recovery to a floor, but politics reign supreme."

"Has he seen his wife?"

She shook her head. "We rolled him down to see her, but he just looked in, said the machines and pumps overwhelmed him and he didn't want to see her like that. He asked about her later, but only after I mentioned that she'd had surgery for a decompression craniectomy to help relieve the pressure on her brain, not that it will change the outcome. Poor thing. Like I said, he's a jerk."

"I guess he is. Hey, thanks for the donut," Jessie called as she turned to go. Rob Hart looked up at the sound of her voice, catching her in his gaze, and smiled. He actually smiled! *Or was it a smirk?* Her face flushed red, and she forced herself to walk away. Something was wrong here, very wrong. She knew everyone processed things differently, but this was too much, no matter how you looked at it.

She headed back to the ER, restocked the trauma room, went out to Triage, which was a waste of time considering how few walk-ins were showing up, or maybe being allowed in, and sat there evaluating only a handful of patients until it was time to go. A waste of a day, but the easiest overtime she'd ever do. At two o'clock, she grabbed her sweater and her keys and headed home, her thoughts still consumed by the curious behavior of Rob Hart. She chided herself. Maybe he didn't understand the gravity of his wife's condition, but the poor woman was pregnant. *Why wasn't he at least asking about the baby?* She caught herself and tried to shut off those thoughts. It was none of her darn business; she just had to stop being so judgmental.

With overtime pay in her future, she stopped to pick up a sandwich for dinner. Her good luck continued when she found an open spot not far from her building. Once home, she changed out her scrubs for sweats, surveyed the pile of dirty laundry in her bedroom and felt her shoulders sag. It was now or never. She stuffed her clothes into a garbage bag, plucked quarters and detergent from her counter and headed to the basement laundry room where her luck held. Both machines were available; she sorted towels from her clothes, slid her quarters into the slots and as soon as she heard the washers click on, she headed back upstairs.

With her laundry out of the way, she tidied up, before clicking on the television just in time for the early news. Once again, the

Harts led the broadcast, their smiling photos on full display as reporters tried to craft "exclusives" out of thin air. "Both victims remain in critical condition," one anchor droned. Another focused on the robbery, though since more was left behind than taken, that seemed to Jessie an unlikely motive. Rob Hart had become the center of attention, an almost-hero just for calling nine-one-one. He'd apparently spearheaded a group for inner city youth, and photos of him shooting hoops with the boys flashed across the screen. She could only shake her head. Seemed as though everyone else thought he was some kind of prince. Ann Hart was described briefly as a beloved first grade teacher, but mostly she was referred to simply as Rob Hart's wife, as if she didn't really exist beyond that.

Jessie clicked through to another channel and a different perspective. "Aside from a Spanish accent, there is little to go on. Police report that surveillance cameras in the area were being changed out. Few were in working order and only one caught the young couple as they walked to their car, a block from the shooting. In those shots, there is no glimpse of the shooter, who was likely lurking in the shadows. Whoever he is, the police assure us they will find him. For the victims, and for the rest of us, perhaps it's time to reconsider the death penalty in Massachusetts," he finished.

Another news report described the police harassment of young Hispanic males. The police commissioner and the mayor were both quoted as saying that getting the shooter off the street was the city's first priority, but that they remained mindful of everyone's rights.

Jessie finished off her sandwich, took a quick shower and curled up on her couch with a cup of tea and a new book—a mystery, her favorite. She was engrossed in her book when her iPhone rang and without checking, she hit accept.

"Oh, Jessie, you finally answered," a familiar and unwelcome voice crooned.

Damn it! She almost said it aloud. It was Bert, her stalker; at least, that was how she thought of him when she was forced to think of him at all. He'd been a reporter with the Associated Press when he'd shown up in the ER one morning after a large airliner had slid from the runway, its nose smashing into one of the concrete barriers along the perimeter during an ice storm. The only injuries had been to the pilot who was admitted to the ICU. The ER had been deluged with phone calls, requests for interviews and queries about the pilot, and then Bert arrived, looking rumpled and weary. His gray hair was combed over but did little to hide a shiny, balding scalp. "I'm here about the plane," he'd announced.

"Yeah, you and everyone else," Jessie had answered, her hand on her hip, her impatience with all of the questions surrounding the incident clear. "No information is being released. You should have called. The operator could have saved you a trip." She'd turned to walk away when he spoke up.

"You don't understand—he's my brother," Bert had said.

She turned back, the half-smile on his face telling her it was a lie. She hesitated, thinking how to get rid of him. "Really?" she asked. "He's black," she said, to call his bluff.

Bert cringed. "Caught," he said. "Touché. Won't you take mercy on a reporter and just give me a crumb?"

She'd laughed. He seemed like a decent guy. Still, she shook her head. "You've heard of HIPAA, right? The privacy act? I can't tell you anything. I can't even tell you if he's here."

Bert had handed her his card and boldly asked for a date. "No," she'd answered too quickly, his droopy eyes drooping even more. He was too old. He must be fifty, or more, but she didn't want to hurt his feelings. "I have a boyfriend."

"So, you'll call me if you break up with him?"

She flashed him a mischievous smile—a move that would turn out to be a big mistake. But she didn't know that then. "You're the first person I'll call."

Bert called the ER regularly over the next few months, and finally Jessie gave in and accepted his invitation to have a drink after work. He'd been overjoyed, and she didn't quite get his eagerness to impress her. He was a national reporter after all, and though too old for her, he also seemed out of her league.

Until she got to know him.

CHAPTER SIX

Over drinks, Bert had said he was just back from a professional break after years as a war correspondent covering conflicts in Afghanistan, Iraq and too many other dicey spots to remember. He'd won a Pulitzer Prize and then fallen on hard times, and was just now, he'd said, working his way back up, writing a novel, too. Jessie had been intrigued and accepted a second date and then a third to hear more of his story. But it was after that third date, when he'd tried to force a flurry of wet kisses on her, swearing loudly when she'd rebuffed him, that she knew he was a creep. She'd stopped taking his calls, told security at work about him, and he'd finally seemed to take the hint, disappearing for almost a year.

When Jessie had googled him, she'd found his story wasn't quite true. He'd won some awards but not the Pulitzer, and the hard times he'd mentioned were actually episodes of plagiarism for which he'd been fired. These days, he was a freelance reporter, scrambling to get back into the business, but he apparently had lots of free time. Her phone regularly lit up with his messages, at first declaring how much he cared for her, then saying she was making a big mistake by avoiding him. She tried blocking him, but he changed his number so frequently, it just seemed easier to ignore him.

But here he was once again. "Bert, please don't call me again." She moved to end the call.

"Don't hang up," he pleaded. "I won't bother you again. I just wanted you to know that you've helped me to move on. With everything. I'm freelancing for the Associated Press, I have a publisher for my novel, and I'm moving to London for a job. I just wanted to say goodbye. That's all."

"Good luck," she said softly, though what she wanted to say was good riddance. At least he was going away, and she'd be free of his endless calls.

She slept soundly, waking to the calming patter of rain on her windows. She rolled over intending to go back to sleep, and then her phone began to ring. She pulled a pillow over her face hoping to block out the sound, but it was no good. Whoever was calling wasn't about to give up. She reached one arm out from under the covers and picked up the phone. "Hello," she mumbled.

"Oh, thank God you answered," Donna said.

"What time is it?"

"Ten. Hate to ruin your last day off but Sheila's having a debriefing, and you have to be there."

Sheila was their ghost of a nurse manager, invisible on most days except for the edicts she issued by email—*no acrylic nails, no eating or drinking in patient areas, no cell phone use on duty, sign your notes by the end of your shift*—all rules well known already by staff. But Sheila liked to think she was a force to be reckoned with, and so the emails continued. A tallish woman with brassy, overly processed blonde hair and a little too much eyeliner, she walked with a haughty gait, her shoulders back, her head high, a click above anyone else. Or at least, she liked to think that she was.

"Not coming. You're right. It's my last day off and I'm sleeping." It was no secret that she hated the touchy-feely flow of those damn debriefings. And what was the point of them anyway? Debriefings were held after major traumas so those involved could get in touch with their feelings and share any angst they felt. *Wasn't that what Foley's was for?* "I don't need to be soothed. I'm fine."

"Sheila says it's mandatory. Sorry. She asked me to call you."

"So, tell her you couldn't reach me."

"Can't. You have to come in. We're headed in shortly. Just get here. You'll be paid."

"You can't pay me enough, but I'll be there," she said, reluctantly pulling away her blanket and clicking on her television as she shivered her way to the shower. She was just drying off when she heard it.

"The Associated Press is reporting that an ER nurse has told them that Rob Hart's last words before being rushed to the OR were, '*Please forget about me. Just save my wife!*' Heart-wrenching words from a loving husband whose own life hangs in the balance. The Boston Police Department plan to hold a press conference later today to update their search for the shooter. We'll bring you that update as it happens."

Jessie fumed. That lie must have come from that little weasel, Bert. She threw her towel to the floor and dressed hurriedly, grabbing her rain slicker as she wrenched open her door and raced to her car. She navigated the roads by memory alone, slipping through one red light and nearly going through another until a car horn blared loudly, breaking through the narrow pulse of anger that shut out everything else. She pulled into the garage and walked swiftly through the corridors and into the main entrance before turning into the ER, swiping her ID across the sensor to gain entrance.

"Whoa! Slow down, where are you rushing off to?" It was Cheryl, the infinitely kind clerk, always smiling, always reminding staff to take it easy.

"The debriefing. A command appearance."

"Poor you," Cheryl sympathized. "They're all in the conference room out back."

"Conference room?"

"Brace yourself. There's a crowd in there."

"Oh, hell," Jessie mumbled to herself. "I should have stayed home." She hadn't even had coffee yet. And now this. She sighed and headed for the conference room.

The conference room doors were wide open, people spilling into the hallway. She could hear voices from within but, at the back of the crowd, she was too far out to make any sense of what was going on. She elbowed her way through the crowd of strangers, not a familiar face among them until she spied Donna in the center. "Ahh, here she is," Donna said, relief dripping from her words.

The room fell silent as Jessie made her way to a chair that Donna held out for her. Finally, she saw a few familiar faces. Besides Donna and Sheila, there were Carol and Elena, nurses who were also working the night of the shooting, Tim Merrick, the surgeon, Neil Doherty, the surgical resident, a few administrators and, tucked into a corner of the room, the detective from that night. He smiled broadly, and raised a brow as if they were in on something together. He'd given her his card, but she couldn't remember what she'd done with it. It was probably in the pocket of her scrubs. *What the heck was his name anyway?*

"So, to bring you up to speed," Sheila began, looking around the room, leveling her razor-sharp gaze on Jessie. "We know," she continued, her prissy voice grating on Jessie's ears, "that this type of case can wreak havoc on our staff's personal lives, and we've brought you all together, in this safe place, to share your feelings." She leaned forward, her elbows on the table, a look of genuine concern on her face. The ER staff knew that look was contrived, designed to fool onlookers. The real Sheila didn't care what the staff thought. "Jessie?" she asked. All eyes were suddenly trained on her. "Anything you'd like to share?"

Jessie folded her arms across her chest, and sank further into the chair. "No," she said shaking her head to emphasize her answer.

"Are you sure?"

"Positive. I'm just here to listen."

"Well, Dr. Merrick, will you continue?"

The surgeon cleared his throat, mostly to make sure he had everyone's attention. "As I was saying, the Hart shooting was a tragedy. The victim believes the shooter was an immigrant, and that affects all of us since, as you know, the community we serve includes a large number of Hispanic immigrants."

He droned on, and Jessie let her mind wander, her gaze falling on the detective. He sat stiffly, his fingers drumming on his leg, his eyes scanning the room.

"What about the wife?" Carol asked. "How is she?"

"Hanging on by a thread," Tim replied. "Neurosurgery says it's only a matter of time—days, maybe hours."

"So, no chance of speaking with her?" The detective sat forward as he spoke.

"None." Tim's voice was harsh, dismissive as though he'd had enough, and as if to underscore that, he stood, pushing his chair away from the table. "I have to get back to the OR. You all know where to find me."

The room went quiet. "Any questions, thoughts?" Donna asked, her eyes scanning the attendees' faces.

Jessie raised her hand, her curiosity getting the better of her bad mood. "Why all the attention for this case? I understand that they're a nice young couple, but we have shootings almost every day. It seems, I don't know... unfair maybe, to make this case a priority when there are so many others we forget about the next day. I know that sounds weird to ask, but, well, that's my question."

The detective, whose name still eluded her, nodded. "Last night's victim is the mayor's chief of staff. The mayor has personally pushed this up to the highest level. I wish we had these resources for all of our victims, but the reality is we don't."

Jessie felt a flush rising from her neck. She hadn't meant to put him in the hot seat, and she wondered if he was trying to put her in her place. "I didn't mean to direct that to you. I just, I don't know. This whole thing..."

"I understand. Can we have a word after the meeting?"

"Uh, sure." There were days she wished she'd kept her mouth shut. Today was one of those.

"Okay, everyone," Donna said. "If there are no more questions or comments, that's it. If anyone has trouble sleeping, or dealing with their feelings, we have help for that. Okay?"

The detective stood. Jessie hadn't realized until just then how tall he was—well over six feet—with the muscular, angled build of an athlete. "Just one more thing," he said, "a quick reminder—we don't want any information about the Harts, or any description of their wounds, released." He paused, probably for effect, Jessie thought and then he nodded.

"Hey, Jessie, right?" The detective came up behind her.

She nodded. "Hate to admit it, but I forgot your name."

"Sam. Sam Dallas, Homicide." He loosened his tie and ran his fingers through his hair, a tiny tuft at the back standing straight up, which made him seem somehow boyish despite the holster and badge on his belt.

"Jessie? A word?" Sheila's eyes bored into her.

"Sure." She turned to Sam. "Sorry, maybe later?"

She didn't have to wonder what Sheila wanted to say. She was only surprised that she didn't get a public lashing at the debriefing. Grateful at least for that, she followed Sheila to her office, a room larger than the staff lounge and just a tiny bit smaller than her apartment. A polished mahogany desk rested on an ornate Persian carpet, and a tiny desk lamp gave off a gentle glow as if to soothe anyone who was invited in. Jessie slid into a straight-backed wooden chair.

Sheila flicked on the bright overhead lights just before she dropped into one of those cushioned ergonomic chairs that had become so popular. "So," she leaned forward, tenting her hands as if about to pray, "can you tell me about this morning's headline?" She held up a copy of the *Boston Globe* with the headline: *Please forget about me. Just save my wife!* "Do you know anything about this?"

CHAPTER SEVEN

Jessie fidgeted in her seat. "No. I just heard it on the news."

"Really? It says here that the reporter's source is an ER nurse. Is that you?"

"No, and it's not Carol or Elena either." She sat a little straighter, folding her hands in her lap.

"And how would you know that?"

"Because Hart never said that, or anything even remotely close to that."

"Mr. Hart is not denying that he said that. In fact, he said he has no complaint with that headline. But we in Administration, of course, do."

"Just speak to the reporter then. Whoever it is will have to admit that he, or she, was never told that."

"We did speak with him—Bert Gibbons. I believe you know him?"

A flush rose to her cheeks. "I *knew* him. I don't see or speak to him these days."

"Really? What would you say if I told you he showed me the call thread on his phone?" Sheila leaned back in her chair, her gaze tight on Jessie.

Hmm, Jessie thought, *now there's a perfect pair: Bert and Sheila.* A match made in heaven, or more likely, hell. "He is not even remotely a friend. I do not pick up when he calls." And then she remembered: she had picked up—just last night. He was a devious son of a bitch.

"Well, obviously, we have to deal with this. This is a HIPAA violation, but because the patient was pleased with the headline, and confirms that he said that, the hospital will not be fined. Still, we must make it clear to all of the staff that violating HIPAA is a grievous act." She picked up a pen from her desk and held it as if poised to sign a document. "I could suspend you."

Her words hung in the air, the threat clear. Jessie had almost no savings and no idea how she'd even pay her rent. Her mouth felt dry as cotton and her mind raced trying to formulate a plan. It would probably take longer to find a job than to wait this out. She sat perfectly still; she neither frowned nor smiled; she didn't react at all. Not reacting was the only way she knew to fight back. Her dad had once said, "*Never* let them see you cry, honey. You just gotta toughen up." And she'd made it a point to follow his advice. She swallowed the hard lump in her throat and remained silent.

"But I won't," Sheila finally said after a long, dramatic pause. "I will, however, transfer you to the ICU for a week or two. I'll check with the critical care team and see where you're needed."

Jessie could only nod, afraid that if she did try to speak, she would cry. She was a damn ER nurse, not a friggin' ICU nurse. Administrators never seemed to understand the difference.

"Report to the ICU manager at seven a.m. She'll be able to assign you then."

"I work evenings, three to eleven, not days."

Sheila stood then, dismissing her. "Seven a.m."

The first stirrings of a headache pricked at Jessie's eyes. She blinked at the harsh lights as she stood. She considered, only for a moment, saying something snarky, but decided against it. She'd only make matters worse. She didn't deserve this, but at least she still had a job.

She pulled up the hood of her slicker, and exited through the ambulance bay hoping that Sam Dallas had hung around. She wanted to share her lingering questions about Hart. She stepped out of the ER and into a glare of cameras, the bright lights bouncing off the nearby puddles, almost dissolving the day's steely grayness. The mayor and police commissioner stood under the building's overhang away from the rain facing a crowd of reporters. Sam was just behind them. The reporters were huddled under shared umbrellas, the rain drumming softly, in contrast to the rapid-fire pelting of questions they aimed at the commissioner and mayor.

"Who was first to arrive on the scene?" one reporter shouted, holding her microphone out. The police commissioner, Jim Conley, a thin, almost frail man who seemed lost in his suit, motioned to Sam to step forward. "Sam Dallas, our chief investigator on this case, can best answer those questions."

Sam stepped up and cleared his throat. "A patrolman was the first to arrive. He confirmed immediately that we needed two ambulances for two critically injured victims."

"Where were they?"

"As we've said, they were in the alley behind the theater on Warrenton Street."

"I actually meant, were they sitting, standing, sprawled on the ground?"

"Mr. Hart had pulled himself up to a sitting position. Mrs. Hart was lying face down next to him."

"He hadn't turned her? Tried to help her?"

Good question, Jessie thought, heaving a satisfied sigh. But then there was silence. No one else dared to follow that line of questioning.

"Do you know any more about what happened?" another reporter asked.

"Not much more than what we've already told you. Mr. Hart and his wife were heading to their car after a night out when a man walked up behind them and forced them into the alley where he shot and robbed them."

"Just one shooter? Do we have any description?"

"Well, we've been told he had a Spanish accent, and Mr. Hart thinks he caught sight of a tattoo on the man's face and right hand, the hand which held the gun. So, it's not much, but it's something."

A tattoo, Jessie thought. *When did Hart remember that?* He hadn't mentioned it that night. Which now that she considered it was actually thirty-six hours ago, though already it seemed a lifetime. She folded her arms against the chill and moved closer.

"A Hispanic man with a tattoo on his face and right hand? Won't that description fit hundreds of men in Boston? Are you going to target the Spanish community?"

"We're going to go where the evidence leads us," Sam replied stonily. "This is a fluid investigation."

"Is there any physical evidence?" a reporter shouted, holding her cell phone out to catch his reply.

"The gunman shot three times. One shot hit Mr. Hart in the side, the second missed him as he fell, and the third hit Mrs. Hart in the head. Mr. Hart's fall, by the way, likely saved his life. That bullet that missed him was found lodged into a window casing in the alley."

"And the Harts. How are they?"

"Still critical," the mayor replied.

"Was there any evidence at the scene?"

"We have the third bullet and the one that struck Mr. Hart. Unfortunately, the doctors were not able to remove the bullet that struck Mrs. Hart."

"What about surveillance cameras? Anything valuable from them?"

"Again, unfortunately, the city was in the process of upgrading cameras in that area. The only footage we have is from a block or so away, and that video only revealed images of the Harts walking towards their car. No sign of a gunman."

"Isn't that a bit of a coincidence? Could the gunman be a city employee? I mean most days those cameras capture everything.

Kind of convenient for the shooter that they were out of commission on that night."

Jessie wanted to raise her hand. She had questions, too, but asking them here risked her job, and that was a chance she couldn't take. At least not right now.

The mayor stepped to the center of the crowd. "I want to announce that a twenty-five-thousand-dollar reward for any information leading to the arrest of the shooter has been posted." He paused and turned to the police commissioner. "We all thank you for coming today and for any help you can provide in this investigation."

"That's it," the commissioner announced as he stepped to the microphone.

"Nothing else?" someone else called.

Sam nodded. "We continue to develop information and will release what we have when that is appropriate."

The group began to break up. One reporter and a cameraman headed towards the ambulance bay for a live shot. Jessie moved out of the way quickly, shoving her hands in her pockets. She'd have to go through the walk-in entrance to find her way back to the garage.

"Hey, Jessie! Wait!"

She turned to see Sam Dallas approaching her. "I was afraid I'd missed you," he said. "Were you watching?" He motioned back to the area where the glut of microphones was being cleared away.

"Just the last bit."

"What did you think?"

"Interesting." She adjusted her hood to keep the rain from her hair.

He opened a large black umbrella and held it above both of them. "I'd like to speak with you about the case. Off the record. I have a feeling you have something to say. I could be wrong, but my gut is usually right."

"I probably shouldn't say anything. I'm already in trouble."

"The headline? That was you?"

She shook her head. "It wasn't me. It wasn't any of us. Hart never said that. But I knew that reporter, and he apparently told them it was me."

Sam's jaw dropped open. "What a louse."

"You don't know the half of it."

"How about you tell me the rest over at L Street?" He flashed an easy grin, the rain failing to dampen his smile or the sudden sparkle in his eyes.

Once again, she was charmed. At least they weren't outside a trauma room while lives hung in the balance. This seemed more natural. She nodded. "I'll meet you there. My car's in the employee garage and I live just around the corner from L Street." They arranged to meet in thirty minutes, giving her a chance to untangle her curls, apply some eyeliner and a splash of color on her lips. Sam Dallas would be a nice change of pace.

And maybe, just maybe, he was just what she needed.

CHAPTER EIGHT

Jessie found an empty spot right in front of her building. She raced upstairs, inserted her key in her lock, expecting the usual tussle with the aging tumbler mechanism, but instead she'd barely turned the key and the knob when the door eased open. She froze. She'd locked her door this morning; she was sure of it. It was almost second nature—turning to lock up before she left. Every time.

Had she forgotten, or was the lock just loose again? It wouldn't be the first time the lock had failed to engage. But today, with everything going on, it seemed somehow more than a lousy lock. She pulled the key out and gently pushed on the door and peered in while she stood outside. That was the beauty of a small apartment; she could see almost everything from the doorway. But there was nothing to see.

"Hello?" she called out, her voice echoing back to her. She stepped inside but kept the door open in case she needed a fast escape. Nothing seemed to be missing or even disturbed. She looked around the corner and into her bedroom and inhaled deeply. She hadn't even realized she'd been holding her breath.

She retraced her steps, closed and locked the door, and flicked on the light in her windowless bathroom. She didn't want to overdo her makeup; after all, this wasn't really a date. It was just lunch, but there was nothing wrong in looking good, because maybe it would turn into something more. She lined her eyelids with a smoky black pencil, applied a sweep of mascara to her lashes and ran a wash of pink color over her lips, then stood back to have a look. The liner brought out the gray flecks in her hazel eyes, the mascara made them sparkle just a little, and the lip color somehow gave her skin, usually so pale and dull, a dewy appearance. She pulled her hair into a high ponytail, leaving a few tousled curls loose to frame her face. Not bad, she thought, heading to the kitchen for a bottle of water.

She reached for the refrigerator handle and stopped, puzzled. Her work schedule, which she always kept under a magnet on her fridge, was gone. She wouldn't have thrown it out. That was how she knew week to week what days she was working. Without it, she'd be lost. She searched the floor, the wastebasket, even the inside of the refrigerator, but it was nowhere. Inexplicably, it was gone. She shook her head. She must be losing it; she may have forgotten to lock her front door and she'd lost her schedule. At least there was something of a bright side. She wouldn't need that schedule. Tomorrow, she'd start days in the ICU.

She took a long swig of water, grabbed her slicker and headed out, careful to check that the lock on her front door was secure this time. Outside, she took a deep breath and turned towards East 8th Street, the familiar streets lined with brick rowhouses and narrow three-deckers, perfect little neighborhoods tucked into the heart of the city. From there, the L Street Tavern was just a block away. She assumed that was the place he meant. At least the rain had stopped. Despite her banishment to the ICU, this day just might turn out okay after all. There was a decided bounce to her step as she turned onto L Street, but it was there that she stepped into the street without thinking. A horn blared, someone shouted and a screech of tires filled the air. "What the hell, lady!" someone screamed.

"Sorry," she said, backing away, willing herself to pay attention. She stuffed her hands in her pockets. Maybe the day shift would turn out to be a good thing after all.

*

Sam Dallas was standing outside when she arrived. "You weren't waiting long, I hope?" she asked. "I wasn't sure if you meant the Tavern or the Diner."

He laughed. "And yet, here we are—at the Tavern." He held the door open and then led her to a pub table along the side wall. The lights were dimmed; there was a hum of conversation, the tinkle of glasses, and a small group of older men huddled together at the long mahogany bar, speaking in hushed tones.

"Handy that you live so close," Sam said, pulling his stool next to hers. "Do you come here often?" Then, before she could answer, he laughed, the hearty laugh of a man comfortable with himself. "I don't think I've ever used that line before." He raised a brow in amusement and motioned for the bartender, who nodded. "Beer?" Sam asked.

And Jessie was charmed once again. "Yeah," she replied, trying not to sound too eager. "That sounds good. I'm not working today, so yeah—a beer."

The bartender served their beers and nodded towards the group at the bar. "They're calling in an order to Sal's. They wanted to know if you wanted to order, too." One of the men turned and waved.

"Pizza?" Sam asked. "We won't have to leave."

"Perfect."

Sam strode to the group, placed his order and peeled off some bills from his wallet. He turned back to Jessie and reached for his beer as he sat. "So, back to business. I was watching you today during the press conference. It seemed to me as though you didn't believe a word."

"I'm that easy to read, huh?" She took a sip of beer, studying him over the rim of her glass.

"No, not at all, except where Hart's concerned. You seemed a bit cynical at the staff meeting, too."

She licked the foam from her lips. "Skepticism is healthy, right?"

"Won't deny that. But why are you skeptical?" He raised a brow.

"The question is—why aren't you?"

"Maybe I am, but I've been doing this for a long time, and my gut tells me Hart is a victim. You seem to think otherwise. Tell me why. I've learned enough to know that sometimes an observer sees things more clearly than me." He put his hand on her knee. "I want to see what it is that you see."

Jessie's thigh was hot where Sam had placed his hand, and he made no move to pull it away. She wasn't sure she could pay attention to his questions just then, and she wanted to—no, she needed to share her thoughts. Even if it was all for nothing. At least she'd have shared what she knew. "You were there. You saw him in the trauma room. Elena said he never asked about his wife. The only person he was worried about was himself."

"He was in shock. You gotta give the guy a break."

"Everyone's giving him a break. How about giving his wife a break?" Sam moved his hand from her thigh and reached for his beer, and Jessie couldn't help but notice that there was something almost graceful in his movements—his long, tapered fingers, like those of a pianist, and the way he held his glass, his hands wrapping around and gently caressing the bottle. It was hypnotic. She forced her eyes away.

"Tell me what you mean," he said.

And she was grateful to get back to the subject at hand. "So, a robber forces them into an alley. Tells the husband to hand over his valuables and then shoots him in the side. He falls to the ground. Then, without asking for anything from the wife—tell me if there's something I don't know here—he turns to her and shoots her in the back of the head. As a parting shot, he shoots one more time, but apparently just into the air. You said today that bullet was found in the window casing. Correct?"

Sam shook his head. "No, Hart said that shot was fired as he was falling. The shooter probably thought he'd hit him. It wasn't fired into the air. The third shot was the one that hit the wife."

"Okay. I see that, but you saw the wife's valuables. Why didn't he take those? He left too much behind for it to be a robbery."

"We're looking at everything, and we're waiting on Verizon to hand over Hart's cell phone records—see if the shooter is using the phone. You, on the other hand, are only looking at Hart. You don't like him much, do you?" He stood to remove his suit jacket, placing it on a nearby stool.

"It's not that. I don't even know him. I just don't trust him. Yesterday in the ICU he was flirting with an intern and he smiled at me! His wife was right down the hall—dying. He saw her, but from just outside her room. He didn't even go in. I mean, come on."

Their pizza arrived, momentarily interrupting their conversation, which was probably a good thing. Jessie could feel a flush rising to her cheek. She was starting to sound obsessed with this and she really wasn't. She just thought there was something more to the story.

"Darn, I should have asked earlier. Do you have a signed release from him so that you can see his records?"

"We do." Sam bit into his slice, grabbing a napkin to catch the drip of tomato sauce that hovered over his perfectly pressed white shirt. "Why?"

"HIPAA. I probably shouldn't even be discussing this."

"It's okay. It's between you and me. I'm not going to the *Globe*. Who was that reporter anyway?"

Jessie nibbled at her pizza, picking the cheese away and dropping it into her mouth. "He was a creep who wanted to date me, but my God, he's old."

Sam's head bobbed back as though he'd been struck. "Whoa. Hold on here. How old is too old?"

"I don't know. Fifty?"

Sam swiped his hand dramatically across his brow. "Jeez, ya had me worried there for a minute. I'm thirty-six. Never felt old until just now."

Jessie smiled. "You're not old and you're not a creep. This guy is. But at first, it didn't matter. He definitely wasn't my type, but he seemed interesting when I first met him in the ER. He said he was a war correspondent and Pulitzer Prize winner. At least, that's what he said, but it turned out not all of it was true. When I told him—again and again—that I wasn't interested in dating him, he called me, texted, showed up at work. He was relentless, but finally, almost a year ago now, it stopped. All of it. It just stopped. And that was the end of it, or so I thought, until he started texting and calling again last week. I answered his call last night without meaning to. He said he'd only called to say goodbye, that he was moving to London for a job, and his novel had found a publisher. I told him I was happy for him. Until today, when I saw the headlines." She took a sip of beer and picked at her pizza.

"And because of him, you're in trouble at work?"

"HIPAA, the privacy act. My manager says I violated it, but the headlines are a lie. Hart never said that, and by the way, he apparently has no complaint with that headline. It kind of puts him in a good light, don't you think?"

"I'm not so sure he cares about the headlines, though it sounds as though your boss does, huh?"

She nodded, swiping a piece of crust around the box to pick up any stray bits of cheese. "Bert never asked about the Harts. Not one question. He made that story up, probably for a byline and a paycheck."

"I can look into this guy for you."

"Thanks, but he's on his way to London, he said, so I think I'm all set." She popped the sliver of crust into her mouth, a satisfied smile on her face.

"So, let me get this right. You don't trust Hart, by all accounts a stand-up guy, but you trust this slimy little Bert."

She laughed. "Well, when you put it that way, I do sound as though I trust the wrong people, but really, just think about it. I know I'm beating a dead horse, but you saw him in the ER—he was worried about himself. He never even asked how Ann was, which I guess is why he's happy about that crappy headline. As of yesterday, he'd only glimpsed her through a doorway in the ICU. They're only a few rooms apart. It's just too weird. The shooter shoots him in the side and the wife in the head. Wouldn't it be more likely to be the other way around? The wife is not a threat to the robber but he might be. And the bullet that missed him. Not to mention that the surveillance cameras were out. Come on. No one's that lucky." She took a deep breath. She had to learn not to prattle on. Talk about ruining the mood.

Sam nodded. "This guy seems to have been that lucky. I tend to believe him, though we always hold onto a little bit of skepticism until we have an arrest. This investigation is active—everyone's a suspect right now, including Hart. Nothing is off the table, but I understand your suspicions. It's the nature of our business." He angled his chin towards her. "Will it help if I tell you we are looking into both Harts, checking to see if there's anyone who might have wanted to hurt them? I'll tell you though, so far I think that's a dead end." He took a swig of his beer. "You and I, we really don't really trust anyone. Am I right?"

He was probably right, and by her third beer, she tended to agree with him. Working in the ER had made her suspicious of the wrong people. But there was one more thing she'd forgotten to mention, and it seemed everyone else had, too. "Ann Hart is pregnant. I understand why it's not in the news, but I wonder if Hart has mentioned it to you guys."

Sam shook his head. "No, he hasn't mentioned it. Maybe he doesn't know. Maybe she didn't know yet. Which I guess makes this that much sadder."

Jessie felt her shoulders tense. "Nonsense," she said, shaking her head. "By the numbers, she's about ten weeks pregnant. She definitely knew, and he's the first one she'd tell. He has to know. Will you ask him?"

"I will, but it's not going to help solve the shooting. As far as I can tell, it had nothing to do with the robbery. Just a sad footnote to the story."

"Footnote? What if it does have something to do with the shooting?"

A wrinkle appeared in Sam's brow. "We'll look at that, but tell me why you think it has something to do with the shooting."

"I don't know. Probably nothing. Forget I said it."

"Would it help you to know that we have a couple of suspects?"

"You do?" She picked at the label on her bottled beer.

"Yeah, similar crimes. Similar MO, just not well-connected victims, so it never made it to the news. No one really noticed. We were still following up on those when the Hart shootings happened. We have a couple of guys in our sights."

"Why not say that at the press conference?"

"It's better to keep some things quiet, at least for now." He tipped his bottle against hers. "What do you say? One more?"

"Don't you have to go back to work?"

"Not today. I'll be back at it tomorrow, but today, I'm free."

They had another beer and then another. The afternoon flew by. It was almost six when Sam looked at his watch. "Whoa, look at the time. Sorry to break this up, but…"

"No worries. I should get going, too. I'm on days tomorrow and I'm not used to getting up early. Thanks for the beer and the conversation." She stood to go.

"Hey, hold on." Sam threw some money on the table. "I'll walk you home."

"You don't have to." She slipped her arms into her slicker. "I'm so close."

"All the more reason. To tell you the truth, I'd like to get your number, too. I hope we can do this again. Minus the crime updates."

She laughed and tucked her arm into his. "I'd like that, too."

The rain had stopped; the early dark sky of Fall was sprinkled with distant stars, the perfect backdrop to what had turned out to be a pretty good day.

After a chaste kiss goodnight, Jessie pulled away and climbed the stairs to her apartment. She smiled as she unlocked her door. She probably hadn't locked it earlier, she thought, and as for her missing schedule, she'd likely crumpled it up and thrown it away. She had to remember not to overthink things. She shrugged out of her slicker and went to close her blinds before flicking on her lights, and it was there, while standing in her window, that she saw a shadowy figure below, looking up and right at her. On this moonless night, it was too dark to make out who it was. There was a streetlamp right there, but the light was out. She hadn't even noticed that before. She backed away quickly from the window and took a deep breath. She was imagining things. That's all this was. Maybe it was Sam. She shook her head as if weighing the possibility. No, she'd seen him walk away. It wasn't Sam.

She peered from the window once again, and there was no mistaking it.

Someone was watching her.

CHAPTER NINE

She slid back away from the window, keeping the lights out. With visions of the movie *Psycho* in her thoughts, she forfeited her shower and slid into bed where she slept fitfully, tossing and turning, darkness filling every corner of her apartment so that no one could see her through the filtered light of cheap plastic blinds and flimsy curtains. She fell asleep just before her alarm sounded. Six a.m. She groaned as she reached out to shut it off.

Six a.m. was barbaric.

She crawled to the shower, dressed for work, stopped for coffee and a muffin, and slid into a parking spot a block from the hospital, saving the twenty dollars the garage would set her back. Already, the fear she felt last night seemed stupid and unfounded. She lived on a busy street. Why wouldn't people be standing around and even looking up? Christ, all she needed now was a cat and she'd be one of those skittish single women who jumped at everything.

She took the elevator to five, and when she stepped out, her phone pinged with a text. *Medical ICU today.* The text was from Sheila. Jessie groaned and headed there, stopping first for a look out the long windows that lined the hallway. There were no windows in the ER, and even if there were, she'd only see concrete sidewalks and blacktopped streets. From here, though, she could see clear to downtown: cobblestone streets flanked by grand old brownstones and glittering skyscrapers. Nearby rooftops, some with grilles and deck chairs, were strung with twinkling lights, still glowing in the dim early-morning light. All of it fit together perfectly in this charming old city. Further on, the lights of the Prudential Building flashed a signal for the weather; today a steady blue meaning a clear day. She smiled. It was a pleasant reminder that life existed outside of these walls.

She reported to the nurse in charge, who greeted her with a smile and her assignment—just one patient. He was, she learned as she read his chart, critically ill. He'd suffered a heart attack complicated by a bleed into his brain. He lay perfectly still, a thin sheet covering him while a ventilator forced air into his lungs, a bevy of pumps injected medicine into his veins, and a host of machines which checked his heart rate, blood pressure, oxygen levels and cardiac output monitored it all. She sighed and introduced herself to her patient. She was never sure if these patients could really hear her, but it made her feel better. And if he could hear, the sound of her voice was surely more welcome than the whoosh, buzz, whir and beeping of all of his machines.

Her day flew. At three, the evening nurse appeared. "You've been stuck in here all day?"

Jessie nodded.

"So, you haven't heard the news?"

Jessie stopped. Those were the words that sent a chill through the heart of every ER nurse. "Heard what?" she asked, willing herself to be calm.

"Ann Hart died. A few hours ago. There's a big commotion in the hallway. You might just want to take the stairs."

"Why is there a commotion?"

"Her family's blaming the husband. Saying it's his fault. Well, shouting, really. Merrick is out there trying to calm them. Strange scene, I'll tell you that."

Jessie gave a quick report, grabbed her sweater and her keys and walked into the hallway to see for herself just what was going on. The small space by the elevators was packed. Tim Merrick stood in the center of the crowd.

"We tried to save her, but her wound was just too serious. I... well, all of us really, tried to save her, but the damage was irreversible. I am so sorry for your loss."

An older man, his eyes red, tears still running along his cheeks, stepped forward. "Why would someone, anyone, shoot our Ann in the head and only shoot Rob in the side? Can you tell me that? It doesn't make any sense." He broke down then, his face crumpling as sobs wracked his shoulders.

Though looking uncomfortable, Merrick placed an arm over the man's shoulder. "I don't know. I just want you to know that we tried."

A younger woman, who bore a faint resemblance to Ann, a sister maybe, spoke up. "Rob Hart is barely injured and our Ann is dead! Why wouldn't he protect her? We never liked him, never trusted him, not for a minute, but we never thought..." She turned away, silent tears spilling from her eyes. "It's his fault that she's gone. I'm sure of it."

Jessie watched as the group huddled together getting ready to leave. Merrick stood quietly and caught Jessie's eye, nodding before he turned back to the Surgical ICU. The doors closed with a thud, leaving only the family and Jessie in the hallway.

"Miss," one of them called to her. "Did you take care of her? Of Ann?"

She froze. Would she be in trouble if she told them she had? An older woman took her hand. "Did you?" she asked, gripping Jessie's hand tightly.

She nodded. "In the ER," she said softly. "I took care of her when she came in."

"Oh, Arthur. Come here and listen," the woman said.

Suddenly, Jessie was surrounded. "Please tell us. Was she awake? Was she afraid? Did she speak to you?"

Jessie couldn't tell who was asking the questions, but it didn't matter. If she were in trouble again for soothing this family, then so be it. "I was with her until she went to CT scan. She wasn't awake."

"Was she in pain?"

No one could answer that question with any certainty, but she wanted to comfort this grieving family; that was all anyone could offer now. "I don't think so. It was as though she was sleeping."

"Did you speak to her?"

"Yes, I did."

"Did she hear you?" The woman locked her gaze onto Jessie. "Did she?"

"I think so. I always speak to my patients, no matter how grave the injury or prognosis." She bit back the tears that pricked at her eyes. "I think she heard me. She knew someone was with her."

The older woman wrapped her arms around Jessie. "Thank you for that, my dear. Thank you for watching over our Ann." At that, the woman's shoulders heaved with her sobs. The group gathered in around the old woman and Jessie backed away, their pain almost too raw to witness. She made her way to the stairwell and ran down the five flights and out to the street, leaning against the building's brick wall and breathing in great gulps of cold air. She walked the block to her car, releasing her sadness for Ann Hart and her family with every step she took. By the time she slipped into her car, she was ready for a sandwich and a glass of wine.

At home, she settled in front of the television, balancing a glass of wine and a tuna sandwich on her legs. She turned on the early news, and just as expected, Ann Hart was the lead story. The poor woman was finally getting noticed.

"This is just a tragedy," the reporter announced. "A young woman, a teacher beloved by all, senselessly killed in a robbery gone wrong. Police tell us they do have a suspect but they remain tight-lipped on details." The camera panned to an aerial view of a neighborhood that was the center of the Hispanic community. "Community leaders complain they are being unfairly targeted, that the police need to share their evidence with the community. The Boston Police Department declined to comment."

Jessie tuned to a love story on Hallmark, and before the expected happy ending, she clicked off her television, took a quick shower, set her alarm yet again for the ungodly hour of six a.m., and crawled into bed, where sleep overtook her in minutes.

She never heard the tapping on her door or heard the creak as it swung open.

CHAPTER TEN

Jessie slept through the night, and woke refreshed and smiling until, ready for work and hitching her backpack over her shoulder, she pulled open her door to head out—and froze. The door was unlocked. She wouldn't do that. Not again. She was sure of it. She remembered locking the door. *Or did she?* She'd been dog tired and hungry, her mind on food and wine. Maybe she did forget. Or, maybe the damn tumbler was still loose. That was probably it. The door was old, the lock probably flimsy. She'd had trouble with it before, but then it was usually stuck, the mechanism too tight to open with a simple rotation of the key. She sighed. Time to ask the super to get her a new lockset, or adjust this one. With that thought in mind, she walked briskly to the corner store for her usual black coffee and muffin.

"Morning, Patrick," she greeted the owner as she stepped inside. There was no need to order. He nodded, poured her coffee, tucked a muffin into a bag, and turned. "That you?" he asked, pointing to the newspaper on the counter.

Jessie's eyes fell to the bold headlines. *Ann Hart's Family Grateful to Angel Nurse.* She lifted the paper and read. The family, the story continued, never got the name of the kind nurse in scrubs they met just outside of the ICU. "*'In our grief, she gave us comfort,' Mrs. Hart's mother said. 'We want her to know she is an angel to us.'*"

"I figured it was you," Patrick said, interrupting her thoughts.

She smiled. "You can see it right here. They said she was an angel, so you know it's not me."

"Ahh, go on. Here ya go." He passed her the coffee and muffin. She reached into her pocket, and Patrick shook his head. "Not today, Jessie. Angels don't pay here. It's my pleasure to serve you." His brogue seemed somehow deeper today.

Jessie's eyes welled up. "Thanks, Pat. I owe you. Have a good day."

She checked her watch. Twenty minutes to seven. She couldn't be late, and she was cutting it too close. She sprinted to her car, pulled into the damn pricey garage and raced to the elevator. She pressed hard on the up button. "Come on," she panted.

"You're not late, are you?" a familiar and grating voice asked.

She turned to see Sheila, a tight smile stretching across her thin lips. "No, actually, I'm not." She hit the button again.

"Well, I'm glad I caught you. You're in the Surgical ICU today."

"Thanks for letting me know," Jessie replied as the elevator door slid open, allowing her to beat a hasty retreat from Sheila. What she wanted to say was, *What the hell? Can't you let me get used to one ICU before sending me to another?* But she didn't. Instead, she took a sip of her coffee as the doors closed.

The surgical ICU was strangely quiet when Jessie buzzed herself in. She found the charge nurse—Ellen, according to the name on her ID—at the main desk peering at a computer screen. "Hi, Ellen," Jessie said and introduced herself. Ellen pulled away from the computer. "We're pretty quiet today. I'm not sure why they sent you to us, but I guess you can take Hart. Everyone else is pretty sick of him. He's over there." She pointed to the room right across from the desk.

"What's he still doing here?" Jessie whispered.

Ellen shrugged. "Your guess is as good as mine. But it's Merrick's decision, and he seems intent on protecting this guy."

"From what?"

"From the press, from his in-laws. From the police, most of all. Hart does not need to be here, but no one is going to overrule Merrick, especially since the wife died yesterday."

"He must have been pretty upset, though, right? I mean, it's his wife."

"One would think so, but he never went in to see her. Just stayed outside and looked in. And the only tears I saw were crocodile tears. I could do better if I learned I had to work Christmas."

Jessie stifled a laugh as she put her things away and sat down to read Hart's file. Ellen was right. This guy really was fine. The bullet that caught him had only grazed his kidney, accounting for the bloody urine that first night, but the injury was so minor, he didn't even require a major repair. The nursing notes described a difficult patient who wanted the ICU nurses to rub his back, get his coffee, and hold his hand—literally—as he walked the halls. "Give me a break," Jessie murmured as she tried to ready herself. This really was going to be punishment, but if she wanted to get back to the ER—and she did—she'd have to just suck it up. She stood and walked the six feet to Hart's room. She paused, pulled her shoulders back, forced herself to smile and rapped on his door before entering.

"Morning, Mr. Hart. I'm Jessie. I'm assigned to you today."

He pushed himself up in bed and set aside the newspaper he'd been reading. She hadn't noticed before how young he looked. His full, round face framed by a crop of brown hair, the trace of a blush on his cheeks, the scant bit of fuzz on his face, all made him seem younger than his thirty-two years.

"Good morning," he said cheerily, though Jessie couldn't see what he had to be cheerful about.

She hit the button on his monitor and the blood pressure cuff tightened around his arm. "Ooh," he said. "You could warn a guy before you do that."

"Sorry, just getting your vital signs, and then I'll leave you alone."

"Please don't. Have a seat. Talk to me. Tell me about yourself."

What was this? A dating bar?

"Hey, that came out wrong," he said as if he'd just read her mind. "I'm just hungry for company. It's been a tough few days."

"I'm sure. I'm so sorry about your wife."

He nodded but looked right at her. Almost right through her. "Do I know you?" he asked. "There's something so familiar about you, or maybe it's just that you look so like Ann. You do, you know."

Jessie cleared her throat, hating that he'd noticed the resemblance. "I was in the ER the night you and your wife came in."

"Ahh, so this is you." He held up the newspaper with today's headlines.

"Well, it's…"

"Thank you for being Ann's angel. And now for being mine." His voice cracked, but only for a second before he regained his composure and flashed a friendly grin.

"Do you want to get up, maybe walk in the hall?" Jessie asked.

"Not yet, but how about a back rub?"

This is a damn ICU, she wanted to shout, *not a massage parlor.* She caught herself and forced a smile. "Let me see what I can do." She backed out of his room and went in search of Ellen.

"What did everyone else do about the back-rub request?"

Ellen chuckled. "Tell him we're out of lotions, and the gloves you'd have to wear will only irritate his skin."

Jessie nodded and headed for the break room where she poured herself a second cup of coffee, and nibbled on her muffin. When enough time had passed, she went back to Hart's room and, suppressing the smile that threatened to break through, she repeated what Ellen had suggested.

"I'll have to have someone bring lotion in, I guess," he said.

"Well, maybe you'll just be discharged," Jessie replied. "You don't really need to be here."

He frowned. She could have kicked herself. She'd gone too far. Again.

He shook his head. "No one understands what I've been through. I'm just not ready to go home. To go anywhere."

Jessie forced herself to keep her mouth shut. She only nodded in reply. Assuming that her nod was a sign of understanding, Hart continued. "I've lost my wife. We were planning a future together. I'm just lost." His tone was flat, his face expressionless. He did not look or sound like a grieving man should, not that she'd really know what a grieving man should look like. Still, there was something not quite right about Rob Hart.

"I'll see if I can find some lotion," she said, though she had no intention of looking for lotion or anything else.

"Thank you, Jessie. You're really very sweet."

What the hell was she supposed to say to that? She retreated to the nursing station, where she pulled up his chart again and scrolled through his past medical history. There must be a psychiatric diagnosis in there somewhere. His medical history was pretty benign: appendectomy, ear infections, and then she reached the final entry, dated two years earlier. *VASECTOMY—patient had no complications.*

A chill ran up her back. After she'd discussed it with Sam, she'd somehow forgotten about Ann Hart's pregnancy. She took a long, deep breath. There were just too many strange twists to this story.

She stood up straight, willed herself to be calm and walked back to his room.

He was sitting in a chair by his bed, a plush robe draped over his shoulders, the picture of relaxation, despite the fact that his wife was across the street lying on a cold, hard slab in the morgue.

"Anything else you need?" she asked, hoping to draw him out, to learn something, anything, about that night.

He smiled. "Just sit with me." He patted his bed. Jessie pulled a plastic chair up instead and sank down.

"It must be hard. Losing everything so unexpectedly. Do you want to talk?"

"Aside from the police, you're the first one to ask me if I want to talk about it. The truth is, I'm not sure talking will help."

"It might," she said, a false worry in her voice. He was silent. This wasn't going to be easy. "Tell me about her, your wife. What was she like?"

He sighed. "She was the love of my life," he said. "She made every day better. I'm not sure what I'll do without her."

Jessie sat silently. She wasn't sure what she'd expected him to say. He hadn't described her at all—just his own feelings. He was the center of this drama, not his wife. On the other hand, she hadn't expected this—the soft tone, the loving words. Maybe she was wrong after all. God knew, she'd never been a great judge where men were concerned. She reached out and gripped his hand. "It must be hard."

He squeezed back and flashed a tentative smile. "Knowing there are women like you out there gives me hope for my future."

What the hell? Just when she thought she might be wrong. Why weren't the police looking at him? She wanted to dig deeper, but that wasn't her job. She was supposed to provide nursing care—nothing more, nothing less. But didn't she have a duty to his wife as well? She cleared her throat and pulled her hand away. "Do you have any children?" she asked.

His eyes seemed to glaze over and he shook his head. "We never wanted children. I guess it's for the best now. I don't think I could raise a child by myself."

"Did you know…?" She paused, not sure she could ask about the pregnancy, but he must have known. "Never mind. It's none of my business."

"I'm your patient. Ask whatever you'd like."

Right, she thought, *and then I'll be fired for sure. Violating HIPAA once again.* She shook her head, changing her tactic. "Is it hard for you to think about that night?"

"I don't think about it," he said. "It's behind me now."

CHAPTER ELEVEN

The day dragged. Hart was a royal pain. Jessie forced herself to hold her tongue and to smile when she really wanted to scream. Just before three—as she was getting ready to hand Hart off to the evening nurse—the mayor, clad in a black overcoat which barely hid his bulk, and his entourage appeared, all looking solemn and dour. They went into Hart's room, closing the door behind them. *This is it*, she thought. *They're closing in*. But where were the police? Where was Sam? As if he'd heard her, he appeared as well.

"Hey, you," he said, stopping at the nursing station. "How's it going up here?"

She shrugged. "I'm doing my time. How about this case?" She nudged her head towards Hart's room.

"We have a suspect that we're looking at. The DA likes him, the rest of us aren't sure yet. We'll be announcing it outside. The mayor just wanted to speak to Hart first, make sure he knows we're close."

"Who is it?" she whispered. "Is Hart involved?"

"You're still suspicious of him?"

"Yes. He's my patient today. I'm pretty sure he's involved."

He raised a brow. "Really? Tell you what. I'll call you after the announcement. Dinner?"

She smiled. "I'd like that."

She watched through the window as the group spoke to Hart, his face an unreadable mask as they gave him their news. She turned away, gave report to the evening nurse, retrieved her jacket and keys and headed for the garage.

She arrived home just in time to click on her television and watch the early news. The mayor spoke first, thanking the police for their hard work and inviting the police commissioner and Sam to the microphone. The commissioner revealed the suspect was one Jose Ramos, a twenty-five-year-old Salvadoran and a member of MS-13, the most dangerous gang in the world.

Sam stepped forward next. "He has a long rap sheet, including an active warrant for the murder of a young man in Lawrence, which is less than thirty miles north, last year. He has the tattoos on his face and right hand which Rob Hart noted."

A hand shot up in the crowd of journalists. "But how does that get you to Jose Ramos? Surely there are others that fit the description?"

Sam nodded. "We haven't released the description of those tattoos but the details of those really narrowed it down for us. That's all we can say right now. If anyone knows of the suspect's whereabouts, please do not approach him. Please call the Boston Police." A number flashed on the screen. "Our call line is anonymous. Thank you for your help."

The report ended and Jessie jumped into the shower. Tomorrow was Saturday. She was hoping to be back in the ER in a few days. Things could only improve. Sam called and offered to pick her up. "I'll never find a spot, so I'll call when I'm close."

She pulled on a suede pencil skirt, a pair of boots, a slinky buttoned sweater, and her soft-as-butter black leather jacket. If she looked good, she'd feel more courageous about sharing her thoughts on Hart. When Sam called, she grabbed her purse and her keys, locked her door and raced down the stairs. His car, a police-issue black Crown Victoria, idled at the curb. He beeped and waved and opened the door. "You look great! How about the North End?"

"Sounds perfect," she said, taking in the dashboard computer, radio handset, Bluetooth phone and GPS. His suit jacket, badge and gun rested on the backseat. "This car is pretty impressive."

"It is, isn't it? I'm on call tonight, but I'm hoping things stay quiet."

"Don't you think there'll be a lot of calls after your press conference?"

"There will be, but most will be junk calls and texts. Still, they'll all have to be checked. We'll sift through them and my team will have a second look at the most promising."

"So, you won't be the one to go through them?"

"Not at first. Too many for one person. And we are pretty sure this guy is the one. So, you saw the announcement?"

"I did. Did you speak to Hart?"

He nodded as he navigated the backstreets to the North End. "I did. He's not much of a talker, though, but you gotta give the guy a break. I mean, he's been through so much."

Jessie grunted. "Have you looked at his medical records?"

He nodded again.

"And you saw the description of his gunshot wound?"

"I have. Are we going to go over this again?"

"Just listen to me, that's all I ask." And she recounted again Hart's attitude regarding his wife, first in the ER, and then in the ICU. "He's just too calm. He told me he's looking to the future and not to the past."

"Being a jerk doesn't make him a killer."

"What about his gunshot wound? Pretty benign. He could have done that himself, you know."

He shook his head vigorously. "We did consider that, but Dr. Merrick says that although it's possible to shoot yourself there, he thinks it would take an experienced gunman. And he should know—he served in a couple of war zones. I served in the Marines in Afghanistan, and I tend to agree with him, but I'll take it a step further. As someone very familiar with guns, I think there's no way that wound is self-inflicted."

This time, Jessie shook her head. "It absolutely can be self-inflicted. I'll show you!"

The car swerved as he slowed and pulled to the curb. "What the hell do you mean? Do you have a gun?" A trace of anger flashed in his eyes.

"No, calm down, I don't have a gun." She twisted in her seat and held her hand against her right side at the area where Hart suffered his wound. "See. It's easy to hold something—including a gun—right there and press the trigger. Merrick is wrong about this. He gets up on his high horse about one thing or another and no one has the courage to disagree with him. Well, I disagree. Just say you'll look into this."

"We are looking into that, believe me, and we'll continue to, but remember he might just have been lucky."

"No one's that lucky. No one. And a shot missed him as he fell? I agree with her family. None of it makes sense. None of it."

"OK, so where's the gun, the wallet, his phone? They've disappeared. You think he committed the crime, raced to a dumpster, got rid of the evidence and went back to call nine-one-one? We have looked at that. There's just no evidence right now to support Hart as the shooter. That doesn't mean we've cleared him—it means we have no evidence that it was him. And ultimately, that is what the DA needs."

"When you say it that way, it does sound absurd, but I don't trust him. I think he was involved. I don't know how. But I'm sure of it."

"I promise we searched all the nearby dumpsters and trash cans and alleys. We searched the whole area and came up empty. The shooter has Hart's stuff. When we find him, I think we'll find it all."

She hugged her arms around herself and sank further into her seat. "I know I'm not trained in this, but I know I'm right." She could see it in his eyes and hear it in his voice; he was convinced there was a bad guy out there. She was equally convinced the bad guy was in the ICU.

Sam pulled back into traffic and placed his hand on hers. "I understand that you believe this, Jessie. I do. There's just no proof of that, no motive, and the fact is when husbands kill wives, it's usually in a moment rage. None of that is here. None of it. He'd just bought her flowers. How many men do that before shooting a wife?"

She shrugged. "There's one more thing, though, and since you have access to his medical records, you've probably seen it, so I'm not violating HIPAA. He's had a vasectomy."

"Yeah? Him and about a million other guys."

"His wife was pregnant."

"I remember. When was his vasectomy?"

"Two years ago."

"But couldn't they have that fixed? Reconnected, whatever you call it?"

"It would be in his chart."

"Hmm. Well, that's interesting."

"It's more than interesting, don't you think? It's a motive. She's pregnant. He's not the father."

"Hmm," he said again. "I'll have a look at his chart, talk to him. See what he says. He may not have known about this, especially if he's not the father."

"He lived with her. Men know women's cycles. He had to know."

"Okay, okay. I get it."

Jessie finally relaxed. "Sorry for bombarding you. Maybe I watch too much *CSI.*"

"Maybe." He grinned. "Your comments got me wondering, though. Are you married?" Sam asked as he turned down a side street, his gaze shifting back to the road.

"No, you?"

He shook his head and shot her a grin. "We probably should have gotten that out of the way that first night."

Sam slid the car into an open spot in a dark alley in the North End, a historic neighborhood not unlike Southie with closely clustered old brick buildings, but here the sidewalks were lined by Italian pastry shops and old men sitting in lawn chairs. Though the area had been gentrified a bit, as had almost every other part of Boston, the feel of the North End, not to mention the scents of simmering spices and sugary treats, made it all feel old world and comfortable, as welcoming as any small town might be.

Sam led her around the corner, and stopped in front of what looked like an apartment house, but tucked into the first floor was the restaurant. "This place is Mother Anna's. Ever eaten here?"

She shook her head.

"You'll love it. Best Italian food you'll ever eat." Sam slipped his arms into his jacket and retrieved his gun and badge, clipping both onto his belt. They made their way inside, the brick walls and dark wood tables as inviting as the scents—garlic, oregano, and aromatic spices—all mingling in the air.

"Hey, Sam, long time no see. How are you?" The speaker, a heavy, balding, bespectacled man, approached them and drew Sam into a quick embrace.

"Hey, Vinnie, good to see you. My friend and I are here for dinner. Got a table for us?"

"Your friend is pretty, Sam," he said, glancing at Jessie. "Too pretty for you."

Sam introduced Jessie, who held out her hand. Vinnie leaned in and kissed her once on each cheek. "We kiss beautiful women when we meet. Handshakes are for old men, like Sam." He led them to a table in the back. "I always keep one table open for special visitors. He handed them menus. "Enjoy yourselves."

Over a dinner of pasta, shrimp and veal soaked in rich sauces, as well as crusty bread loaded with butter, all washed down with red wine, they began to reveal a bit of themselves. Sam loosened his tie as he spoke. "I sometimes wish I'd married, and God knows my mother wishes I would. There's still time, but this is a tough job for families, and I suppose that's what holds me back. More than half the cops I know are divorced. Makes it a big decision. I've been close once or twice, but, well… I'm still looking." He winked. "What about you? Why aren't you married? Seems like you're the type to have had a few offers."

She dabbed her mouth with the crisp white napkin. "Engaged once," she said, and it all came flooding back. *What's-his-name*, as she called him these days, since she'd vowed never to say his name aloud or even to think it, had left her for her best friend. Jessie, who'd loved him and was longing to belong to him, to be a part of his life, was broken. "I met him after my father died. My mother left when I was a baby, so it had always been just my dad and me. I have no other family, so I was well and truly all alone. I fell for his promises that he'd love me forever."

She paused, remembering the feel of his arms when they were wrapped around her. Looking back, she knew part of why she'd loved him was her desperate need to free herself of her loneliness. But that was three years ago, a lifetime almost. She was long over him, and it was best never to think of him again. "And then he cheated on me. With my then best friend." She said it with an uncharacteristic sneer. "So, that was the end of a friendship and an engagement."

"Ooh, that must have hurt." Sam took her hand across the table. "I had no idea you had no family. I'm sorry, Jessie."

Jessie shrugged. "No need to be sorry. I'm fine with it now. Really, I'm okay." She pulled her hand away. The last thing she needed was sympathy. "Anyway, it was better to find out that he was a totally self-absorbed loser before, rather than after, the wedding. To tell you the truth, I think it was harder to lose my friend than it was to lose him. I haven't had a really close friend since then. It's difficult to trust people. I guess that's why I'm suspicious of Hart, too. No one's as good as they seem at first glance."

"Oh hell, we're back to him."

"No, no," she said. "We're not. As long as you keep an open mind on Hart, I'll keep an open mind on everything else."

"Everything else?"

She flashed her most mischievous smile.

"Oh, God, Jessie. I wish I weren't on call tonight."

"Well, you are, and I'm back to work at seven, so we'll have to call it a night."

Once home, he walked her to her door and leaned down to brush his lips softly against hers. When he smoothed her hair behind her ear, she swore she felt her toes tingle and her heart race.

"I'll call tomorrow," he said as he turned for the stairs.

CHAPTER TWELVE

Jessie was relieved to find that the lock on her door was secure. She let herself in, washed up and peered through her blinds onto the street. The streetlamp was still out, but at least there was no one lurking outside. Feeling safe and exhausted, she slid into bed and drifted off to sleep.

She felt like she'd been asleep for only moments when a shrill blare broke the still of the night. She sat bolt upright, sweeping away the threads of her dream, the noise coming again and again. She rubbed her eyes and spotted her phone, the source of the insistent sound. A call in the night is never good.

That was how she'd learned her father had died. "Quietly," the nurse had said. "In his sleep." And though it had been expected since his stroke, the news had almost broken her. Without him, she was alone. Her mother had long ago just up and left, leaving Jessie with only a vague memory of a laughing woman with bright clothes, dark hair and dimples. Her dad had been perpetually angry but somehow stoic, and always there, but he was gone, and there wasn't anybody else in her life right now, so whatever this call was, *how bad could it be?*

She reached for the phone and hit *accept*. "Hello," she said drowsily.

"Oh, shit. You were sleeping. Sorry, Jess, I thought you'd be just getting in from work."

The voice, at once so familiar and yet so strange, caught her off guard. She swung her legs over the side of the bed. "Who…?"

"Nick. I looked for you in the ER tonight. Thought I'd try to catch you for that drink."

"Ahh, I knew your voice sounded familiar. What time is it?" Her voice was thick with sleep, the synapses of her brain not quite connecting.

"It's after midnight."

She'd only just gotten in, it seemed. "I'm on days for a while. I have to be in at seven."

"Why are you on days?"

"It's a long story. I'll tell you all about it another time."

"How about tomorrow?"

"Sure. Call me then." She hung up, curled back under the covers and woke only when the alarm shrieked in her ear. She rose quickly and went through her new morning routine—find clean scrubs, pull up her hair, splash water on her face, run a hint of liner along her eyes and a swipe of color on her lips—and she was ready to go. She stopped at the corner store for coffee and a muffin and was grateful that Patrick wasn't there to gush over her again. She glanced at the headlines—*Funeral Details for Hart to Be Announced Today*. A smiling photo of Ann Hart filled the first page. Jessie shivered. She felt as though Ann Hart was looking straight at her. She turned away, but the discomfort stuck with her. It was almost as though Ann Hart was drawing her in, asking for something.

At work, she was directed once again to the Surgical ICU, and she walked in crossing her fingers that Rob Hart would have been discharged or at least transferred to the floor, but as soon as she stepped through the door, she saw him, through the glass of his room, curled up on his side sleeping the sleep of the innocent, or, in his case, the guilty.

She spied Ellen at the desk. "Please tell me he's assigned to someone else."

"I wish I could," Ellen replied, trying to hide the smile on her lips. "But he requested you."

"What the hell?"

"That's what we said, but in a different, lighter tone of voice."

"Very funny. I can't refuse?"

"No. Merrick says he's been through a tough time, and to just give him whatever he needs. At least for now. He actually said that Hart reminds him of a young soldier he couldn't save in Afghanistan, so apparently, based on that, Hart gets a pass." She shook her head. "Who knew that Merrick has a heart? Unbelievable, but true."

Jessie mumbled as she put her things away, swigged her coffee, picked at her muffin and took report from the night nurse who was happy to announce that Rob Hart had slept through the night. She hadn't heard so much as a peep from him, which likely meant, she told Jessie, that he'd be wide awake and looking for company all day.

"Why doesn't he get visitors? Why do we have to entertain him?"

"He's announced that he doesn't want visitors. Not yet."

"Morning, Jessie," Rob said, pulling himself up as she stepped into his room.

"Morning, Rob," she said, stonily turning on the bright overhead lights. He blinked and turned away. It was juvenile of her, but at least she'd made him uncomfortable, if only for a moment. One small victory at a time. "How about we get your vital signs and then I'll leave you alone?"

He nodded and held out his arm.

She hit the blood pressure button and watched him wince as the cuff tightened against his arm. "Would you like me to call some friends in for you?"

"No. I don't want to see anyone."

"You must be tired of answering the same old questions from the police, huh?"

"Not really. I spoke to them that night in the ER and then the next morning, when I remembered the tattoos, and maybe once or twice again. They came in with the mayor to tell me they have a suspect, but since then, no, I haven't seen them. I asked Dr. Merrick to tell them I need rest, and anyway, it all happened so quickly, there's just nothing else I can add. I don't much feel like visitors either."

"I'll leave you alone then."

"Please stay for a while. Tell me about yourself."

Jessie made it a point to never share personal stuff with patients. She shook her head. "Not much to tell."

"I bet there's lots to tell. Are you married?"

"No."

"A beautiful girl like you. Come on." He flashed what could only be described as a flirtatious grin.

She wanted to tell him to screw off, that she knew he was a creep, but she couldn't. She backed out of the room, telling him she had another patient. She didn't have another assignment, but she couldn't bear to be near this jerk. And in her mind, he'd been involved in his wife's murder. If she could figure out a way to expose that, she would, but in the meantime, just as Sam said—it wasn't a crime to be a jerk.

She stretched her neck this way and that, hoping to ease the knot of tension that had settled there. It was Saturday, five days since the shooting, two days since Ann Hart's death, and Jessie couldn't figure out why this case had stuck with her the way it had. She'd cared for hundreds of shooting and stabbing victims, some she remembered, most she forgot. That was how ER nurses and staff dealt with the tragic incidents they encountered, but she couldn't let this one go. It didn't help that she had to see Rob Hart up close. If anything, that compelled her even more. She was no detective, though like most ER nurses, she fancied herself one, though she had to admit it was a bit of a stretch to go from triaging confusing symptoms to solving crimes. But this time, she felt as though she was seeing what the police were missing.

Jesus. She had to stop thinking about this.

Or convince Sam to listen to her just one more time.

CHAPTER THIRTEEN

She spent her day avoiding Hart. She volunteered to accompany an intubated patient, who was hooked up to three infusion pumps and two fancy monitors, to CT scan. That killed two hours. She mixed antibiotics and the blood thinner heparin for another nurse, flushed an arterial line and finally looked back in on Hart, who smiled broadly.

"Hey, you," he crooned. "Where've ya been?"

She wished he'd stop speaking. That might allow her to be a little less suspicious, but clearly, he was well aware of HIPAA. He knew she couldn't talk about his frisky, flirtatious ways. "Busy," she said. "This is an ICU. Most people are very sick. You're the exception."

"You don't think I should be here, do you?"

Oh, Jesus, don't let me be fired for what I'm about to say, she thought. "No. Same as yesterday—you don't need intensive care."

"I do," he said. "Just not the way you think. I need the safety this space provides me. I don't mean to be a burden."

And she almost felt sorry for him, but he was smiling again, that sappy, sweet, flirty smile that made her sick to her stomach and knocked some sense back into her. That's how men like him got away with things. "You're not," she said, hoping to salvage her job. "You're really not."

She took an hour for lunch and then covered another nurse's patients so she could have lunch, and finally her shift was over. She gave report on Hart and poked her head in to tell him she was leaving. He held his newspaper up. "Have you seen this?" Funeral arrangements were set for Monday, two days from now, she read. "They never even told me. I had to read it here." He passed the paper to Jessie.

She glanced through the story quickly. A Mass would be held at the Cathedral. Burial would be private, but friends and family were invited to attend the celebration of Ann's life. She handed the paper back. "You'll be going?"

He shook his head. "I'm not strong enough."

"Yes, you are," Jessie blurted before she could stop herself. "But of course, it's up to you."

"Her family never liked me. I'm sure they blame me for Ann's death. I heard them shouting the day she died that it was all my fault. They're not very sympathetic to me. I mean, I know that when a wife is killed, police look first at the husband, but I'm a victim here, too. They've forgotten that." He paused and took a deep breath. "I have my own wounds to heal, and anyway, I think I'd be a distraction. To tell you the truth, I just don't want to do that to Ann, or to myself."

Jessie wanted to scream. He'd made himself the center of this drama, not Ann. He was a sociopath. *Why couldn't the police see through him?* "Don't you want to say goodbye?" she asked, hoping he'd take the bait and say something, anything, that she could take to Sam.

"I did," he answered. "That night in the alley."

Jessie felt the blood drain from her face. She hadn't expected this. "That night? You knew she was dying?" she asked, her voice cracking.

"Well, no… not exactly." His voice was a whisper as though he'd caught himself saying more than he'd intended. "It seemed pretty clear to me that she probably was. That's all I meant." He looked away; it was as though he'd drawn a curtain. The conversation was over.

There was nothing she could say to that. "Maybe I'll see you tomorrow," Jessie said.

That evening, the nightly news reported that an insider had divulged to the Associated Press that Hart would not be attending his wife's funeral. Jessie sat forward, her jaw tight. "The Associated Press added that Mr. Hart is too ill to attend. He will be sending his love, and if he has the strength, a final note to his dear wife." The announcer cut back to the reporter who was again in front of the hospital. "The police and the mayor's office have said they are still searching for the prime suspect—Jose Ramos. If you have any information at all, they are asking that you call the number scrolling at the bottom of your screen."

She clicked the television off. "What the hell? Bert said he was leaving! How the hell did he learn this? And a note to his wife? Hart never mentioned any note." She shook her head in disgust just as her doorbell chimed. "What?" she shouted into the small receiver.

"It's Nick. We have a date?"

She buzzed him in, and laughing, she pulled the door open before he could knock. "I'm so sorry. It's just that... Never mind."

Nick stood there quietly, his blue eyes focused on her, his shoulders—usually so strong and sturdy—sagged just enough to notice. "You forgot, didn't you?" His gaze dropped away; those shimmery blue eyes suddenly hidden under a fringe of thick brown lashes.

Jessie nodded. "But your timing is perfect. I'd love to get out, away from the news, and if you give me five minutes, I'll change. Beer and wine in the fridge," she called over her shoulder as she looked through her closet. She stepped out of her sweats, pulled on a pair of jeans, a turtleneck sweater and a pair of leather boots. She ran her fingers through her hair, swiped on a coat of mascara and grabbed her jacket.

"Ready," she announced.

Nick turned and whistled as he caught sight of her. "On second thought, let's stay in."

"Another time," Jessie answered. "Tonight, I need dinner and someone to talk to."

He stood, all six feet four of him towering over her five feet three. His hand on her chin, he nudged her face up to his until his lips found hers and lingered there with the softest, gentlest yet most insistent kiss she could ever remember. She let herself sink into his arms. When she could pull herself away, she traced the lines of his jaw with her finger. "But feed me first," she whispered.

"Where to?"

"Anyplace that's quiet and has good food."

They wound up at the Playwright, a popular pub within walking distance of Jessie's. The afternoon football games were over, the rowdy crowds spilling into the street as they approached. It was early Saturday evening, that quiet time before the dinner crowds arrived, leaving the place almost entirely to Nick and Jessie.

They chose a quiet corner booth, and ordered dinner and beer. Even in the dim light of the pub, or maybe because of it, the penetrating blue of Nick's eyes bore into her. She felt her heart race and she reminded herself again that he was exactly the kind of guy she should fall for. And what was not to like? He had it all—good looks, good job, a quiet confidence, and if that weren't enough, there were always his eyes. *Paul Newman eyes*, Donna had said once when she'd seen him in the ER.

Nick tipped his mug against hers. "To more evenings like this," he said, his eyes flashing seductively. Or maybe she was just reading that into this moment.

"So, tell me," he said, "what's going on? You seem so jumpy."

"You're sure you want to hear this?"

He nodded. She leaned into her seat back. "It started the night of the shooting."

"The Harts?" He seemed to stiffen as he leaned forward.

"Yes. That whole thing is just so strange, but there's more, stuff that affects me directly." She told him about the feeling that someone was watching her, the intermittent trouble with her unreliable lock, the odd disappearance of her schedule, the news report that supposedly came from a nurse.

"That was you?"

"No. It wasn't me, or anyone else, but I was blamed because I knew the reporter."

"Who is this guy?"

Over steak tips and mashed potatoes, she told him about Bert, and his penchant for lying, this time about her. "I've been banished to working days in the ICU, which is why I wasn't in the ER when you were looking for me. Tonight, there's another AP story in the news. I can't seem to win."

Nick's eyes shimmered in the dim light. "That reporter again?"

"Probably. I haven't seen the newspaper yet, but I'd bet it's him." She shrugged. And as she considered the events of the last few days, she wondered if maybe they were connected—if Bert was watching her, if he'd gotten into her apartment somehow. She shivered at the thought and quickly dismissed it. He was a creep, but not that kind of creep. "Not much I can do about it except hope my manager doesn't see it."

"She's still there?" Nick had met her once when he'd run into Jessie in the ER when he'd escorted a prisoner who'd needed stitches. As they'd stood in the hallway chatting, Sheila approached. "Socialize on your own time," she'd warned Jessie, who'd rolled her eyes and told Nick she'd see him later.

"Why can't they get rid of her?" he asked.

"She comes to work, our numbers are good, and they're too lazy to look for someone else. She and Bert have combined to make my life miserable. I just wish I could make them both go away."

"Really?" he asked, his forehead crinkling.

She shook her head. "No, just wishful thinking."

Nick laughed, his eyes suddenly twinkling. "So, on to other things. How is the ICU?"

"As if being there on days isn't bad enough, I've been assigned to Hart. The final nail in my coffin."

"That's why you're spending time with that detective?"

"Huh?" Jessie asked, a forkful of potatoes halfway to her mouth. How would he know that? "I…" She swallowed her food, wondering what to say.

"I saw you speaking with him at the hospital, that's all," Nick said hurriedly as if to answer the question that hung in the air between them. "I figured he was asking about the Harts."

"You should have stopped to say hello."

"I know you're busy. I was, too. Next time I'll be sure to stop, as long as that manager isn't around. But while we're on the subject, did he say if there's anything new with the Hart investigation?"

"No. Nothing that hasn't been on the news."

"Hmm," he muttered, taking a long draw of his beer.

They chatted about the weather, the upcoming holidays, her runs by Castle Island.

"I should start jogging again myself," Nick said, running his fingers through his thick brown hair. "I haven't been working out much lately. Maybe I can run with you sometime."

"I'd like that. I'm hoping that I'm back in the ER on evenings this week. I'll have more time to run in the morning. I just hate working days." She glanced at her watch. "And since I'm on tomorrow, I'll have to be home soon."

Nick pulled his chair closer and leaned in. "Let's do this again then. Soon. And I want you to know I've been transferred to South Boston, so I'm nearby all the time. If you're nervous, just call me. Don't even bother with nine-one-one. Just call me. I think you know I like you, Jess. A lot. I'll always look out for you." He kissed her then, a gentle graze along her lips, the softness of his lips rich with the promise of more. Much more.

And for the first time since the shootings, Jessie felt every muscle in her body relax. Nick had a calming effect on her. She smiled and kissed him back, this one deeper, more intense. Finally, she pulled away. "Walk me home?"

At her door, Nick checked the lock, which seemed secure, and kissed her goodnight. "Want me to come in?" he asked. "Have a look around?"

She smiled. "If I let you in, I'll never let you out."

He waited until she stepped inside and locked her door before he bounded down the stairs, his footfalls echoing in the hall. From the other side of the door, Jessie listened as the entryway door banged shut, and then there was only silence. She leaned against the door and sighed. He was exactly the type of guy she needed. Much as she liked Sam, he was older, still single and seemed happy that way. Nick was young, eager and definitely into her. She smiled to herself. It was Nick she needed. It was Nick she wanted. Which was probably why it would never work out.

CHAPTER FOURTEEN

Sunday mornings offered an easy commute. It always seemed that everyone was off on Sunday, and that made finding a parking spot outside the hospital easy, too. Jessie slid into a spot by the ER and cut through the ambulance bay into the Trauma hallway. The back elevators were her destination but she lingered for a moment by the trauma rooms, one of which had clearly just emptied, the floor littered with the debris of one more life in the balance.

"Hey, Jess," Elena called, her arms laden with IV bags. "Are you back?"

"Not yet. I'm still in the ICU. Just taking a short-cut to the back elevators."

Elena shrugged. "Well, we need you. We're so short-staffed, Sheila's forcing us to do mandatory overtime. We're pretty fed up."

"You know I'd be here if I could be. You have no idea how much I miss this place."

"This place misses you." She nodded towards the mess in the trauma room. "Gotta get this mess cleaned up and restocked," she said, disappearing into the room.

"See you," Jessie muttered to the air. In the ICU, she was assigned to Hart again, but luck was with her. She was also assigned to the trauma victim who'd just left the ER—a fifty-four-year-old man who'd been assaulted. He'd been beaten with a bat, and had bruising around his skull, abdomen and back. The charge nurse gave her report. "Head CT's negative but he was confused in the ER. Belly CT showed a retroperitoneal bleed, but he's clotted it off; his hemoglobin is stable at ten so we're waiting for Merrick to come in. He's intubated, typed and crossed, and sedated with a Propofol drip. He's stable. For now." She handed a stack of paperwork to Jessie. "And Hart is fine. Maybe you can ask Merrick to move him out of here."

"Yeah, right. Like I might ever."

Jessie read the notes on her new patient, checked his IVs, vital signs and ventilator settings before poking her head into Hart's room. "Morning," she said. "Listen, I have…" She was about to say he'd see very little of her today, but he interrupted her before she could continue.

"Jess, good morning." He sat up straighter in bed, fluffing his own pillow behind him. "I'm so glad you're here. I need your help." He held up a pen and notebook. "I want to write something for the service tomorrow. Can you help?"

"Not today," Jessie said. "I have another patient. He's critical, so I'll be poking in only every now and then."

Hart's face crumpled. "I was hoping… Never mind then. It sounds selfish."

Yeah, not to mention creepy, Jessie thought as she flashed an insincere smile. "Maybe later." She ducked back out and spent the next three hours with her trauma patient.

At ten-thirty, Merrick and his band of residents appeared. A resident recited the patient's vital signs and results of the CT. Merrick pulled the sheet away and examined the patient's abdomen. "Any thoughts?" he said to the group, who remained silent, feet shuffling in place.

Jessie stepped to the bedside. "Your residents don't have the latest information, so I'll just tell you his hemoglobin's dropping, and his abdominal girth has increased. You can see for yourself how tense it is."

Merrick's eyes swung from Jessie to the small group of residents. "Next time, I'd like one of you to have that information." They seemed to shrink away from him. "Thanks, Jessie. Think you want to stay here in the ICU?"

She shook her head. "Hell, no. I want to get back to the ER where I belong."

"Well, we'll see what we can do about that. In the meantime, is he typed and crossed? I want to get him to the OR within the hour."

"He's typed and crossed for five. I'll call the blood bank and ask them to make sure they're available."

Merrick turned and headed for the door, his band of not-so-merry men right on his heels.

Jessie checked her patient's vital signs again, called the blood bank and asked that the first three units of packed cells be sent to the OR, and then rechecked his hemoglobin with a simple pinprick. It was still dropping. She drew blood from his IV directly into a small blood tube, bagged it and sent it to the lab to confirm the numbers.

Twenty minutes later, the resident reappeared. "I'm going to take him to the OR." He wiped a bead of sweat from his pasty brow and began to transfer the patient's wires and tubes to portable equipment for the trip to the OR.

"Tough day?" she asked, stepping in to help.

He nodded.

"You'll get used to him. He just wants you to prove yourself. When you get to the OR, tell him you just rechecked his hemoglobin and it's six-point-five. Tell him the blood bank is sending the first three units to the OR. Got it?"

A little color seemed to return to his face. "Thanks." He peered at her nametag. "Jessie Novak. Thanks, Jessie. I owe you."

She helped him guide the gurney to the elevator, and then they were gone. She stretched, trying to work the kink from her back. Unless she was assigned a new patient, she'd have to go back to check on Hart. She heaved a sigh and strode into the ICU. There seemed no way to avoid him. His room was still across from the nursing station.

"Hey, Jess," he called as she tried to slide by. "Got a minute?"

"Oh, please God," she mumbled, "get me back to the ER where no one knows my name." She paused just outside his door. "I just need to get ready to get another patient," she lied. "And then I'll be back."

He sank back into his pillows and smiled.

Jessie went through her trauma patient's room. He likely wouldn't be back until she was off duty. She'd just have to suck it up and go in to see Hart. "Sorry that I haven't been able to see you today," she said. "Let's check your vital signs and see how you're doing." She already knew how he was but she had to play this game.

"Have a seat," he directed her once she'd recorded his numbers. "Like I said before, I want to write something for the service. Can you help?"

She shook her head. "I don't have any idea what you should write."

"I don't either, but I'd like to say something."

"So, you're going to the funeral?"

"No. I'm going to see if the mayor will read it for me."

"No close friends or relatives who could do it? I mean, having a politician read it makes it... I don't know... strange?"

"I don't have any really close friends, just work friends and acquaintances, and the mayor has been so good to me. Ann always liked him. I think she'd be happy about that."

She'd be happy, Jessie thought, *if her creepy husband just showed up at her funeral.* "Well, then, try to write something."

"You think I should?" A shadow seemed to pass over his eyes.

"I don't think anything. This is your call. Not mine." His face was a mask once again. He seemed to have two expressions: flirty smiles and blank, empty stares—the police, she was sure, read those stares as grief, or quiet stoicism. Jessie thought they seemed more like restrained relief. He was trying to hide his real feelings. But no one would believe her wild imaginings, so she might as well forget it. She smiled weakly and nodded before standing and smoothing the creases from her scrubs. A smile draped his lips. He was about to speak, to ask another favor, so she rushed ahead. "Listen, since you're all set here, I'm going to get myself some coffee, and help the other nurses with their patients."

His smile faded. Again.

"I'll be back," she said cheerily. She found her way to the break room where she poured herself a cup of coffee, grabbed a stale donut and sank into a chair. Today couldn't be over fast enough.

Her phone buzzed with an incoming text. She pulled it from her pocket and read. Sam was asking if she was off tomorrow and if so, was she interested in going to the funeral. He explained:

Odd request, but sometimes the bad guys show up. Thought it might help you to be there. See things for yourself.

Hell, yes! Call me later.

She might not choose as Sam as a boyfriend, and maybe he wasn't entirely interested in that either, but she definitely wanted him as a friend even if he was just humoring her with his investigative expertise. She stuffed her phone back into her pocket and headed back to work. Hart seemed subdued when she poked her head back in. "I think Merrick's going to discharge me the day after Ann's funeral," he said, sweat trickling along his forehead.

"That's good news, isn't it?"

"No. I'm not sure where I'll go. I don't want to go home, not yet anyway. A friend called and said he'd clear Ann's things out for me, but he can't do that until later in the week." He looked away, seeming sadder than she'd seen him.

"Can't you stay at your friend's?"

"I don't want to be around people. Maybe I'll just go to a hotel."

"That's a good idea." Jessie wasn't sure what he'd expected her to say but he was clearly disappointed with the plan to discharge him. She almost told him she'd be off the next two days and wouldn't see him again, but she didn't want to invite any more personal or weirdly flirty questions.

The rest of the day flew. She started an IV for another patient, hung a bag of platelets, bagged a patient who was being intubated, and stopped to check on Hart who was curled under his covers sound asleep, and before she knew it, she was giving report on Hart and her patient who was still in the OR.

At the desk, her phone buzzed again. She excused herself and stepped into the lounge expecting another message from Sam. Instead, the text was from Bert.

I need to speak with you. Please call me at this number. It's IMPORTANT! Bert

She shook her head. He was still at it, trying to create more problems for her. He'd show the call thread to Sheila, and she'd be on the hot seat once more. "Screw you, Bert Gibbons," she mumbled as she deleted his text and blocked his number.

CHAPTER FIFTEEN

Jessie headed home, stopping briefly to stock up on essentials: wine, coffee, eggs, bread, chips, frozen meals, and Diet Coke. By the time she turned onto K Street, the orange glow of dusk had slipped away, replaced by the deepening shadows of night. The streetlamp in front of her apartment was still in darkness. She'd have to remind herself to tell someone about that. She found a spot close by, unloaded her car, and lugged her bags to her building.

At her door, she set her bags down and as she fished for her key, one of her bags fell over, the contents spilling down the stairs. She fumbled with the damn lock, the key jamming, refusing to release the tumbler. She kicked the door and shouted: "Stupid lock." She might as well just pick up her groceries before they rolled to the basement. She ran down the stairs, collecting apples, a bag of now broken cookies and—distracted by her mission—she ran right into the elderly man who occupied the first-floor apartment.

"Whoa," he said, holding out his hands before she could knock him over. "What is it, girl? You look like you're on fire."

She stopped to catch her breath and adjust the apples in her hands before they fell again. "Oh, I'm sorry. I can't get into my apartment. My damn lock is stuck, and now my groceries are everywhere." She caught a rolling orange with her foot. He reached down and picked it up.

"Okay," he said, opening his own door. "I can have a look at that lock for you if you want." He reached in and pulled a heavy metal baseball bat from behind the door. Jessie's eyes widened at the sight. "If you live in the city," he said, "you've got to be ready for anything—a baseball game or a bad guy who's up to no good." He ran his hand—the skin loose, the veins full—along the length of the bat as if checking the weight of it.

Jessie's eyes opened wide. "You're not thinking of breaking the lock open with that, are you?"

He laughed and reached behind the bat. "No, just getting my tool kit." He turned for the stairs, an old tackle box in his hand.

Suddenly, Jessie's frustration evaporated, helped along by her neighbor's reassuring calm. "Wait for me," she said, picking up the last orange, "I'm coming too."

She hurried up the stairs and watched as he squirted a bit of oil into her lock before taking her key and wiggling it to and fro, his hand on the doorknob, a smile on his face as the door swung open. He lifted her last two bags and laid them down inside her apartment.

"Well," he said. "Time for introductions, I guess. I'm Rufus Buchanan..." He narrowed his gaze and chuckled. "I was just waiting for you to say something. Rufus—terrible name for a boy, but just about fine for an old man." He ran his hand over his scalp, flattening the sparse bits of hair that stood up.

She laughed. "Thanks, Rufus. I'm Jessie Novak." She held out her hand. "I'm not usually so skittish."

"But you work over there at Boston City, right?" He gripped her hand tighter than she thought possible, his own so bony and frail.

She nodded.

"Reason enough to be skittish, Jessie. Just be careful." He helped her get her bags into the kitchen and reminded her that he was close by. "I'm right downstairs. If you ever need me, knock or just holler. For anything. Anything at all."

"Thanks, Rufus. Same goes for you." It wasn't lost on her that she'd been here for almost two years, and had never spoken to him; she'd only waved in passing. Never asked how he was, never asked his name. That was the thing about the city, you could live right above someone and never know them. She gave him a quick peck on the cheek, and he smiled.

"Don't forget to lock up behind me," he said, turning for the door.

And she took his advice, turning the lock and slipping the chain into place. She brewed a cup of tea, put her groceries away, stuck a frozen meal into the microwave and settled onto the couch. She needed to get back to her routine. She clicked on the television and, same as every day this week, the shooting was the top story. This time, the news anchor reported that some kids from Hart's youth group were asking to be pallbearers at the funeral. A Facebook photo appeared, showing Hart surrounded by a cluster of teenagers, all smiling. As the photo faded to a weather map, Jessie reached for her iPad.

"Facebook, of course. Everyone's on Facebook." She typed in Robert Hart and followed the links to the Facebook page she'd just seen. He didn't seem to have a private page, just this work-based page that touted his work with minority youth and the city's initiatives to ensure successful futures for these kids. It was hard to argue with that. It seemed as though he did great work. No personal posts or photos, though; not even his wife made it to his page.

She ate her dinner while searching Facebook for Ann Hart, and there she was—smiling, cheerful, and bearing that same striking resemblance to Jessie. Ann had four hundred-plus friends. She'd shared holiday photos of herself and Rob, photos of her students, her family, and her last post—a photo of teachers standing together outside of a school. It was dated just three days before she was shot. Ann was standing next to a young, fresh-faced man whose arm was draped around her shoulder. He was looking, not at the camera, but at Ann. It was all the sadder for its ordinariness. That may have been the last day her co-workers, her friends, saw her. Jessie sighed. Maybe she shouldn't go to the funeral.

While she was pondering that idea, her phone buzzed and she hit *accept*. "Hey, Sam," she said. "About tomorrow…"

"I'll pick you up at ten. The service is at eleven at the Cathedral."

"I don't know if I should go. I mean…"

"They won't even know you're there, and the word is Hart might show up."

"I don't think so," she answered. "He was trying to write a goodbye note to his wife today. He said the mayor's going to read it tomorrow."

"I wouldn't be so sure about that. Seems the mayor's not as enamored with him as we thought."

"Really?"

"Really. I'll see you at ten." And the phone clicked. No goodbye, nothing. But now, her misgivings forgotten, she knew she had to go.

She washed her cup and her fork and curled up on her couch where she fell asleep, waking to the sound of sirens screeching outside her window. She peeked through the blinds but there was nothing to see; the sirens faded, moving to someplace else. She checked her watch. It was six a.m.—she'd spent the whole night on the couch. She stretched to get the kinks out. She could get a run in, she thought, if she moved quickly. She pulled on her spandex leggings, top and a sweatshirt before slipping her feet into her running shoes. She hadn't run in the last week, and she needed that release, those endorphins that kicked in when she hit her stride. It had been one week since the shooting, since the world and everything else had seemed to turn on its axis. She needed her routine back; she needed to get back to the ER, her runs and her regular life, and then, just maybe, she'd stop thinking about the Harts.

It was still dark, a cold November nip in the air, when she stepped to the street, but already the city was rousing itself from sleep.

Morning commuters filled the roads, irate drivers sat on their horns at lights, and an occasional truck thundered by. The crowds ensured safety and she warmed up quickly, a jog in place, a stretch, and she was off. She turned onto L Street and crossed Day Boulevard to the beach, running her old familiar loop to Castle Island, the biting wind hitting her full in the face, her lungs burning with the effort, her ponytail swinging, sweat trickling down her neck, her heart pounding in her chest. By her first half mile, she'd settled in, her heart rate leveling off, matching the pace of her feet as they hit the pavement. She ran by Kelly's, the famous burger and clams place, the center of Castle Island's universe for the seven months or so that it was open. And as she ran by, the scent of yesterday's clams and fries hung in the air and her mouth watered.

She finished the loop, a mile and a half, and checked her time. A disappointing twenty minutes. She'd slowed down considerably. She reset her watch and turned for home, the beach to her left as she took it all in—the salty air, the sound of her footfalls, the sun hovering just on the horizon, an occasional runner moving past. This was her idea of the perfect morning. By the time she turned back onto K Street and checked her time, she'd made the last mile and a half in fifteen minutes. *Better*, she thought, stopping to stretch. She took the stairs to her apartment two at a time, clicking on her television as she stepped into her shower.

She could just barely hear the voices filtering in from the television. "Robert Hart," the announcer said, and Jessie turned off the water, leaning out to hear. "He may…" and then the voice faded. She grabbed a towel and headed for the living room. The anchor was just finishing up. "We'll have a reporter at the funeral and we'll keep you posted." She grabbed her clicker and tried to get the story, but the national morning shows were doing their cheery daybreak dialogue. She gave up, brewed her coffee, and grabbed her iPad. She scrolled through the news stories until she came to Rob Hart. Sam was right: the headlines confirmed that

Hart might attend the funeral. She sat back. Today was going to be interesting.

She pulled on a black dress, black nylons and shoes, knotted her hair into a slightly messy bun and applied the palest lipstick she had. She stood in front of the bathroom mirror and nodded at her reflection. She'd fit right in. No one would ever know that she didn't belong there.

Sam arrived promptly at ten and texted her that he was outside. Jessie slipped into her coat, locked her door, wiggled it to be sure it was secure, and satisfied that it was, she pounded down the steps.

"You look nice," Sam said as she slid into the front passenger seat.

"Thanks. I'm trying to look as though I belong. You look pretty good yourself."

He adjusted his tie as he pulled into traffic. "Thank you. I look like this every day, though."

"Then I guess I'm saying you look nice every day." She smiled and smoothed her coat, picking at a piece of lint that had appeared. She did like this guy. She liked the soft fullness of his mouth, the hard angle of his jaw. She liked the way his suit jacket pulled snugly over his broad shoulders. She liked… and she turned away. *God, what was wrong with her?* She'd met him in the ER over shooting victims and decided that maybe, just maybe, she really liked him on the way to a funeral. She had to get a grip, and remember that she liked Nick a little more—he was exactly the kind of man she needed in her life, and that was why she'd chosen him. Life was strange. At least hers was.

The Cathedral was a ten-minute drive away, but in the morning's heavy traffic, it would probably take longer. "You really think Hart will be there?" she asked as Sam maneuvered through long-forgotten side streets, past a crumbling housing project, its residents spilling out to watch the event, a likely change of pace from the petty crime and misery of the neighborhood. He pulled up in front of the church, a majestic old Gothic Revival building, at ten-fifteen. The usually crowded side streets had already been emptied of cars and marked with orange traffic cones. Reporters and photographers were busy setting up cameras, a few mourners waited outside while others headed into the church, and passersby stopped to take it all in. It all had the feeling of a holiday instead of the solemn memorial it was intended to be.

Jessie twisted in her seat to watch the early arrivals. "I know him," she said, at first in a whisper and then a shout. "I know him!"

CHAPTER SIXTEEN

"Who? Who are you looking at?" Sam unhooked his seatbelt and turned his head, his eyes following her gaze.

Jessie pointed him out, the fresh-faced young man from Ann Hart's Facebook page. His face was streaked with tears as he walked slowly towards the church, two young women alongside.

"Who is he? And how do you know him?" Sam swiveled to face her, his gray eyes as flat and cold as the sidewalk.

"I don't *know* him," she said defensively. "He's on her Facebook page, looking at her with… I don't know… love, lust. Haven't you seen it?"

"Her Facebook page? One of the guys checked it. Said there was nothing there."

"You never thought to look yourself?"

He raised a brow. "Why did you?"

"The husband's Facebook page was on the news last night. His page was work-based. Showcased his youth group, but nothing else. Not even a picture of her."

"I saw his page."

"So, has anyone spoken to those kids?"

He nodded. "Yeah, we have. Turns out, it's more of a drop-in center, no regular activities. The center is open for pickup basketball games, or just to talk. Nothing formal, and apparently Hart wasn't there much. Seems like he went for photo ops. They haven't seen much of him lately."

"Have you spoken to Hart again?"

"No. The good doctor says to give him some time."

"Give me a break. He doesn't need to be in the hospital, never mind the ICU. Hart told me he's being discharged tomorrow. Don't know if that'll happen, but he thinks so."

"Good. Maybe we'll get another shot at him."

Jessie raised a brow. "Thought you had your eyes on Jose Ramos. Is that still the case?"

"We look at everything and everyone. It might not always appear that way, but we do."

"Have you searched Hart's house?"

"For what? He and his wife are the victims. The shooting didn't happen there. And we have to make a case to the DA to get inside someone's house. This isn't television." There was a decided edge to his voice.

She scrunched her face into a frown and slumped in her seat.

"We've looked at Hart. Really. But he seems to be squeaky clean. Grew up in the Charlestown housing projects, single mother, and by all accounts, he was a good kid. Never got into trouble. Went to Harvard on a full scholarship and then was hired by the mayor after he volunteered on his first campaign. He's worked his way up. Doesn't have any close friends, but no enemies that we can find either. Any way you look at it, hard to figure he had any part in this."

She rolled her eyes. "All very impressive, but even good guys go bad."

"True," he said looking at his phone. "The procession will be here in five minutes. Let's go."

Despite the full bank of clouds that had swelled with the promise of imminent rain, the crowd of onlookers had grown. Sam took Jessie's hand and led her through the throng and up the stairs to stand at the church's entrance. "We can watch everyone up close as they arrive. See if anyone looks out of place."

The hum of sirens could be heard in the distance, and as it moved closer, Jessie stood on her toes and watched as a caravan of black sedans, looking like a queue of black beetles, inched closer. Police cruisers and motorcycles guided the procession, blocking streets and traffic as they went. Even from a distance, it was a solemn procession, and as the first cars arrived, the police broke off, the sirens dying to a drone, the silence spreading like a soft whisper. Even the birds seemed to pause as the cars ground to a stop, parking right there in the street.

As the car doors slid open and the family and close friends emerged, those who had already gathered stepped back almost in unison as the casket, draped in white, was pulled from the hearse and carried into the church. Reporters and their cameras moved closer, their flashes almost chasing away the shade of the clouds. Jessie peered through the crowd of reporters, pencils or cameras or both in hand, for any sign of Bert. When she realized he wasn't there, she heaved a sigh of relief.

As if he had just read her mind, Sam leaned in. "Any sight of that crazy old coot, that reporter?"

Jessie shook her head. "He texted me yesterday—said he needed to speak to me, that it was important."

"You didn't call him, did you?"

"I hit *delete* and blocked him. I thought he might be here today, but so far, he's not."

She looked around again and caught sight of Ann Hart's family, her mother and father and the others she'd met in the hallway of the ICU. Today, they were expressionless and stoic, backs straight, eyes dry and fixed straight ahead. The only clue to their pain—they clutched hands so tightly, Jessie could see the whites of their knuckles. She bit back her own tears, and stood tight against the entrance, willing herself to be invisible, but Ann Hart's mother had noticed her and stopped. She nodded, a trace of a smile crossing her lips before it slipped away and she moved into the church. The mayor and his entourage, all dressed in somber black, were close behind the family and shuffled in soundlessly, until the first strains of "Amazing Grace" filled the air, the singer's voice rich and strong enough to carry to the street.

Jessie and Sam stood quietly and watched as the mourners filed in, an endless line snaking into the church. The group she'd noticed earlier—the teachers from the Facebook post—moved slowly to put their arms around the young man whose head was bowed, his shoulders heaving with silent sobs. Jessie nudged Sam. "Look at him," she whispered. "He's heartbroken."

The music continued, the mourners filled the church and Sam and Jessie moved inside, hugging the back wall, watching everything. Once the introductory rites and prayers were recited and psalms were read, the priest announced that a dear friend of Ann's would be delivering the eulogy. The woman, dressed in black, a red scarf draping her neck, stood, the click of her heels echoing as she approached the altar. She placed a photo of Ann on the podium, smoothed a sheaf of papers, cleared her throat and began. Jessie stood on her toes to get a glimpse of the photo, but the image was too small, the distance too great. Still, she could imagine it—Ann smiling, her dark hair, her hazel eyes. Jessie shook her head to release the image. This was Ann Hart's funeral, not hers, and Ann's friend was speaking.

"For our beloved Ann, there are no words to describe our heartbreak, our extraordinary and so unexpected loss. Ann was the one we could always rely on—for a laugh, for advice, for a reminder that love was all that mattered…" She continued on, spinning a picture of a wonderful young woman. The sniffles and sobs from the mourners punctuated her words, and every few minutes, she paused to let the weight of the moment sink in, to let the church echo with the lonely sound of weeping. "We will never forget our beloved Ann," she said. "Rest in peace, beloved friend. You will forever be our angel."

The funeral Mass continued, the scent of incense, a woody, pine-needle fragrance, reaching even to the back of the church where Jessie and Sam stood. Her eyes watered and she blinked away the remnants of the smoky fog. And soon it was over, the casket was led back down the center aisle, the family close behind. As Ann Hart's mother neared, Jessie couldn't help but notice the streaked eye makeup running down her face, the tears still coursing over her cheeks. She elbowed Sam and gave a sideways glance to the mother. "See that," she whispered.

He nodded and they stood quietly as the remaining mourners filed past, more women with the running eye makeup that Jessie had noticed on Ann Hart the night of the shooting. And when the church had almost emptied, the man from Facebook, who had wept so openly, now looked simply shell-shocked, his eyes red with tears, his face a frozen mask of misery. He moved slowly, supported on each side by equally sad-faced women. It was a sharp contrast to the smiles and dry eyes of Rob Hart.

As the crowd broke up, and the funeral procession continued on to the private burial, Jessie and Sam lingered at the top of the stairs. "Did you see what you came for?" Jessie asked.

He shook his head. "No one even remotely out of place. No Jose Ramos either. What about you?"

"I saw plenty. First, that man who's so broken. That's the way a person reacts when they lose someone they love, but it was Ann's mother and the other women that really struck me."

"How?" Sam reached to his pocket, pulling out his iPhone and checking the messages.

"Put that down for a minute and listen to me. Really listen."

"Sorry," he said, tucking the phone back into his pocket. "Force of habit. Go on."

"Did you notice their faces? The eye makeup running in black streaks through the tears?"

"I did. Seems pretty normal, right?"

"Right. After a woman's been crying for a while. Most eye makeup doesn't run with a few tears. And you saw her mother. She was dry-eyed when she arrived. But she's been crying now for at least half an hour, the same for the others."

"And your point?"

"Ann Hart's face was streaked with tears and eye makeup that had run. Rob Hart says everything happened in an instant. That doesn't fit. A woman can't cry so much that quickly to ruin her makeup. Do you understand what I'm saying?"

"I do, but there's no proof of that."

"I'm a witness. I'm the proof."

"I hear what you're saying. I do. It's a chilling thought that she had time enough to cry like that, but it's not evidence of anything, and even if it were, it's gone. I can't take that to the DA or a judge. *Your honor...*" he started, his voice a falsetto, the corners of his mouth turning up. "*Her eye makeup...*"

Jessie heaved a long sigh. "Never mind. How about Foley's?" she asked. "A quick lunch?"

CHAPTER SEVENTEEN

Just blocks from the Cathedral, Foley's looked somehow different in the harsh glare of daylight, even on this cloudy day. Located in an area once filled with warehouses and decaying brick buildings, the neighborhood had been restored to its long-ago glory of brick office buildings and newly restored loft apartments. Jessie had only been here long after night had settled over the city, and she wasn't sure she would have recognized this street or the building if not for Sam.

A few smokers lingered on the sidewalk taking last drags of cigarettes before hurrying back inside. But however different it looked on the outside, it was as familiar and inviting as always on the wood-paneled inside. A long mahogany bar greeted visitors, but bar stools did not. Patrons had to stand at the bar or snag a seat at one of the high pub tables which forced people to move along and perhaps mingle a little more on a crowded night.

Off to the back, in a likely nod to the millennials who'd gentrified the neighborhood, full dining tables and menus lined the back wall. In the old days, Foley's was for drinking; the only food you could find was potato chips and maybe a hot dog, but these days you could get a sandwich or a full meal. They slid onto stools at one of the pub tables by the bar, and watched the day-drinkers, a few reporters, a politician or two and the locals, swig down beers and shots.

Jessie settled onto the stool as Sam went to the bar and ordered burgers and beer. The beer was frosty, and slid down Jessie's throat more easily than she would have thought for this time of day.

"So," Sam said, "tell me your whole theory. I know you have one."

"First, tell me about the mayor. You said he wasn't as keen on Hart as you'd thought."

"Yeah. Seems Hart's been using his clout as a top mayoral aide to grease his own potential campaign. Word is, he wants to run for Congress and has been trying to line up some of the mayor's big donors to support him. Any money they give him will likely come off the top of the mayor's donations, so that's a problem. It's just a rumor, but there's enough of it that the mayor was apparently ready to fire Hart. Just a chink in his armor, though, not enough to get from there to murder." He took a slow swig of his beer, his gray eyes sparkling over the mug. "Your turn? Tell me what you've been thinking. I know there's plenty going on in that mind of yours."

She smiled, trying to avoid the magic in his eyes. She knew that she'd forget everything she wanted to say if she was lost in those deep pools of shimmering gray. She looked away long enough to remember what she wanted to tell him. "You're right. I've been thinking about this plenty, and I think I've seen enough of people at their worst to have a credible theory." She ran her finger along the rim of her glass. "I think someone must have helped him."

"Where did that come from?" Sam offered a wry smile.

The bar was starting to fill up. Jessie guessed people actually did come in for lunch. "Because I really believe he was involved, for all the reasons I went over before. He's not even a little sad, and those tattoo details—where did they come from? He conveniently remembered them the next day. Come on. And the pregnancy? Not one hint that he cared about that either. He even mentioned that police usually looked at husbands first, but he said that because he was a victim, too—he was beyond suspicion. Then there was that guy today, who was so heartbroken. He showed more emotion that Rob Hart has."

"I have to remind you that Rob Hart is not a primary suspect right now. He's still a victim of a crime. There's nothing, despite what you think, to suggest otherwise. Satisfied?"

"No. That's what he wants you to think. I'm still convinced that Hart shot himself."

He rolled his eyes. "There's no evidence of that. And your own Dr. Merrick doesn't think it all that likely that the wound was self-inflicted. The DA agrees."

"But have you tested that theory? Tried it out with a blank weapon the way I showed you?"

"Ballistics is working on that. Doesn't give us any real evidence, though. Remember, we have to focus on the facts of the crime, and those facts are few. A robbery gone bad does not point to Hart as the shooter. There is nothing to support any charge, let alone murder."

"I just think there's a big piece missing."

"Jesus," he said, swiping a hand dramatically across his brow. "We know how to run a murder investigation. We did speak to his co-workers and the few friends he has to see if anyone had it in for him, but it seems, despite the rumors of him trying to skim away some of the mayor's donors, he's a pretty benign kind of guy."

His voice had grown testy. He was tired of her questions, but she couldn't help herself. "No girlfriend?"

He shook his head. "Unless you've seen one at the hospital?"

"No, but he flirts as if he's trolling for one."

"Not a crime. You're beating a dead horse," he said, taking a bite of his burger. "Everyone's an armchair quarterback these days."

Jessie swirled the dregs of her beer in the bottom of her mug as if she could read them like tea leaves. "Maybe I should flirt back, get him to tell me something."

"Jessie, no! Promise me you won't do that. If it turns out you're even remotely right, that would be dangerous. Please, just leave this to us."

"I don't have to promise. If he's discharged tomorrow and I'm back in the ER Wednesday—and God knows that's where I want to be—I'll never see him again." She raised her empty glass and nodded to the bartender, who poured two more frosty mugs and delivered them to the table. Jessie tipped her glass against Sam's. "And once I have my life back, maybe I'll stop thinking about this and tormenting you about it."

"Cheers to that," Sam said, giving her a reluctant smile.

That evening, the Harts were again the lead story on every newscast in Boston. Video of the funeral focused on the family as they left the church. The camera had narrowed in tight on the mother's tear-streaked face, her shaking shoulders and the crowd behind her. Photos of Ann flashed on the screen as the anchor announced that Rob Hart had released a statement from his bed at Boston City Hospital:

"*I want to thank Mayor Reilly,*" the anchor read solemnly, "*his staff, and the Boston Police Department for their efforts to support me and to find the ruthless thug who took away my beloved Ann. And of course, I am forever grateful to the team of doctors and nurses here at the hospital who've worked tirelessly to save me. Without them and their expert care, I would not have survived. And finally, I thank you for trying to save my dear Ann—a beautiful, smiling woman who was beloved by all and will never be forgotten.*"

The anchor, clearly moved by Hart's words, paused for a moment before continuing. "Rob Hart released that statement from his bed in the ICU at Boston City Hospital where he remains in critical condition."

"What the hell?" Jessie shouted at the television as the weatherman appeared. She jumped up and paced, trying to calm herself. "Critical condition! What a piece of work he is. I have to get out of the ICU or I'll wind up in the loony bin." She checked her watch—four p.m. The sun would be setting soon, but Mondays guaranteed heavy car and pedestrian traffic on the roads, offsetting any risk of running in the dark. And she needed to run again. That would clear her head. She donned her running gear, laced up her shoes, and headed out just as darkness was settling into the sky.

Jessie ran her familiar loop to Castle Island, passing other runners along the way. Before long, she was lost in the rhythm of her run, the sky at dusk, the scents of evening—of cooking smells and wood fires and as she passed the beach—the salty, clean aroma of the ocean and the soothing sound of the waves. She could almost feel the tension and anger ease from her muscles.

At the midway point, she checked her watch—twelve minutes. She smiled. Being pissed off was at least good for her running time. She headed back, her head clear, the sound of her footfalls lost in the early-evening sirens and car horns and neighborly shouts. By the time she turned onto her street, her mood was improved. She stopped for a long stretch, balancing her legs one at a time on the steps to her building.

And she froze, one leg suspended in midair.

Was someone watching her?

CHAPTER EIGHTEEN

She dropped her leg and turned quickly, but no one was there. The street was still filled with traffic and a few pedestrians, and nothing else. It was only her imagination. She heaved a sigh and wished that Nick or Sam would call to take her mind off things, but both were probably working.

Once home, she showered, heated a can of soup and curled up on the couch, clicking on the television for company. Thanksgiving, she was reminded during a commercial, was just days away, and as she had in the five years since her father had died, she expected to work, maybe a double shift, so someone who had a family could be home with them. Jessie felt happiest on those family holidays in the ER surrounded by the homeless and lost souls who would surely crowd the waiting room that day. Being with them allowed her to forget that she had no family, that holidays were days to get through and get past.

By ten p.m., she was beginning to nod off on the couch, and she forced herself to get up, determined to get into bed tonight. She put her dishes in the sink, turned off her lights and, just to be sure no one was out there, she peeked through her blinds. The streetlamp was still dark, but at the corner, a Boston police cruiser sat idling. A small glow from within the car revealed that it was Nick, his eyes on the street. A warm rush flooded through Jessie's veins. Nick—keeping an eye out for her. It had been a while since she had two men interested in her at the same time, but she knew that Nick was the right one for her. His being here proved that.

Nick would quietly take care of her. She'd be his priority. His only priority. She couldn't quite imagine that same scenario with Sam. His job was everything to him. She slid into bed with images of Nick watching over her swirling through her mind.

The following morning, Donna called from the ER. "You're back here tomorrow!"

"Thank God! Evenings?"

"Actually, Nurse Ratched wanted to know if you'd do a day-evening double tomorrow and Thursday—Thanksgiving Day. Do you mind? I can tell her to kiss off. Well, not exactly in those words, but you get my drift."

Jessie laughed. "Oh, I've missed you guys. I'll do both doubles. I'll do anything to be back where I belong."

"See you tomorrow. Now go out and have some fun. This is your last day off!"

Jessie knew that to get back into her own routine, a thorough house cleaning and laundry were the first order of business. She pulled on sweats and socks, dragged her vacuum out and ran it around her tiny living room, the lines in the carpet a comforting kind of testament to a clean apartment. Once her laundry was spinning in a machine in the basement, she slipped on her running shoes and did a slow jog to Patrick's corner store for coffee and a muffin.

"Morning, Patrick," she called as the little overhead bell tinkled her arrival.

"Morning, angel," he answered.

She rolled her eyes. "Are we still on that?"

He held up a newspaper whose headlines declared: *Hart-Less Husband a No-Show but Angel Is There*. A grainy photo of Jessie standing next to Sam was underneath.

"Oh, no," she muttered. "Now I'll be back in the ICU for sure."

"What's that, love?"

"The usual coffee and muffin," she answered. "And I'll take this too." She reached into her pocket, pulled out her money and passed it to Patrick, who pushed it back to her. "Told ya, your money's not good here. I'm happy to know you, Jessie. Wish there were more like you. The world would surely be a better place."

She stuck the newspaper under her arm, took the coffee and muffin and turned to go. "Thanks, Patrick, but I'm no angel. Remember that."

"Ahh, go on. You'll never convince me of that."

She walked back to her apartment, bolted the door behind her and sat to drink her coffee, eat her muffin and read the story—afraid that Bert had written this one as well. But his name was nowhere to be found. The story was written by a local reporter who noted that Ann's family had called him to express their thanks to the people of Boston, and especially to the nurse who'd cared for Ann in the ER and then took the time out of her busy life to attend the funeral. The implication was clear: where was Rob Hart?

The next story took that implication a step further, hinting that something was amiss in the marriage of Ann and Rob, asking why he hadn't attended.

The police attended along with at least one nurse. Where was the husband? Too heartbroken to attend or too ill? Or just not interested?

The writer didn't answer his own questions, but that anyone else had wondered at all buoyed Jessie's suspicions. At least she wasn't alone. Maybe this article would change things.

She spent the morning finishing up her laundry and laying out her hospital-issued light blue scrubs for work. By one o'clock, she was finished and looking for something to do. She sank into her couch and was about to curl up for a nap when her phone rang. The caller ID flashed Nick's name. Smiling, she answered. "Hey, how are you?"

"I'm great, but better if you're off today and interested in going out for lunch and maybe drinks later?"

She sat forward, unpinning her hair and letting it fall to her shoulders. "Just name the time. I'll be ready."

"See you at two," he crooned, or maybe she just imagined it was a croon.

By the time Nick rang her doorbell, she was ready. She'd showered, pulled on her favorite jeans, a clingy sweater, and boots. She'd managed to draw the perfect line along her eyelids and to swipe a fresh trace of color along her lips. When she pulled her door open, Nick stood back and whistled.

"You look beautiful," he said as he drew her in and kissed her, his tongue lingering there before moving on to her neck and chest. His hands slipped under her sweater as he pulled her closer, a sudden urgency in his moves. He moaned softly in her ear.

She felt that same longing deep inside, but it was too soon, too fast, for that. "Hey," Jessie said, pushing him gently away. "It's good to see you, too, but let's at least get lunch first."

"Sorry," he said, stepping back. "I got carried away." He kissed her cheek. "Where to?"

"Quincy Market," she answered. "We can wander around, see some of the decorations that are up, do a little bar hopping."

At Quincy Market, a news hawker held newspapers up high and shouted, "Read it here! Hart a no-show at wife's funeral!"

Nick moved closer. "Hey, that's you," he shouted, snatching a paper. Jessie tried to shrink back as people turned to look.

Nick passed the seller a ten-dollar bill and walked away reading the story as he went. "Hey, mister. Thanks!" the newsboy shouted.

Nick was engrossed in the story, or maybe the photo. Jessie couldn't tell. "Isn't that the detective I saw you with before?" Nick asked as he tapped the paper. "Are you seeing him?" he pressed, his usually steady blue eyes flickering with uncertainty.

Jessie knew that telling the truth—that she'd been attracted to Sam—was not the answer that Nick wanted to hear. Neither did she want to share that bit of information. It would doom their relationship before it even got off the ground. A fib was required here. "No," she said, the lie slipping through her lips as easily as a sip of wine. She slid her arm through his. "Now feed me before I faint."

They stopped at one of the food stalls in the market and shared a lobster roll and an order of oysters before moving on to one of the pubs where they drank tequila shots before Jessie called a halt. "I'm not really a tequila drinker. One more of these, and you'll have to carry me home. And I'm not ready to go home just yet." They headed back outside, watched the workers decorate the Christmas tree which would be at the center of a lighting ceremony in just a few days.

"We should come back for that," Nick said, draping his arm around her shoulder. Jessie felt herself melt into him. He was exactly the type of partner she needed—reliable, sweet and easy on the eye. She turned and planted a kiss on his lips. "What was that for?" he asked.

"Felt like it. That's all."

He smiled. "Hey, Jess," he said, "hate to break the spell, but any word from that reporter who bothered you?"

"He texted me the day before yesterday. Said he had to talk to me."

"Did you? Did you talk to him?" he asked, his brow knitted into a tight frown.

"No," she answered. "Why?"

"Just asking. He was the one who got you kicked up to the ICU, right?"

"Right. I even thought he was the one watching me, but I don't think it was him. It probably wasn't anyone, just my own imagination, but it doesn't matter. I'm back in the ER tomorrow. As a matter of fact, I can't stay out late, I'm doing a day-evening double tomorrow and the next day."

"The next day's Thanksgiving. You're working a double? No dinner?"

"No, I prefer it that way. So, back to business—how about one more drink and we head home?"

At her door, Nick pulled her into an embrace, tilting her chin up. "Tonight was perfect. I'll see you soon?"

"It was perfect, and yes—soon." She stood on her toes and kissed him before pulling away. "Hey, I forgot to thank you."

"For what?" he asked, his eyes crinkling in curiosity.

"Last night. You were outside my apartment in your cruiser. Made me feel safe. Thanks." She planted a quick peck on his cheeks. "I hate to end this night, but I've got to get some sleep. See you soon?"

He nodded. "Go on in," he said. "I'll wait until you lock up before I leave."

And if she were the type of woman who swooned, she would have. "Goodnight," she whispered.

CHAPTER NINETEEN

The following morning, Jessie was greeted like a long-lost friend. "Welcome back! We missed you!" echoed in the still-quiet halls. The flurry of walk-in activity wouldn't likely start until at least nine. Their usual patients—"clients" they were supposed to be called—were still asleep. It would be a while before they woke and decided that their aches and pains, however chronic, needed immediate attention in the ER. The ambulance entrance, on the other hand, was always busy. Heart attacks, gunshots, stab wounds, car accidents—none of them kept to any identifiable schedule, and that was likely the attraction of working in the ER. You just never knew. Quiet as a morgue one minute, and overwhelmed with trauma patients the next.

"Morning, Jess," Donna greeted her. "Do you mind doing charge for both day and evenings? I have to get the next schedule done."

"No problem. I'll wash the floors too if you need that. I'm just so glad to be back."

The crackle of the C-med radio interrupted their conversation, the whir of static filling the air. "C-Med to Boston City. Over."

Jessie picked up the line remembering the last time she'd done this; it had been to get notification of the Harts' imminent arrival. This morning, it was just a test. Jessie confirmed that the transmission was clear and hung up. She made out the day's assignments and added herself to the trauma team. There weren't enough nurses to fully staff the place. They'd just have to do the best they could, which was what Administration always reminded them. Today, she had no complaints about poor staffing as long as she was here, right where she belonged.

The first trauma of the day arrived shortly after Jessie did—a forty-year-old driver who'd had his left arm hanging out the door when a truck veered too close and crashed into him, severing his arm in the process. The patient arrived with his arm laid gently on top of the sheet that covered him. Luckily, he was in shock and didn't seem to notice.

The team moved quickly—IVs were inserted, X-ray was called, Vascular Surgery and Reconstructive Surgery were paged stat. Labs were drawn. Jessie ran the hemoglobin test herself. "It's nine," she said. "But I'll still order five units. Okay?" No one answered. Everyone was busy taking care of their own assigned tasks. A technician was doing an EKG, the other nurse was drawing up sedatives, and pushing them gently into the patient's IV lines while the surgeon intubated the patent. Respiratory appeared just in time and began to bag the patient. The social worker pulled out the man's ID. "I'll try to reach his family," she said hurrying from the room.

Thirty minutes after the patient's arrival, Cheryl, the reception clerk, poked her head into the room. "OR's ready," she called. "Jess, welcome back and when you have a minute, come to see me, will ya?" Jessie nodded and turned back to the tasks at hand: packing the patient, his IV drips and pumps, his monitors and his belongings, for the trip to the OR. And when he was gone, and the team had scattered, she restocked the room, and paused by the intercom.

"Housekeeping to Trauma One," she said smiling. They were suddenly the sweetest words of her day. It really was another day in paradise. The pace of the ER picked up quickly. Walk-ins crowded the waiting room and ambulances filled the ambulance bay, jockeying to slide in as one pulled out. She spent most of her morning in one or another of the trauma rooms helping to manage a heart attack, a stroke, and a stabbing victim whose injuries turned out to be so minor, he was discharged home after a few quick sutures.

Suddenly, it was two p.m., the day shift almost over. Jessie had been able to ignore the grumblings of hunger in her stomach as the day wore on, but they'd grown exponentially and now, she knew she had to eat. "Cheryl," she called as she passed by the reception desk. "I'm just running to the cafeteria for some food. Want anything?"

"Nothing for me, but don't forget—I want to see you."

"Oh, no. I did forget. Sorry. I'm here now. Can you tell me what it is?"

"It's that reporter who was bothering you."

Jessie's hunger pains were suddenly replaced by a swell of anger that threatened to burst from within. "What about him?" she snapped.

Cheryl's eyelids fluttered as she stepped back. "I'm sorry," she said, her voice soft.

Jessie reached out a soothing hand and gripped her shoulder. "*I'm* sorry. I didn't mean that. It's just… never mind. When was he here?"

"A couple of days ago. It was your last day in the ICU, I think."

And she remembered the text he'd sent that afternoon. *I need to speak with you. Please call me at this number. It's IMPORTANT! Bert.* "You didn't tell him anything, did you?"

Cheryl shook her head. "No. I just said you weren't here. I didn't know who he was until Donna saw him leaving and asked what he wanted. She told me then that he was the one who'd been bothering you. I'm sorry, Jess."

"That's okay. No harm. Just let me know if he shows up again."

"There's something else. I haven't told anyone, but I think I have to tell you."

"What is it?"

"He came here the morning after that shooting. Said he was with the mayor's office. He looked the part—overcoat, suit, official. You know what I mean?"

"I do. That's his scam. Pretend he's someone else to get a story."

"Well, I believed him. I sent him up to the ICU."

"Oh, hell," Jessie muttered. Cheryl seemed to wither at her words. "Sorry. Don't worry, and don't say a thing to anybody. He probably never got in to see Hart. No harm done."

Cheryl forced a weak smile. "Sorry, Jess."

"Cheryl, he's the problem, not you. Don't worry about it. I'll be back shortly. Okay?"

Jessie had lost her appetite but knew she'd need something to eat to get through the rest of her double shift. She took the stairs to the second floor and arrived at the cafeteria just as they were closing. "Please," she begged. "I just need a sandwich. I'll be quick." The lady waved her through and offered her the last of the lunch selections—a roast beef sandwich with chips. "You, my friend, are an angel," Jessie called as she headed back to the ER.

She inhaled the sandwich while she clicked onto the internet and searched for a photo of Bert. It didn't take long before she recognized him—his beady eyes, balding pate and crooked teeth filled her view. She hit *print*. She'd run up to the ICU later to ask if they'd seen him.

C-Med sputtered to life once more, reporting the imminent of arrival of a gunshot victim, the wound in his buttocks. Jessie met the ambulance in the bay and directed them into Trauma One for a quick assessment by the surgeon. The superficial wound was nowhere near life-threatening, but as a precaution, they X-rayed him, started a line for antibiotics and sent labs, all while their patient, a fifteen-year-old covered with gang tattoos, cried for his mother.

An hour later, C-Med buzzed once more, this time reporting that a sixteen-year-old male with a gunshot wound to his thigh was en route. "It's non-stop. The gang of midgets is back," the surgeon muttered.

Jessie laughed. "Seems like it." She wondered if the gang unit would be in—those undercover cops dressed in tight jeans and leather jackets, their silver shields hanging from chains around their necks. The very sight of them made every nurse stop what she was doing for a look. It seemed that model good looks were a requirement for the job, not to mention a sense of humor.

It was the cops who'd dubbed the shooters and their victims "the gang of midgets." They were nuisance shootings, the wounds never serious just an inconvenience and a likely badge of honor for the victims, but a nuisance for the ER staff and police who had to deal with them. The shootings, the police said, were likely part of gang initiation and subsequent retaliations—a vicious cycle that, once started, would go on for months until the bitter cold of Winter would put an end to it. In the Spring and Summer, the shootings might start again, but you never knew. This could be the waning days of the gang of midgets. At least she could hope, Jessie thought.

It was seven p.m. before Jessie had a chance to catch her breath. Walk-ins and even the ambulances slowed down. Tomorrow was Thanksgiving, and everyone was out shopping or at home cooking, preparing for families to celebrate. For Jessie, it was just another holiday to get through. By Friday, the Christmas spirit—decorations, shopping—would be underway and she'd have to somehow manage to navigate the whole month of family holidays—late November through late December, which might have been pretty simple except for friends and co-workers who were eager to include her in their plans.

"We'd love to have you," Donna said every year. "I don't want you to be alone."

"I won't be alone, I'll be working and then seeing friends." Jessie repeated the same lie every year, knowing full well that she chose to be alone rather than with strangers. Someday, she'd have her own family.

In the meantime, she had things to do. The calm that had settled over the ER allowed Jessie a quick respite, and with her pager on, she took the elevator to five to see if anyone there had seen Bert. The police guard was gone, the entry quiet as Jessie slid her ID over the sensor and walked into the unit. Ellen sat at desk typing into a computer. She turned at the sound of the door. "Hey, Jessie. Are you coming to give me a heads-up on a new patient?"

"Not this time. But I'm glad you're here. I want to ask you something."

"About where your favorite patient is?" Ellen laughed and nodded toward the room across from the desk, Rob Hart's room.

Jessie's gaze followed Ellen's. The room was empty, the monitors quiet, the lights off, the bed ready for another patient. A wide smile broke onto her lips. "When?" she whispered. "And how?"

"Yesterday. Administration said his insurance wouldn't cover his stay any longer, and the hospital couldn't afford to keep him. And that was that. He did ask me to tell you how much he appreciated you. He actually asked for your number. Said he wanted to tell you himself."

"You didn't…?"

"No, but don't be surprised if he shows up in the ER, or calls looking for you."

"Oh, God, that's all I need. Another stalker."

"Another stalker?"

She shook her head. "Sorry, I'm just being dramatic, but I do want to ask if you've seen someone."

"Who?"

Jessie pulled the photo from her pocket, smoothed the folds and passed it to Ellen. Have you ever seen him? Maybe visiting Hart?"

Ellen peered at the image of Bert and bobbed her head up and down. "Yeah. He came in the morning after the shooting. Said he was with the mayor's office. He spoke to Hart. Why are you interested?"

"He's not with the mayor's office. He's a reporter. His article is the one that got me into trouble."

"Jessie, I'm sorry. I'm the one who let him in. He seemed legit. Hart even asked what the direct number to his room was so this guy could call him."

She clenched her jaw. "That son of a bitch," she muttered. "He had a hand in planting those stories, and stupid Bert went along." She folded the photo again and jammed it into her pocket.

"Huh?" Ellen asked, her eyes narrowing.

"Never mind, but thanks, Ellen. I've got to get back to the ER. I'll catch up with you later."

"Hey," Ellen called as Jessie pushed open the door. "Happy Thanksgiving!"

She felt a thickness rise up in her throat. "You, too," she said softly. "You, too."

When she got back to the ER, she texted Sam.

I have some information about Hart. Call when you get a chance.

By the time Thanksgiving morning dawned, Sam had yet to reply. *Maybe he's away for the holiday. Seems everyone is*, she thought, her fingers tapping the steering wheel as she drove towards the hospital.

The streets were deadly quiet, and except for true emergencies, she expected the ER would be too. And she was right. A handful of walk-ins arrived, all with minor complaints. The regulars were at the shelters or drop-in centers where politicians and local celebrities would serve them dinner early enough so they'd make the evening news.

Jessie knew that her distrust of just about everyone's motives was a problem. Once she'd lost her dad, and without a mother to comfort her, she'd found herself resentful of everyone else's happy families. She'd developed a great big chip on her shoulder. She might have already found someone to share her own life with, but instead of being open and loving, she inevitably pushed the good men away and pined for the impossibly bad, bad boys. She was probably doing that again with Nick and Sam. She knew that Nick was the best man for her. He just might be the one to help her knock that chip off. She smiled at the thought. It was definitely Nick she wanted.

As if he'd known what she was thinking, Nick showed up, in uniform, at seven p.m. with a homemade turkey dinner in hand. When he peeled back the foil, the steam and scent spiraling into the air made her stomach grumble.

"Thank you," she said, planting a kiss on his cheek. "I was just going to make a cafeteria run. You have perfect timing."

"You're not so bad yourself. What are you doing after work?"

"Are you kidding? After two doubles, I'm going home to bed."

"Want some company?" he asked, the penetrating blue of his eyes holding her tight in his vision.

When he stroked her face and tucked a stray curl behind her ear, she felt weak in the knees. She needed this. She needed him. "Yes," she whispered. "Bring wine."

Jessie arrived home with time—or so she thought—to spare. She stepped into a hot shower, the steam rising in a smoky mist around her. She scrubbed away the melancholy that had so enveloped her earlier, stepped from the shower and lathered a scented cream over her skin. With a towel draped around her, she stood in front of her pencil-box-sized closet to decide what to wear.

And then she heard it. Someone was jiggling her doorknob.

CHAPTER TWENTY

Jessie froze, every muscle in her body tensing up, her heart slamming hard against her chest. She slipped her arms into her bathrobe and crept softly toward the door. She could see the knob moving back and forth. "Who's there?" she shouted, reaching for her phone, her finger hovering over the emergency call tab.

"Jess, it's me," Nick answered.

She slumped against the door before pulling it open. "You never heard of knocking?" she snarled.

"Hey," he said softly, ignoring her anger. "Are you okay?"

"I thought someone was breaking in. You scared me."

"Oh, baby, I'm sorry." He ran his fingers through her wet hair, working out the tangles. "I did knock, and when you didn't answer, I tried the door handle to see if you'd left the door open for me."

She began to laugh, almost giddy with relief. "I'm just glad you're here." She nestled herself into his arms, the steady thump-thump of his heart soothing her. "Hey," she pushed herself back. "I didn't get to greet you the way I hoped."

"Well, that was pretty close," he said, planting a kiss on her forehead. "But do you want me to go out and knock again?"

"No," she laughed, standing apart from him, her eyes wandering over his body. "I wanted to say—is that a gun in your pocket or are you happy to see me?" She doubled over with laughter. "I've always wanted to say that."

"I've always wanted to hear it, and the answer is—both." He pulled her back into his arms, his lips grazing the top of her head.

Jessie stumbled and then toppled onto the couch, Nick falling on top of her. He pulled himself up on his elbows. "Well, this happened even faster than I'd hoped."

She pushed him away, and sat up. "Not yet. Let's have some wine, listen to music, maybe dance?"

"You're on," he said, reaching for the wine. "I'll get this opened and I'll find some music."

He kissed her once more before heading to the kitchen. Jessie slipped into her bathroom where she pulled on sweats, wound her hair into a loose braid, pinched her cheeks for color and joined him back in the living room where he was fiddling with her old iPod.

"Try this," Jessie said, opening her phone and choosing a playlist she'd created on those nights she needed to decompress after work. As the first strains of the Righteous Brothers' "Unchained Melody" began, Jessie sighed contentedly. They sat back, sipped the wine and before long, they were locked in an embrace, Nick's lips searching for hers. He pulled her up and held her close as they danced slowly, their shadows close, their bodies closer. Jessie's heart began to race once more, her skin growing hot. She tugged at her sweatshirt, at the sudden heaviness of it. He slipped his fingers under the fabric and played with her breasts before bringing his mouth to them, her hand cupping his head. Jessie arched her back to him before taking his hand and leading him to the bedroom.

They hurriedly pulled at each other's clothing before sharing a slow, deep kiss that Jessie knew she'd remember for the rest of her life. His hands gripped her buttocks as they fell onto the bed, his fingers and then his tongue sliding from her lips to her neck and then to her nipples where he lingered, his touch teasing, light as air. "Oh, Jessie," he moaned. "You have no idea how long I've wanted this, wanted you," he whispered, his breath hot on her skin.

She was smoldering in her center, almost like the flicker of a small flame. She could only moan as his hands reached between her legs. His touch grew more insistent, an urgency in his lips and fingers, and she felt it too. She lifted her hips to him, and when they joined, she gasped at the pure pleasure of it, of him, of their bodies moving in rhythm. They moved together, at first slowly and then building with a sudden urgency until she could wait no more, a fiery explosion erupting inside of her, the thrill spreading out to every inch of her body. Nick shuddered with his own final release and collapsed on top of her, the weight and feel of him its own unexpected pleasure. They both lay there, slick with sweat and satisfaction.

Nick rolled away before pulling her close, her back snuggled against his chest. "This was great, Jess," he whispered as he drifted off to sleep, the weight of his arm holding her close.

Butterflies flickered in her stomach, but the steady rhythm of his breathing told her he was fast asleep. She'd almost forgotten the magical power of leaning into someone at night, the closeness so soothing, such a perfect end to the day. She was certain that Nick was the one: solid, dependable, and he cared about her. Sam, on the other hand, was older and unattached, and it seemed more likely that what he was looking for was an affair, not a relationship. And as proof of that, he hadn't even responded to her text.

She woke late the next morning, stretching the kinks out of her curled-up body, but holding onto the warmth of last night. When she reached for Nick, his side of the bed was empty, the sheets cold. She sat up and swiped her hand across the pillow where his head had lain. "Nick?" she called, throwing off the covers, her voice echoing in the emptiness. She reached for her robe, and then she saw it—a note on the small table.

Had to leave for court. Call later.

He'd drawn a big heart and signed his name. Jessie sighed and held the paper close to her chest. How could one night have made her feel so happy?

Her mood lasted through the morning and when she arrived for her three p.m. shift, Donna noticed. "What's gotten into you?" she laughed.

"Huh?" Jessie asked.

"You're humming. 'Unchained Melody', isn't it?"

She laughed. "I guess I am humming. I'm just happy, I guess."

"I can see that. Want to tell me why?" Donna, who seemed stuck in the nineties and hated computer charting, stuck her all-too-familiar pen behind her ear.

"Not yet. I don't want to jinx this."

She took report from Donna, and made her rounds. So far, things were, if not exactly quiet, then neither was it too busy to handle. The pace of walk-ins picked up as the ambulance arrivals slowed. It was Black Friday, and most people would be out searching for the next great bargain. Tomorrow, they'd remember their aches and pains, but that was another day and she'd be off. Today would be a good day in the ER. There was a lot to be happy about.

At six-thirty, just as the staff were making plans to order pizza, Tony, an assistant to the state's Chief Medical Examiner, arrived. "Hey, Jessie," he said, his voice velvety, "how's things going?"

Jessie shook her head. He did make her laugh. His real name was Edgar Anthony Jones, a name he'd rejected early, adopting the nickname Tony because it evoked a toughness that Edgar never would. He was solidly built and incorrigible; he looked like he might have been a boxer instead of a technician with the ME whose job involved dealing with dead bodies. More than once he'd asked her to come and see the ME whom she'd helped out with last-minute equipment or medical records, or a description of how a wound had looked before the ER staff had probed it or opened it wider. "He wants you to work with him. Thinks he needs a forensic nurse." Tony had passed the message more than once. "You're the perfect woman for the job, for him, if you get my drift."

"Why am I the perfect woman for the job, or him?" she'd asked.

"Think about it, Jessie. This is not rocket science. You have a pulse. It'd be a nice change of pace for him."

She'd laughed so hard she'd almost fallen over. But today, Tony wasn't laughing. "Is it about the job?"

"Not this time, Jessie. Not this time."

"Did you come for pizza? We have no patients for you."

He shook his head. "That's tempting, but the ME sent me to get you."

"I can't just leave. What is it?"

"We need an ID on a body."

"Why are you looking for me then?" she asked, her voice cracking. "I don't know anyone who's died."

"The ME asked me to get you. That's all I know."

"Come on, Tony. You know everything."

"Honestly, I don't know anything." He stuck his hands in his pockets. "What time are you off? Wanna go out later?"

"You never give up, do you?"

He smiled, his coal-black eyes shimmering in the fluorescent overhead lights.

She shook her head. "Let me tell Elena where I'm going. I'll be right back."

She grabbed a piece of pizza and walked across the street, shivering in the cold air and cursing herself for leaving her coat behind. She followed Tony into the morgue, an old brick building that might have gone unnoticed except for the two stone lions at either side of the entrance. He held the door open and she stepped inside, depositing the last of the pizza into the nearest trash bin.

Even here in the large, open lobby, the stench of formaldehyde and sadness, which carried its own peculiar scent, created a fog of sorts. Jessie coughed and wondered how long she could hold her breath. They took the stairs to the second floor where the bodies were stored and the autopsies were done. She trailed Tony along a corridor to the room at the end, and she knew before he even pulled open one of the heavy double doors that this was the autopsy suite, though why it was called a suite as if it were in a fancy hotel escaped her. She paused, trying to steel herself, and passed through the door into the room.

As soon as she crossed the threshold, she could feel it—a distinct chill in the air, even colder than outside. "Bodies like it cold," Tony whispered. She turned and made a face.

"Stop," she whispered as a short, wiry man walked towards her. He put his hand out and then, just as quickly, pulled it back and peeled the rubber gloves that covered both hands.

"Jessie," he said. "Good to see you again."

Jessie smiled and reluctantly took his hand, the flesh wrinkly and damp. She felt herself cringe, and she slipped her hand away. "Good to see you, too, Dr. Dawson."

He tilted his head, his neck disappearing into the folds of his autopsy apron, and smiled, pulling his eyeglasses up to his forehead, revealing deep amber eyes that shone brightly, almost too brightly, so that they were almost the yellow of a cat's eyes. "Just Roger, please."

Jessie nodded. "Roger."

He ran his ungloved hand through his hair, the thick graying strands unruly and resistant to his attempts to smooth them down. "Well, well…" he said. It was clear that Roger couldn't make small talk. Tony was right—too much time around the dead had rendered him socially awkward and timid.

"I can't stay long," she said, pointing to her scrubs and hoping to rush this along. "I'm working."

"And I don't want to keep you, Jessie," he said, his eyes glowing, "but someone's come in that we think you might know."

Her forehead crinkled. "I don't think so…"

"Just follow me," he said, motioning her forward. "Don't be afraid."

Jessie took a tentative step. To her right, two male corpses were sitting upright, the metal gurney supporting their backs. They might have been chatting but for the fact that they were deceased, their bodies wrapped in plastic shrouds, their heads poking through. Jessie looked away. She followed Roger into the autopsy room, the shape of a body lying there under a white sheet. Her chest tightened. This was some kind of mistake. She was sure of it.

Tony lifted the sheet up as Jessie moved closer. And she gasped, her mouth falling open, her hand fluttering there as she stumbled back.

"You know him?" Tony asked.

She could only nod.

CHAPTER TWENTY-ONE

"Do you need a minute? Would you like to sit in the other room?" Roger asked.

She shook her head. The other room held even more bodies. "No, just give me a minute."

"Can you confirm his name?" Roger asked.

"It's Bert Gibbons. He's a reporter." A tight knot formed in her throat. "What happened?" she asked. "Heart attack?"

"No. His landlady found him hanging. I was told it was a suicide, but…" He looked back to the gurney. "Well, I'm not sure of that. I'm just now having a look."

Jessie moved closer to the table where Bert lay. "Suicide? I didn't know him well, but what I did know is that Bert was not the type to kill himself. Besides, things were going better for him lately. He had a new job in London. He told me he was leaving soon." She flicked through her memories of Bert, searching for any hint of a man who'd decided to end his own life. But there was nothing there. He might have been a pain in the ass, but he wasn't suicidal. This didn't make sense. "Who did you say found him?"

"His landlady. He'd told her he'd be moving out earlier this week. But he hadn't given the keys back, his mail was piled up and she went in this morning and found him. She called nine-one-one but as you can see, it was too late. He'd been there for a day or two, rigor mortis had set in and then reversed, leaving him flaccid. The police called it a suicide and sent him here."

"Why call me?"

Tony came forward. "Your number was on a piece of paper on his desk. There weren't any other contacts that we could find. The landlady said there was no emergency number on his lease either. You were our only lead. Sorry, Jessie." He rested his hand on her shoulder.

She clenched her fingers and moved back to the table where Bert lay, his face bloated and blue, his eyes still open wide as if in fright. Old blood had collected by his nose, his mouth, even his ears. She felt a surge of bile rise to the back of her throat, and she covered her mouth, remembering the text he'd sent just five days earlier. Had he been in some kind of trouble? Might this have been avoided if she'd only answered him?

"Are you okay? An ID was all we needed. You don't have to stay," Roger said gently, moving to her side. For all of his weirdness, he really wasn't a bad guy. "Would you like some water?"

The thought of drinking water from these faucets—probably infused with the formaldehyde that hung in the air—made her feel nauseous all over again. "I'm okay. It's just that, well, he texted me a few days ago. I just didn't expect this." She forced herself to do what she did in the ER—separate herself from the person who lay in front of her. That was what she did to help her provide care for her patients; she distanced herself. But here, with Bert, it was too late to help him. "I've seen hangings before, and, well... do you mind if I look?" Maybe it would help.

"Be my guest." He pulled the sheet away, and Jessie leaned in for a closer look.

"His arms and hands," she asked. "They seem so stiff, so unnatural."

"He was found with his fingers under the rope as if he was trying to loosen it or pull it away. And though the rigor mortis had subsided, his arms were still tightly contracted."

"I don't mean to overstep," Jessie said, her voice a whisper, "but—look at his fingers."

Roger slipped on a pair of surgical gloves and lifted one of Bert's hands. "You have a good eye, Jessie," he said, pointing to the abrasions on his fingertips and the debris under his nails. "They're scraped and cut, his knuckles too, and he seems to have skin under his nails. Three of his fingernails have been broken off as well. All of that, in my experience, is more likely to be found in the hands of someone who's been involved in an altercation. A rope wouldn't cause those injuries."

Jessie moved closer, her hand on her chin, the unpleasant sights and scents of the room all but forgotten.

"His neck wound is very deep," Roger continued, pointing to Bert. "Those lines there in the center are more consistent with strangulation. In a simple hanging, the wounds are not so deep and are a little higher." He turned to be sure she was still listening.

"I've only seen a few hangings," she said. "But I see it, too. This wound looks somehow different."

Roger pulled his glasses back down over his eyes, peering closely at Jessie. "Another good call," he said softly, as though he'd been pleased that she agreed with his findings. "I wish you'd reconsider working with me. You always offer a fresh perspective. With your experience in the ER, you'd make a great forensics nurse. I think we'd make a great team, you and I."

Jessie wondered if, despite his prominent position as the state's Chief Medical Examiner and principal pathologist, maybe he was really looking for someone to offset his shyness, his awkwardness. It was certainly true that no one had ever called *her* timid. "Thanks for the offer, but I don't think I could be here all the time. I mean, this place is just too sad."

"Not if you're helping to unravel the mystery of what really happened to someone. Think of it that way. You already see plenty of murder victims. Sometimes, the whole course of an investigation changes because of what we find over here. It's worth considering."

She folded her hands together. She hadn't realized that her palms had grown so clammy, so damp, probably with guilt. She hadn't much liked Bert, but she'd never have wished him harm. "I…"

"You look as if you need to sit for a minute."

A hard lump formed in her throat, and she could only nod.

"Tony, will you take her to my office? I'll just get started in here." He picked up his rubber gloves and snapped them on.

"Will you let me know what you find?" she asked.

"I'll call you tomorrow. Leave your number in my office."

"Thank you, Roger," she said as she turned to follow Tony through the doors, up a flight of stairs to the third floor and into a place so different from the autopsy suite, she might have been in another building altogether. The floor was carpeted, soft and plush under her feet. The soft gray walls were covered with framed prints of flowers and streams. But the starkest difference was the scent of cinnamon and cloves that filled the space. She inhaled deeply. "It's so different in here."

"This is where we write our reports, meet with police, have lunch. Hell, no one could work down there all the time." He winked, and for the first time since she'd entered the morgue, she smiled. He threw open a door at the end of the hallway and she stepped inside, her mouth agape. The furniture was dark and sturdy, a lushly cushioned couch pushed against one wall, but it was the other walls that caught her eye. They were covered with floor-to-ceiling bookshelves. A rolling ladder allowed access to the highest shelves. She edged closer and saw that he had everything—science, physics, biology, chemistry, forensics—but he had novels, too—mysteries, classics, history. There was more to Roger than she'd thought. It was typical of her to judge first, think later.

Tony handed her a bottle of water. "Take your time," he said, pulling the door softly behind him. She sank down onto the couch and took a long guzzle of water, hoping to clear the taste of bile from the back of her throat.

Her hands trembled as she set the bottle back down, an empty, gnawing feeling erupting in the pit of her stomach. It wasn't hunger. It was fear. *Who would kill Bert?* It didn't make sense. Would a robber stage a suicide? That would take too long. And would the police really investigate this? Sam was so reluctant to look at Hart, though husbands, she knew, were the first suspects when a wife was murdered. Anyone who watched *Dateline* knew that. He hadn't answered her text yet either. She closed her eyes, determined to get her bearings.

These were two separate killings, but they were connected. They had to be. This was too much of a coincidence. Bert knew Rob Hart and now Rob's wife and Bert were dead. She suspected once again that Rob Hart was the killer. Had he killed his wife and then Bert? And if not Hart, then who? Someone was out there, and they must know about her too. A shiver ran along her spine.

Was she in danger too?

CHAPTER TWENTY-TWO

She had to get back to work, but she had to speak to Roger again first. She took the stairs two at a time down to the second floor, taking a moment to steel herself before she pulled open the heavy door and stepped back into the main autopsy suite. Mercifully, the upright bodies by the entrance had been covered over, the stretchers laid flat, but the sharp stench of formaldehyde mingled with the coppery scent of old blood made her wince once again. Although it seemed odd considering where she was, Jessie knocked before she pulled open the door to the autopsy room.

Roger turned as she entered. "I'm glad you came back. I'd like to show you something," he said, gesturing to Bert's body, opened now from his throat to his navel, his lungs and heart and stomach visible even from where she stood. A drain at the foot of the gurney dripped with his body fluids and Tony was arranging metal bowls on a side table to collect organ specimens.

She shook her head and turned away quickly, forcing back the bile that crawled into her throat. "I... I can't," she said. "Can I speak to you outside?"

"Sure," he said. "Just give me a minute here."

Jessie pushed against the door and stepped into the main room, the first hints of a headache pulsing behind her eyes. She backed up to the exit door, so she could leave if she needed to. She whisked away the bead of sweat that erupted on her forehead despite the chill in these rooms.

Within minutes Roger appeared, drying his hands on a towel and throwing it into a laundry bin when he was finished. "Sorry," he said. "That was insensitive. I forgot that you knew him."

"It's okay." Roger seemed somehow disconnected from the real world unless he was talking about bodies.

"Hmm." Roger fished in his pocket for a mint. "Want one?" he asked, holding the container out.

She took one and popped it into her mouth, the taste of bile and the overwhelming scents fading as the mint dissolved on her tongue.

"My trick to make this more bearable."

"Thank you," she said. "I forgot to tell you that Bert knew Rob Hart. I know it's a stretch, but it got me wondering. Do you think Bert's death is connected to Ann Hart's?"

He made a *tsk*ing sound. "Because Gibbons knew Hart?" He shook his head. "That's a big leap, I'd say. That's for the police, not me, but I did find something interesting."

"What's that?" Jessie asked, her nausea, the foul scents all but forgotten.

"His hyoid bone, the little bone beneath the chin, wasn't just fractured, it was crushed. While a person might break his hyoid bone while hanging himself, it's just as likely—if not more so—to be the result of strangulation. His cricoid cartilage—that ring of cartilage around the trachea—was fractured as well. That also happens with strangulation." He rubbed the side of his head as if to help with his reasoning. "Combining the two fractures with that deep wound on his neck, and the small pinpoint hemorrhages in his eyes, I'd say that Mr. Gibbons was most definitely murdered.

"He probably put up a good fight judging by the defensive wounds on his fingers and hands. He had a large bruise on his abdomen, too, as though someone had to kneel hard on him while he had the life choked out of him." He ran his fingers through his hair. "Yeah, I'd say he put up a hell of a fight. The bleeding from his neck wound, and from his ears and mouth and even that bruise, happened before the hanging. He was hung only after he was dead."

"Oh, God," Jessie said stumbling back, the door breaking her fall.

Roger reached out and grasped her elbow. "Do you need to sit?" Jessie shook her head.

"No. I'm alright," she said though of course she wasn't. It was one thing to think something, even to be convinced of something, but to be proven right—there was no satisfaction in that. Not this time.

"It is pretty shocking what one human being can do to another, isn't it? I'm sorry this happened to your friend."

She picked at her fingernails and nodded. They stood in silence until she knew she could speak without breaking down. "The thing is," she said, "he wasn't my friend. I didn't even like him, and I was pretty mean to him myself. Now this. I just can't wrap my brain around it." She shook her head as if to clear the memory. "Will you tell the police?"

"Of course. This is a homicide now. I'll call them to let them know my findings, and so they can pick up his belongings and his phone—that might offer up some information. I'll tell them as well that they should speak to you, that you may have information."

"But I don't really," she said, her tone higher than she'd meant it to be. Once the police had his phone, they'd see his calls and that last text before she'd blocked him. Her stomach knotted up.

"Don't worry. The police will take care of this."

She leaned forward and let her head fall into her hands. *How the hell did she get involved in this? In any of this?* She took a deep breath. Bert knew Hart, he'd even helped him, and now he was dead too. It seemed too much of a coincidence. "Can I ask you something?"

"Anything. If I can answer it, I will."

"You did the post-mortem on Ann Hart, right?"

He tilted his head. "Very sad, that one." He sank into a nearby chair. "I'm old-fashioned. I still write out my reports. It helps me to remember my findings. My secretary transcribes them into the computer. I'm not sure I can share that information, though."

Jessie pulled up a chair and sat down. "I took care of her the night she came in, and I took care of him in the ICU. I just have one question. I know that Ann Hart was pregnant, about ten weeks by the numbers."

Roger pushed his eyeglasses onto his forehead, and sat back. "And?"

"Is it possible for a man who's had a vasectomy to impregnate a woman?"

"Are you saying that Hart had a vasectomy?"

"It's a HIPAA violation if I answer that, but theoretically, is it possible?"

He shook his head. "Less than one percent chance, despite what you see on television."

"So she died from the single gunshot wound to her head? Nothing else?"

"I'm not sure what you mean. But that one bullet caused her death—it ricocheted around her skull. A horrific injury."

"I'm not even sure why I'm asking this, but did her family—her parents—did they know about the pregnancy?"

"According to the medical record, they did. A nurse documented that they'd asked how far along the pregnancy was, and as you know, it was early. She was still in her first trimester. So, the answer to your question is yes. They knew. I'd rather you not share that information."

"I won't. The police have this information, too, right?" she asked, thinking of Sam. She knew that he did, but he hadn't seemed interested in the pregnancy—or her thoughts on that case. She couldn't help but wonder why.

"I'm only assuming here, but if I've read her chart, it makes sense that they would, doesn't it?"

Jessie smoothed her scrubs and stood. "There's so much that doesn't make sense, but that does." She heaved a slow sigh. "I have to get back to work. Thanks, Dr. Dawson. Roger."

"I'll call the police to pick up my preliminary report. I can get one for you as well if you'd like."

"I guess so, but can you hold onto it? I just don't want to keep thinking about this. I need to clear my head, but I'll come by another time for it. I just need a break."

"No problem," he said. "It'll give me a chance to convince you to come work with me. We could fix it so you work part-time in the ER and part-time here."

"I don't think my boss would let me."

"I like to think I have a little clout. Just say the word." He smiled, showing off his perfectly straight, shiny white teeth.

Jessie lingered in the morgue's entry, the thought of the police seeing Bert's phone somehow disturbing. She pulled her own phone out of her pocket and scrolled through her contacts. At least she hadn't deleted Bert, she'd just blocked him. She pressed *voicemail* and then *blocked messages*, releasing any messages Bert might have left. And there they were, four of them.

The first call was last Sunday, just five days ago and only an hour after he'd sent the text that she'd deleted.

"Jessie, please call me back. This is important. I have to speak with you. Please." There was a pause as though he was about to say more, and then a click. The call had ended.

Jessie leaned against the wall, a sudden chill running through her. With trembling fingers, she hit *play* and listened again. "Dear God," she said out loud, "what the hell is wrong with me? Listening to these?" But she couldn't help herself and she scrolled to the next voicemail.

Left on Monday morning, the day of Ann Hart's funeral, the next message was quicker, a total of four seconds: "Jessie, call me. It's important." His voice was firm, demanding, the old Bert, certain he could convince anyone to do anything.

Later that same day, he'd left another message: "I'm leaving for London tomorrow, but before I go, I have to warn you about someone. I might have my biggest story ever, but I'm not sure I can ever use it. Just don't trust anyone. Call me as soon as you can."

His final message came on Tuesday morning. "Call me, Jessie. Please. I think the police might be involved in the Hart shooting, or the cover-up." His voice dropped to a near whisper, and she held the phone to her ear. "There's more, but I need to speak with you. Be careful. Don't trust the police on this. Just call me."

Jessie clutched her chest and slid down the wall to the floor, the phone in her hand. *The police.* Of course, it made sense. Sam was in charge of the investigation, but he wasn't looking at Rob Hart the way it seemed he should. She considered for only a millisecond that Bert might mean Nick, but he had nothing to do with the investigation, or the shooting for that matter. He meant Sam. She was sure of it. Something was very wrong here, and Bert had been on to it.

"Hey, Jessie," Tony said. "You still here? You okay?"

She slipped her phone into her pocket and stood. "Yeah, sorry. Just a shock, you know." She couldn't tell Tony about the messages—if she was smart, she wouldn't tell anyone. Her legs felt wobbly and she felt herself sway. Tony reached down and she let him help her up.

"Come on," he said. "It's not easy to see someone you knew like that. I'll walk you across the street."

She let him guide her back to the ER, gulping in fresh air, hoping to clear her head. Her shift wasn't over yet. "Hey, Elena," she said. "I'm sorry that took so long."

Elena, her brow wrinkled, took a step closer. "What's wrong, Jessie? You look as though you've seen a ghost. Have you been crying?"

She swiped a hand quickly across her eyes. "It was those damn chemicals over there. I didn't realize how toxic they are. I'll be right back. I'm just gonna fix my makeup." It wasn't just her makeup that had suffered; she was suddenly exhausted, drained, as though she'd run a marathon and then worked a double shift. In the staff bathroom, she surveyed the damage. Her eyeliner and mascara were intact, but she was pale and ghostly. She splashed water on her face, dried off with a paper towel and re-applied a fresh coat of lipstick and swipe of blush to her cheeks.

Reassured that she could pass for normal, she pulled open the door and stepped back into the ER and right into the path of Nick. "Hey," he said. "I've been looking for you." He tilted her chin up. "What's wrong?"

"Nothing," she said, not wanting to tell him about Bert or the morgue, or the voicemails. "It's just that it's been busy, I guess."

"Really? It's quiet on the streets. A few shoplifters, and that's about it. That might all change later, but I'll be long gone." He smoothed his hand over her hair. "How about Foley's after work?"

She shook her head. "Not tonight. Another time?"

He grasped her hand. "Last night your eyes sparkled a bright green. Tonight, they're a dull brown. Come on, Jessie. Let me put that sparkle back in your eyes."

And despite her dismal mood, she laughed.

"I've convinced you, haven't I?"

"I don't know…"

"Let me show you off, let everyone there know you're my girl."

Her misgivings melted away. It was probably a good idea to go, to do something that would take her mind off Bert. And Sam. "You know what? Yes. I'll see you there." She made a quick check to be sure no one was watching and planted a kiss on his mouth. "See you later," she whispered, dragging her fingers across his lips.

Nick raised a brow mischievously and strode off, humming.

Just like she had, a lifetime ago.

CHAPTER TWENTY-THREE

At eleven-thirty, Jessie gave report to the night charge nurse, gathered her things and headed to Foley's. It was almost twelve when she arrived, the bar's overflowing crowd spilling into the street. She elbowed her way through and stood on her toes looking for Nick, but try as she might, she couldn't see him. She squeezed by a large group at the bar and felt a hand on her shoulder. She turned, smiling, and then her mouth dropped open.

It was Sam. He gripped her shoulder firmly, and he was speaking, shouting really, to be heard above the noise.

Her heart racing, she shrugged his hand away and shook her head.

"Come outside for a minute," he said. He tugged at her hand and started to lead her through the side door, which led to an alley.

Jessie pulled back. There was no way she'd let herself be alone with him in an alley, not after Bert's messages. She just didn't trust him anymore. There was too much that he'd dismissed, too much about him and his investigation that didn't make sense. "No. I don't want to go out."

A sudden look of confusion clouded his eyes, and he stood for a minute before pointing to the back of the bar. "Down there, then. It's a little quieter. I won't have to shout."

She followed him to the back corner, where the noise wasn't quite as loud, and you could actually be heard without hollering.

"Hey," he started, "sorry for not answering your text. I was at my sister's house for the holiday. Just got back and planned to call you tomorrow. So, what was so important?"

She struggled to remember what it was she'd texted him about. Though it was only yesterday, it already seemed light years away.

"Hart," he answered. "You mentioned him in your text."

And then she remembered she'd wanted to share that Bert had snuck into the ICU and had probably been helping Hart by planting stories favorable to him in the press. But it didn't seem to matter now. Bert was dead. Sam hadn't seemed focused on Hart anyway, and if Bert was right, then maybe Sam was involved. What she needed to do was to unravel herself from this mess, and so she shook her head. "I don't remember. Maybe it was to let you know he'd been discharged."

Sam raised a brow. "The text seemed, at least to me, to indicate that it was more than that. And what's wrong with you? You're so distant. Are you angry that I didn't answer your text right away?"

"No. It's not that. I'm just tired, that's all." Worried that he'd sense her fear, she focused her gaze on the wall behind him.

"Want to get out of here? Find someplace quiet?" He smiled, his gray eyes shimmering in the dim light, and for a moment, she wondered if she was wrong about him. But it was only for a split second, and then she remembered again that he'd been almost too protective of Hart and too quick to blow off her thoughts about his involvement in his wife's death. Then there was Bert. She was with Nick now, anyway. It was a good choice, for once in her life. And she needed to stick with it.

"No. I'm meeting someone here."

"Oh," he said, surprise in his voice.

"Hey, Jessie!"

She turned to see Nick and relief swept over her. "He's here," she said, turning back to Sam. "See you later." She backed away, the confusion in his eyes stealing the shimmer, making it seem that he was glaring at her.

Nick pulled her into his arms and kissed her, almost too slowly for such a public place. "Why were you talking to him?" he asked, tilting his head toward Sam, who still stood alone at the back of the bar.

"Just work stuff. It's not important."

"It looks as though he thinks it's important. He's staring at us."

"Don't pay attention. Buy me a glass of wine." She didn't have to turn to know that Sam was watching her. She could feel his eyes boring into the back of her head.

"Stay right here," Nick said, disappearing back into the crowd.

Suddenly, Sam was beside her once again. "Are you seeing him, Jessie?" he asked.

"What if I am?"

"Be careful. He's a cowboy, a rogue cop some say. I'm usually a pretty good judge of character, and I just don't trust the guy."

Jessie stepped back. "You're a good judge of character," she said, raising her brow and her voice. "This from the man who believes Rob Hart? Listen Sam, Nick is a stand-up guy. He's as solid as they come. Just leave me, leave us, alone." Her tone, her attitude, was sharper than she'd meant it to be. It was Bert, and Ann Hart, and everything else. She slipped her hands behind her back so he couldn't see the tremors. She wasn't sure she was doing the right thing, but she had to take a stand.

Sam's jaw went slack and he shook his head sadly. "I don't understand where this is coming from. I don't get it, Jessie, but if that's what you want, I won't bother you again."

"That's what I want," she said softly. She folded her arms across her chest, her eyes scanning the crowd for Nick. When she saw him, she waved and watched as he made his way toward her and handed her a glass of wine. She took it and guzzled almost half the glass, the alcohol like lightning in her throat. She hadn't eaten. God, she'd be lit in no time.

"You're trembling," Nick said, taking her hand. "Come on, let's sit." He led her into an empty booth and slid in next to her, draping his arm over her shoulder. "You okay?"

She nodded. "Just cold," she answered as she watched Sam, his head bowed, his shoulders sagging, leave the bar.

Nick waved over a couple of his policeman friends, their uniform trousers topped by sweatshirts and jackets. The men smiled over their beers, giving not so discreet thumbs up to Nick, who winked at her. They made small talk, the usual stuff about nothing, the weather—too cold, or maybe too warm, work—too busy, or maybe not busy enough, the new iPhone—pricey, but what isn't? Thank God for Foley's, they all agreed, tapping glasses in unison.

"Another round!" someone shouted, and a third, or was it the fourth round, arrived. Jessie pushed hers away and looked at her watch. It was after one a.m. and she was dead on her feet, the wine sloshing around her brain making her words slur and her thoughts blur, and she laughed aloud at her own cleverness. She nudged Nick and tilted her chin toward the exit.

"You ready?" Nick asked, and after too many goodbyes to count, she settled into her car, Nick at the wheel, and noticed the first of the season's Christmas lights along the way. This year though, would be different. She had Nick. At home, he inexplicably poured another drink for each of them.

"Oh, God, Nick, none for me. I have to get some sleep. I want to run tomorrow."

He pulled her onto his lap. "Thought you might need it. You seemed tense tonight."

She hadn't thought he'd noticed, but he was more perceptive apparently than most men. Still, she didn't feel like talking about Bert or Hart, or even Sam. She shrugged.

He ran his fingers through her hair. "It was that detective, wasn't it?"

"No, not really." But she was a lousy liar after a few drinks, and she watched as he shook his head.

"Just tell me," he said, his eyes pleading. "I don't want anyone, or anything, to bother you."

And she gave in, but not to everything. "Sam said I should be careful with you. That you're a cowboy, and he doesn't trust you. I guess he was trying to convince me that I shouldn't trust you either." She'd just begun to lean in for a kiss when he stiffened and pushed her away.

"What the hell?" he said, his eyes flashing, the once-deep blue of them suddenly cold with anger.

"Geez," Jessie muttered, the last remnants of her buzz fading away. "Why are you so upset? I'm with you, so I obviously do trust you. And I like cowboys, so I don't see any problems, do you?"

"Yeah, I do. I'm no cowboy. I worked my butt off to get on the job. It's all I ever wanted. I joined the Army right out of high school 'cause I knew a kid from Charlestown would never get on the force without that. I even did a tour in Iraq." He took a swig of beer. "Sorry," he said. "I'm no cowboy. I'm a good cop, a good loyal cop."

"You are," she whispered, running her fingers along his hand.

His muscles seemed to relax and he planted a silky kiss on her lips before backing away once more. "I'm going to tuck you in and head home. You can get your run in and I can get some overtime in the morning. Okay?"

She grinned playfully and headed to her bedroom, pulling off her scrubs as she went.

"Oh, God," he muttered. "You're not going to make this easy, are you?"

She shook her head and placed her palm against his chest, wiggling her fingers through the buttons on his shirt, allowing the heat of him to seep into her hand and from there to her very center. Nick moaned and peeled off his own clothes before slipping into bed beside her.

Sleep eluded both of them, but for the best possible reasons. When Jessie finally curled herself into the curve of Nick's body, she knew he was the one for her.

No matter what Sam had to say about it.

CHAPTER TWENTY-FOUR

A headache the next morning was the only reminder that Jessie had overdone it, and with any luck, a good run and a couple of ibuprofen would take care of that. She guzzled water and orange juice and slipped out the door and down the stairs. She was just pulling the entry door open when Rufus opened his door.

"Hey, Jessie, how are you?"

"I'm good," she said, closing the door against the rush of cold air. "And you?"

He nodded. "For an old man, I'm good. But I was wondering—did you get your lock fixed?"

"To tell you the truth, I forgot all about that. But it seems to be fixed, or maybe it's me. Either way, I haven't had any problems in the last few days. So, I guess I'm good. I'm almost afraid that saying it out loud will jinx me." But she couldn't help wondering why her lock troubles had seemed to stop so suddenly. She shook off the thought. "Thanks for asking, Rufus."

"Get that lock checked anyway. Or, get a new lock. Better safe than sorry."

She leaned in to hug him. "I will," she said, planting a quick kiss on his cheek. She pulled open the door and turned back. "Hey, want to have lunch? Maybe go to the L Street Diner?"

His light brown eyes, normally fogged over with the haze of early cataracts, lit up. "I'd love that, but I have leftover turkey and potatoes. How about we share that? Have a delayed Thanksgiving lunch?"

Jessie nodded and headed out, blaming the cold for the tears that nipped at her eyes. She ran her usual loop and managed to block out Bert, Sam and Rob Hart. When she turned for home, she stopped at the corner store for coffee, and couldn't help but notice the Christmas wreath on the door. Maybe this year, she'd do something to decorate, see if Nick wanted to help her out, maybe put up a tree together. She needed to get her real life back. That would be a good first step.

"Well, there ya are," Patrick greeted her as she entered, his brogue as soothing as his smile. "Muffin?" he asked as he handed her her usual coffee—black, no sugar.

"Not today. I'm having a delayed Thanksgiving lunch."

"That's lovely. You had to work the holiday, then? See, you are an angel. The newspapers had it right."

Newspapers? Her eyes nervously scanned the headlines. Hart was gone from the front page, and Bert hadn't made it there either. The poor guy's death hadn't even caused a ripple. "Thank God, those stories are history." She passed him two dollars and raised her cup in salute, turning to wave as the little bell over the door jingled.

She walked home, the brisk air clearing away the last bits of her semi-hangover. At home, she tidied up, showered, pulled on jeans and a sweater and headed out to buy a pie, and maybe another treat or two. She couldn't show up to lunch empty-handed.

Her dad had always said that when invited anywhere, she should arrive with arms so full, she'd have to ring the doorbell with her elbows. And everyone liked pie, right? At this time of year, it was practically required eating. At the supermarket, she chose a fresh-baked apple pie and when the caramel topping of a pecan pie caught her eye, she grabbed that one as well. Warm, crusty rolls enticed her next, and then everyone's childhood favorite—a box of Whitman's Sampler chocolates. She smiled as the cashier scanned her items. Aside from Patrick, who really only knew her for her coffee preference, Rufus was her first friend in Southie, a place where friendships weren't forged over fences and green lawns, where you had to earn your friends one at a time—and that suited her just fine.

She rang his bell with her elbow, a full smile draping her lips when he pulled open the door, his metal baseball bat still at the ready by the entry. "Welcome," he said, ushering her inside his apartment. Jessie passed the packages to him and stopped. It was a little larger than her own, but the rooms, the hallway, and almost every bit of space in her line of sight was filled with stuff. Three piles of newspapers, one almost as tall as she was, narrowed the entryway. To follow Rufus, she had to turn sideways and inch her way through. The walls were covered with fading, peeling bits of wallpaper. The floors were hidden under layers and layers of she didn't know what. Boxes, some filled with clothes, others with old catalogues, still another with old cans and jars, were pushed tight along the wall. The scent of food, long past its expiration date, and cat litter hung in the air. Her eyes stung and her throat burned. She coughed and found herself in a kitchen. This room, though still cluttered, was at least cleaner, the air less pungent. A washing machine hummed in the corner. A stack of dishes dried on the counter.

Rufus pulled out a chair and shooed a sleeping cat away. "Have a seat. Lunch is almost ready. You're my first guest in a while, and as you can see, I haven't had time to clean." He swept his arm up, motioning around the room.

"Let me help," she said. "I can clear a few things away for you."

"Not today," he said. "Another time, I'll welcome your help, but I'll need to go through everything first. Some of that stuff I've saved for a reason. Today, we'll share a meal and get to know each other."

She realized, then, that though he was thin, he wasn't quite as frail as she'd assumed. His heavy flannel shirt hugged his shoulders; his belt was pulled tight on the second hole. He brushed back a strand of thinning white hair from his forehead, the skin there crisscrossed with blue veins. "Haven't had time for a haircut or a shave either." He winked. "There was a time I looked pretty good, but once Mary died, well, things changed. I've just turned seventy-one. It doesn't matter so much how I look these days. No young girls, or old ones, are ringing my doorbell. Well, present company excluded." He winked again.

"I think you look fine," Jessie answered, catching his eye as he set the platter down, turkey and potatoes spilling from the sides. He sat heavily, his knees creaking louder than the chair.

The turkey was the rubbery deli slices they served at the hospital, the potatoes from a box, but all served so lovingly, with a glass of milk, that Jessie shoveled it in. "Delicious," she said through a mouthful of potatoes. "Did you make this?"

"No," he answered, a sly smile on his lips. "Truth be told, it's from the Senior Center. They sent all of us home with plenty of leftovers. Glad you like it. Of course, my Mary would have done better. She could cook like nobody's business." He sank a little further in his seat, his eyes glazing over just enough to let her know his mind was on his dear Mary.

"Tell me about her," she said, and he did. They'd had no children but Mary was a kindergarten teacher, so they lived vicariously through her students. After Mary died, that connection was lost. "I used to drive a bus, but they don't want old men driving, and I understand that. I don't drive at all these days. My eyes aren't what they used to be."

"Well, I drive. I can take you where you need to go."

He nodded. "That'd be nice, Jessie. I appreciate that."

She imagined that if her father were still alive, he'd be as kind and sweet as Rufus, but the reality was he'd been a gruff and angry man, a quiet rage seeping from his pores. He didn't share much about her mother, only that she'd abandoned them both. There were no pictures, no mementoes; it was as though she never existed, so different from here in Rufus's apartment where his wife seemed to be everywhere—in the faded kitchen curtains, the plastic flowers by the sink, the worn linoleum on the floor. This was a home where love still lived. Jessie sighed. She'd been a latchkey kid, her childhood home as empty as a tomb.

"Pie?" she asked, hoping to clear her head of old memories. She stood and began to clear the table.

He raised a brow. "I never met a man who could turn down a piece of pie." He chose apple. "Those pecans look good, but I'm not sure my old teeth can stand up to them." He smiled, revealing a few missing teeth.

Jessie munched on a large slice of pecan pie, before finally pushing away from the table. "I'm stuffed. I'll clean up."

"I'll help," Rufus said, his hands on the table to help propel himself up.

"Oh, no you don't." Jessie placed her hand on his shoulder and gently nudged him back into his seat. "You know the rule—whoever cooks does not have to clean. Today, it's my job."

She cleared the table, washed the dishes, wiped down the counters and swept the floor.

"There," she said, setting the broom in the corner and pushing her hair back from her face. "Thank you for my Thanksgiving lunch, Rufus. This year, I'm thankful for you." She kissed him on the forehead.

"Oh, you dear girl," he said. "You are an angel."

She loathed that word these days; it reminded her of Hart, Sam and Bert, and all of that freaking misery that she needed to put behind her. She opened her mouth to reply when her phone buzzed with a text, and she retrieved it from her pocket to have a look.

WATCH THE NEWS TONIGHT! I made the big time!

She never understood or much liked that sunglass emoji that Nick had used. *First world problems*, she thought, catching sight of Rufus out of the corner of her eye.

"Sorry," she said, stuffing the phone back into her pocket. "I don't know why I had to look."

"No need for apologies, my dear. You're a nurse. Any message could be important."

"Thanks, Rufus," she said. "I'll come by tomorrow to see if you need anything." She squeezed her way back to his door and pulled it open. "Lock this behind me," she called.

Upstairs, her tiny apartment suddenly seemed spacious, but her jeans, after eating her fill, not so much. She clicked on her television and tugged herself out of her jeans before pulling on a pair of comfy, loose sweatpants. Grabbing a Diet Coke, she settled onto her couch just as a breaking news alert was announced. Everything was breaking news these days, but the banner that scrolled across the screen shouted that an arrest had been made in the Hart robbery and shooting.

"Jose Ramos," the reporter shouted gleefully, "the only suspect in the Hart robbery and shooting, has been arrested." The screen filled with a video of a young disheveled Hispanic male being handcuffed and led to a police car. A tattoo—a scrolled capital M—was inked into the side of his face. He was shouting angrily into the camera. "I'm innocent," he snarled.

The camera pulled away for a long shot, and she saw Nick, his eyes determined and cool, leading Ramos to the car, putting his hand on Ramos's head as he was guided into the backseat. Nick slammed the door, his stern façade replaced by a satisfied smugness. "Any comment, officer?" the reporter asked as Nick walked around the police car and opened the driver's door.

"Nothing now. I'm sure there'll be a statement from headquarters." With that, he pulled the door shut and sped away, the camera focusing on the glow of the car's brake lights as they faded from view and the camera turned back to the reporter. "The arrest, we know, was made when Officer Nick Dolan spotted the suspect and followed him here to Day Boulevard while calling in for backup, but before they could come, the astute policeman had cut off the suspect and made the arrest. That's all for now. We'll cover the news conference live as it happens. For now, back to you in the studio." Headshots of the Harts filled the screen—and like a moth to a flame, Jessie was riveted once again by the story.

She checked the other local channels. They were all covering the breaking news of Ramos's arrest. Finally, she paused, rewound and replayed the frames focusing on Ramos. She moved closer to the screen to see if the tattoo on his hand was visible, but with his hands cuffed behind his back, there was nothing to see. She focused again on his face and shook her head.

Though she'd been trying not to think about it, she still believed that Hart was somehow involved, and Bert had probably known that. This arrest didn't change anything.

CHAPTER TWENTY-FIVE

It wasn't long before her phone buzzed with a new text from Nick.

Did you see it? Watch the news conference! I'm getting ready to go out there with the mayor, the commissioner and the DA.

He ended his message once again with that smiley face with sunglasses. This time he included a string of hearts as well.

When the news conference was announced, she turned up the volume and curled her legs underneath her. The mayor stepped forward to a bank of microphones and introduced the police commissioner who stood stiffly, his hands behind his back. The District Attorney, a middle-aged woman with short, graying hair, a rosy complexion, and a suit that shone under the lights, stepped forward, her hands folded demurely in front of her. She tilted her head slightly when she was introduced, and then let her eyes fall to the ground, allowing the mayor to have the full attention of the press. She knew the DA's reputation—quiet and mouse-like at first glance, but a demon and a warrior in the courtroom. It was a rare case that she lost, and if she believed Ramos was guilty, then he likely was.

That would mean her whole stupid theory would come crashing down. What the hell had she been thinking anyway? She was no detective, and neither was Bert. She should just stick to what she knew—nursing. On the other hand, who saw people during their best and worst moments in life? Nurses. Therefore, it made sense that she was a good judge of character, or lack thereof.

The camera panned to the group behind the mayor and Jessie caught sight of Nick, standing just as the commissioner was, stiffly, with his hands behind his back. But his blue eyes were sparkling in the fluorescent lights, and she could almost feel his thrill at being the one who captured Ramos. Off to the side, and too far to see how his gray eyes were responding to the news, stood Sam, his arms crossed, a sour expression—or maybe it was simply disbelief—on his tightly pinched face. Probably angry that Nick was the hero.

Mayor Reilly tapped the microphone as he spoke. "The city has been consumed with this tragedy for almost two weeks now. Many of you likely thought that the case would never be solved, the suspect never caught, but the police have been working on this every minute of every day, and today, Officer Nick Dolan made the arrest that we all have worked so hard for." He rotated and pointed to Nick. "Well done, Officer Dolan. The city thanks you for your bravery and a job well done."

Nick nodded his head, his blue eyes dancing with pleasure at the attention, but his face remained serious. Only someone who knew him would catch that look of satisfaction at a job well done.

"Commissioner Conley?" The mayor turned and invited the commissioner to speak.

The commissioner adjusted his tie as he stepped forward. "We are still in the investigatory phase of the Hart murder and shooting. Ramos, a member of MS-13, has been arrested on unrelated murder charges, but we are looking into his potential involvement with the Harts," he said. "We are not going to comment on the particulars of this investigation and this case just yet. We do not want to risk releasing any information that might jeopardize the process, going forward. Thank you for respecting that aspect of this case."

He wasn't convincing. He seemed as though even he didn't quite believe the facts he was so reluctant to sell to a hungry press. The DA stepped forward and echoed Conley's sentiment. "I'll save my comments for the courtroom when and if we get there," she said softly before stepping back.

Nick was invited forward next for questions from the press.

"When did you first spot him?"

"How did you know it was Ramos?"

"Why did you arrest him alone?"

The questions flew, and Nick seemed shell-shocked. "Whoa," he said, holding up a hand. "I'm not used to this." Laughter rippled through the crowd of reporters. Nick had them eating out of his hand. His eyes sparkled again. "I'll just read a statement, if that's alright."

Mayor Reilly nodded and Nick began. "At about three o'clock, I was driving on Dorchester Avenue when I spotted the suspect. I recognized the make of the car, which we knew belonged to his sister. When I checked the plate number it came back registered to one Iris Ramos. I didn't want the suspect to see me, so I kept a two-car distance behind him, and followed until he was on Day Boulevard. That's a busy street, lots of people and cars about. He began to speed up and I was afraid that he'd made me. I called it in then, and just as he was about to turn into L Street, which is narrow and crowded, I knew I had to corner him. I wanted to avoid being stuck in a tight area. I put my siren on and raced ahead, cutting him off in the intersection with L Street. He didn't resist. I had him cuffed before assistance arrived."

"Why did you wait to call it in?"

"I wanted to have a visual. When he started to make the turn, I could see clearly that the driver was Jose Ramos."

"Did you read him his Miranda rights?"

"I did," he said, remaining unflustered.

"But," one female reporter shouted, "did he understand? Does he speak English? I remember that Rob Hart said he had a heavy Spanish accent."

Jessie could have kissed that woman for her question. She wasn't alone in her doubts.

"He understood. He definitely spoke English today." Nick was reveling in the attention.

"Can you tell us about that tattoo?" someone shouted. "What about the gun? Do you have that? The phone, the wallet?" Suddenly, the questions were flying so fast again, it was hard to make them out. The DA and Commissioner Conley moved forward, blocking Nick from view.

"That's enough for now, folks. Please respect that as we move forward, it's imperative for us to guarantee the integrity of the investigation and ultimately, the case in court." They all turned and headed back into headquarters, but their leaving did nothing to deter the rapid flow of questions. It was almost as if the reporters were trying to outdo one another.

"How can you be sure you have the right man?"

"Is there other evidence that you haven't shared?"

"Does Ann Hart's family know about the arrest?"

She wondered that herself. Had someone called them? What about Rob Hart? Did he know? Jessie stood and stretched. A nap was what she needed. Sleep might just wipe away a lot of her questions. She drew her blinds, crawled under the covers of her bed, and quickly drifted off, waking what seemed just minutes later to the insistent buzz of her phone. It was Nick.

"Hey," he said breathlessly. "Did you see it? I've been texting you. Where are you?" He was so excited he didn't bother pausing so she might answer.

"Nick!" she finally interrupted him. "I saw you. Congratulations! You were wonderful."

"Really? You really think so?"

"I do, and I think anybody who saw that thinks so too. Don't worry. You were great!"

"I'm working till midnight." As if to emphasize that, his police radio squawked in the background. "I gotta go, but maybe catch a drink after?"

"Oh, Nick, I'd love to, but two nights in a row will kill me. You go. Have fun. I'll see you soon."

"Aww, Jess, you're the best. I'll be thinking of you all night."

Jessie wanted to answer in kind. She was definitely in like—in lust, even, but to think of him all night—that was still a bit of a leap for her. But honesty wasn't always the best policy. "Me too," she purred. "Me too."

She pulled the covers back over her head and slept for several hours, waking only when a full-on charley horse gripped her leg. She sat up and reached to massage her limb before stepping onto the floor to work it out. Too much running maybe, or maybe not enough. She rose, ran her fingers through her curls and wandered into the kitchen, where she drank a large glass of water and checked the time. Eight o'clock. Damn it, she'd missed the news. She'd have to stay up late to catch it, or just get up early and watch it then.

Her phone buzzed then, and she answered without looking.

"Glad you answered," the voice said. "Thought maybe you wouldn't."

It took a moment for the fog to clear her brain, and when it did, she heaved an exasperated sigh, her shoulders rising with the effort. "Sam…"

"I need to speak to you, and before you hang up, this is professional. It's not about you and me, or even Hart, though perhaps it's about him peripherally. Anyway, I'm calling about your friend Bert. I've been assigned that case."

She groaned, unwilling to share the voicemails with him. If Bert was right and the police were involved, it would seem a poor choice to give them a heads-up. "He wasn't my friend, and I'm not sure why you need to speak with me. I can't add anything."

"The police at the scene called it a suicide and closed the inquiry. The ME said you were with him when he decided the death was a homicide. And you knew Bert. So, actually, I suspect you can add much more."

His voice had an undercurrent of something and she wasn't sure what it was. Suspicion, maybe? "I barely knew him."

"We have his phone, Jessie."

"So what?" she asked, her voice cracking.

"Jessie, please don't make this any harder than it is. I'll still have to question you," he said, his words growing muffled as he spoke to someone in his office. "Do you want to come in?"

"No! Of course, I don't want to come in. Just ask me what you need on the phone."

"That's not how it works. You know that."

"Are you kidding? Am I a suspect now?" Her heart pounded hard in her chest. This was how people got railroaded.

"God, no. But you are a material witness. You might know something that you don't even realize."

She thought of the ICU nurse saying that Bert and Rob seemed to be friends, and she wondered if Sam had any information about that. Something had been going on; Bert had somehow figured it out, or been involved, at least peripherally, and now he was dead. She'd been a miserable bitch to him, but she did want to help find the person who'd killed him. "Can you just speak to me on the phone? At least for now. I get that I'll need to see you, but it's getting late. I just want to go to bed. And I don't have anything to hide."

"I don't think you do either, Jessie. But Bert had been texting you. Did you get those texts?"

She poured another glass of water and sat down at her small kitchen table, gulping down one long, refreshing swig. "I got one text. I deleted it and blocked him." She wondered if he'd seen the calls.

"Alright, so you haven't seen the later texts?"

"No," she said, her voice quivering. "He texted me after that?"

"He did. I know this isn't easy for you. Can we back up a bit? Back to the text you sent me. Does that have anything to do with this?"

"I don't know. Probably not. I'd learned that Bert had gotten in to see Hart using his old ruse—pretending to be someone he wasn't. He told the ER clerk he was with the mayor's office. The ICU staff bought that story, too. And Rob asked the nurses for the telephone number to his room so Bert could call him directly. If you have Bert's phone, you must have seen those calls. For me, it seemed like more evidence that Hart was a snake and even involved in his wife's death."

"How does that prove anything?" he asked. She could almost see him shaking his head.

"Hart was planting stories with Bert that made him look good, that answered questions before anyone asked."

"Why didn't you tell me this the other night? I don't get it. A man that you despised is killed. You didn't think to share that, or his connection to Hart? Why not?"

A rustle of papers meant that he was probably taking notes while they spoke. "Because I decided I don't want to be involved in this. I don't want to think about that creep Hart for another minute."

"That's a big turnaround, isn't it?"

"Somebody's death will do that to you." She hoped she sounded as sarcastic as she felt.

"Are you worried that I'm protecting Hart?" he asked, his voice almost a whisper.

"It crossed my mind."

"Is that why you were so nervous around me?"

"Maybe."

"I'm not protecting Hart, or anyone else."

"I saw you on the news at the press conference but you seemed to be hiding in the back, almost as if you were distancing yourself from the whole thing."

"It looked that way, huh?"

"It did, and it got me to thinking—what exactly do you have on Ramos? Apart from tattoos and a Spanish accent?"

"*Significant* tattoos. He's no angel. He's a member of MS-13 and he has a long rap sheet, including murder, and he should have been arrested today, but not for the Hart murder. This case is complex, and there's still more than a few holes that we need to fill."

"You'd announced days ago that you were looking for this guy. If you weren't, why was he arrested?"

"Because there is a warrant for his arrest on murder charges," he said with a testy edge to his voice. "Nick should have followed him, called it in and we could have picked Ramos up without all the fanfare."

Jessie took in a deep breath and huffed it out. "Then why have a press conference?"

"The press listen to the police scanners, and they made it to the scene in time to film it. We had no choice, we had to answer their questions, but if you paid close attention, you'd have noticed that, aside from Nick, we were pretty close-mouthed."

"So, is Ramos the one?" Even through the phone she could almost see his shrug.

"I'm not sure. We'll see."

"So, you don't really have anything, do you?" She just couldn't seem to shut up.

"I can't tell you what I do or don't have," Sam snapped. "You're still convinced it was Hart? What exactly do *you* have?"

"Everything I've already told you—about a hundred times. I know it's circumstantial, but Bert texted me last week—said he had to speak with me, that it was important. It had to do with Hart. I know you don't believe a word of that, but I do."

She could hear the creak of his chair as though he was settling in for a long conversation.

"But you never spoke to him," he said, and she couldn't tell if it was a question or a statement.

"Right," she said warily. "A big mistake on my part, but I've made plenty of them. This one I regret more than most of the others. I think he knew something, and now he's dead."

"Good God, Jessie. Take this seriously and don't tell anyone. Bert sent you other texts and we know, too, that he called you. ·He may well have known something. He wanted you to know he thought someone in the Department was helping Hart."

"The Police Department?" She hoped she sounded surprised.

"Yes, and if Bert was killed to keep him quiet, and there's any hint that you know something, too… well, just keep it to yourself. Understood?"

A tiny bubble of fear bloomed in her gut. *But what if it was Sam who was involved?* He'd just asked her to protect him.

What the hell should she do now?

"Tomorrow is Sunday," Sam said. "I can pick you up for breakfast, that lets you avoid coming in to my office at headquarters to answer the rest of my questions. What do you say?"

"I…" Jessie hesitated.

Sam seemed to sense her reluctance. "I can meet you. We'll be in public. No need to worry about me, but I understand your angst."

No, you don't, she thought. "Victoria Diner on Mass. Ave? Nine?"

"Sounds good. I have a date tonight. Nine sounds fine."

An unexpected swell of jealousy burned into her brain. She wasn't even sure why. She had Nick. Sam deserved someone too.

"Are you still there?" he asked, obviously noticing her long pause.

"Yes. Sorry. I'll see you then."

"Okay, and Jessie, please, for your own safety, do not share what you know with anyone."

She took a long, hot shower, dried off, got a glass of wine and the mystery book she'd been reading—which probably explained her seeing suspects at every turn—and crawled into bed. It wasn't long before her eyes grew droopy and her vision hazy with sleep. She turned her light off, slid under the covers, and drifted quickly to sleep.

She woke with a start, a rustling sound coming from the living room. Someone was out there.

CHAPTER TWENTY-SIX

Her heart pumped wildly in her chest, her brain was on full alert, her synapses trying desperately to think of what to do. She slipped quietly from her bed and crept to the door, her ear listening for any other sounds, but there was only silence. She gripped the doorknob and rotated it softly as she opened the door to have a look.

The room was bathed in total darkness, a man's silhouette sprawled on her couch was all she could see, and deep heavy breathing all she could hear. She tensed her muscles and prayed as she inched forward and retrieved a knife from her kitchen and her phone from the table. The man, whoever he was, hadn't moved. Jessie held her breath and in one dizzying action, she clicked on the overhead light, held her knife upright, and suddenly, everything stopped—even the dust motes froze in their hurried flight and hung limply in the air.

She took a minute to understand what she was seeing, her jaw clenched, her fear replaced by anger. Her hand dropped to her side. Nick cowered and blinked at the brightness, his hands rubbing at his eyes.

"Hey, Jessie," he murmured.

"What the hell is wrong with you?" She tried not to shout, not to alarm Rufus, though his hearing likely was not what it used to be. "How did you get in here?" she hissed through gritted teeth.

"That useless lock. You still haven't had it fixed," he said, his speech slurred and slow. "I'm sorry, Jessie. I thought I'd surprise you, but I must have fallen asleep."

"Surprise me? Really? Are you kidding? It's two a.m. You break in here and curl up on my couch? I was terrified, you asshole! I should call the police."

"I didn't break in." He raised himself from the couch, stood shakily and staggered to her side. "I just wanted to see you, Jessie. This was a big day for me. I just wanted to share it with you." He paused to lean against the wall as if to get his bearings. "I missed you tonight," he whimpered, his eyes glassy, his hands shaky as he reached for her.

"Just sit down," she said icily, directing him back to her couch. "I'll make you some coffee."

He walked unsteadily and fell onto the couch. "I'm sorry, Jessie. I really am," he murmured as his head fell back, his eyes closed and his mouth flew open, letting the first of many snores escape.

She threw a blanket on top of him, turned the lock on her bedroom door, climbed back into bed, and with one eye cracked open and her fists held tight at her sides, she lay awake for what seemed like hours.

In the quiet of Sunday morning, he was gone, the crumpled blanket the only evidence of last night. She had a fleeting rush of guilt over the way she'd treated him, but she caught herself. *What the hell had he been thinking?* She shook her head, threw on jeans and a comfy top, and went downstairs to see Rufus.

"You all right, Jessie? You look frazzled."

"Morning, Rufus. I didn't sleep well. I'm here to ask for help with my lock."

"You're going to get it fixed? Finally," he said, relief in his tone. "We'll both sleep better with that taken care of."

"Can you help me?"

"If you'll drive me over to Home Depot in South Bay, I can. We can pick up a new lockset and I'll change it out for you."

Jessie checked her watch. "I'm meeting someone at nine. Can we go after that? Maybe eleven?"

"Just let me know. I'll be here. I'll just get my tools together."

"Thanks, Rufus. See you in a while."

Upstairs, she washed her face, untangled her curls, collected her keys and bag, and headed out. She locked her door and started down the stairs, and stopped. She turned and put her hand on the knob and wiggled and shook and sure enough, with a good push, the lock released. But it didn't really matter. Today, she'd have a new lock and no more surprise visitors.

At the Victoria, Jessie pulled around back and slid into a spot just as another car pulled out. Her phone buzzed with a text from Nick. She glanced quickly at his apology, silenced her phone, and slid it back into her pocket. Once inside, she spied Sam in a booth at the back, reading over a menu. She slid in across from him. "Morning," she said, "how was your date?"

"Morning, Jessie." He laid the menu on the table. "Thanks for coming. And my date was fine. Thanks for asking."

The little twinge of jealousy flared again and she couldn't help herself. She wondered who the woman was, what she did, what she looked like. She was willing to bet that Sam wouldn't be showing up drunk at his girlfriend's apartment at two in the morning. "So, what do you want to ask me?" she said with a smirk, hoping to cover her pathetic interest in his dating life.

The waitress, her blonde hair bobbed, her work smile pasted onto her face, suddenly appeared. She pushed her eyeglasses up with the end of the pencil. "Ready?" She lifted her notepad.

"Coffee, cream with two sugars, and toast for me," Sam said.

She turned to Jessie. "I'll have two eggs over easy, bacon, an order of home fries, and an English muffin, grilled, with extra butter."

The waitress raised a brow. "Coffee?"

"Black," she answered. "No sugar."

Their orders in, Sam leaned forward. "I think Bert Gibbons' death might somehow be tied into the Hart murder. From his texts, Bert seemed determined to tell you something about Hart, but of course, he can't now."

Jessie's eyes grew wide with feigned surprise. "What did his texts say? Do you have his phone?"

"Not with me. Crime Scene Unit has it, but the gist of his messages was that he didn't trust Hart and he thought the police were helping him."

"No names?"

"None. I think if he had a name, he planned to tell you that in person."

She wondered if he was telling the truth about Bert not naming names, and if he was, why wouldn't he bring the phone to show her? A tic pulsed behind her eyes; she blinked it away. "Do you think now that Hart was involved in his wife's death and maybe Bert's as well, or that a policeman was helping him?"

"Right now, that's a stretch, but I will tell you the whole thing's starting to stink. Bert, the whole Ramos thing…" He shook his head. "We did a profile, searched similar MOs and came up with Ramos and a handful of others. When his tattoos matched, it seemed like a score, but in retrospect, we landed on him too quickly, too easily, almost as though it was a set-up. We don't have a strong case against him, and he swears he has an alibi. Once that checks out, we'll move on in the case."

"Who was the first one to name him as a suspect? Or is he an accomplice?"

"We named him as a suspect based on Hart's description, and Ramos's history, his MO, his accent and his tattoos. And before you ask, there's no connection there to suggest that Ramos knew Hart. Nothing at all. Anyway, why would Hart turn an accomplice in? Ramos is not exactly a stellar citizen. Why would anyone with a brain team up with him? Ramos could turn on a dime. No," he said almost to himself, "there's nothing to suggest that."

The waitress slid their coffee cups onto the table. Jessie wrapped her hands around her mug, the heat seeping pleasantly into her fingers. Sam added cream and sugar to his coffee and seemed to take forever to stir it just so. He took a slow, lingering sip.

"So, what now?" Jessie asked, impatience adding an edge to her voice. "What did you want to ask me?"

"Anything at all you can tell me about Bert. Anything."

She recited what she knew of him once again. "I told you how he'd harassed me after I refused his advances, but then it just stopped, and I thought that was the end of it. But he got in touch again after the Hart shooting. He was a total jerk. He was arrogant, I guess, but not in an arrogant way, if you know what I mean. His arrogance was an act. I know that sounds crazy. He just pushed the envelope, you know? He wanted to be successful, make a big name for himself, and he almost did that once, but then he plagiarized an article, and he was fired. After that, he fell on hard times, or so he said. He was trying to get his reputation back. He said he'd written a book that would be published soon, and he had a job he was heading to in London."

She took a sip of her coffee as the waitress returned with their food. She speared the potatoes with her fork. "I don't think he killed himself. It's not just that things were turning for him. I mean, look at the evidence. It looks to me as though he fought back."

"It does," he said, smiling. "You have a pretty good sense of this stuff, Jessie. The ME confirms that Bert fought back. He says that you pointed out the abrasions on his fingers." He paused and took another slow sip from his mug. "We're running the prints we picked up at his place, and we're trying to get any videos of the neighborhood. See if we can spot anyone coming or going to his apartment."

"That didn't work so well with Hart."

"Those were city surveillance cameras that were out of order. In this case, we're asking homeowners for access to their security footage. They're a more reliable lot than government officials." Sam nibbled at his toast. "Not to change the subject, but I just have to say it's unusual to eat with someone while discussing the minute details of murders and bodies."

Jessie swallowed a chunk of bacon. "I'm an ER nurse. We can eat through anything."

"Apparently." Sam laughed. "So, does this mean you believe me? That Bert may have meant the police were involved, but it's someone else? You don't seem to be nervous around me."

She shrugged. "Daylight, even on this miserable cloudy day, gives me courage." *Not to mention last night*, she thought, remembering Nick's drunken break-in. She just couldn't picture Sam ever behaving that way. "I'm not saying I believe you, but just suppose I do. If not you, then who?"

Sam shook his head. "That is the million-dollar question, but you cannot repeat any of what we've discussed, or Bert's texts to you. Not a word. If Bert was killed because he knew something about Hart or the shooter, or because someone thought he did, then you could also be at risk."

An icy finger ran along her spine, and she shivered. She wondered if she was sitting across from the man who posed the greatest risk to her, but she couldn't let him know that. "Are you serious?"

"Yes, and you have to take this seriously, too. Tell no one. Understand?"

She shook her head. "No. If you let some of this information out, maybe you could flush out whoever was involved."

"I don't want any of this information to get out. One person speaks up, and then it spreads like wildfire. Best to just be quiet."

She used the last of her English muffin to soak up the runny bits of her egg. "Then why are you telling me so much?"

"Well, you're involved for one thing, and besides, an outsider's perspective can have real value. As an ER nurse, you might see things that I don't see."

"Have you spoken to Hart?" she asked through a mouthful of food.

"I've called his home number a few times. Stopped by and left messages asking him to call me. But nothing yet."

"Can't you pick him up?"

"For what? He's the victim, the grieving husband, and the DA is still not convinced that he was involved. Aside from that, he doesn't seem to be at home. We're not sure where he is."

Jessie pushed her plate away. "Are you kidding? Shouldn't you be tailing him?"

"That's a little dramatic, but yes, we'd like to know where he is and what he's up to."

"Ahh, you don't sound so certain of his innocence anymore."

Sam raised a brow, his gray eyes losing some of the coldness that had settled there. "Hmm... the investigation isn't nearly over yet. If you hear anything, no matter how insignificant it seems, call me. Agreed?"

She nodded.

"And if Hart contacts you, stay away from him, and call us right away." Sam leaned closer and she caught the acrid scent of old cigarettes, and she remembered noticing that same smell the night they'd first met in the Trauma hallway. "You smoke?" she asked, leaning back.

"Only at work. I found that a cigarette at grisly murder scenes calms me and helps me to focus, and a cigarette after a visit to the ME clears my airways of the smell of bodies and formaldehyde." He sniffed the collar of his suit jacket. "Probably should have changed this. Sorry."

"No need to apologize. I smoked in nursing school when exams were especially tough. I quit once I graduated, but there are those moments after a particularly rough trauma room case that I wish I still did." She inhaled deeply, imagining the rush of a cigarette once more. "Actually, a cigarette might make the ME's office more tolerable. Thanks for the suggestion."

"ME's office?"

"Roger Dawson asked if I'd be interested in working with him as a forensics nurse. He hasn't worked out the details yet, and my boss will likely say no, but it is intriguing—and still a secret, so please don't say anything."

Sam's eyes, ringed by deep bags, suddenly sparkled. "So, I think we have a deal. You keep my secret, I'll keep yours." He reached across and gripped her hand, holding it tighter and for longer than their simple agreement required.

And despite her own misgivings, she felt drawn to him once again.

CHAPTER TWENTY-SEVEN

"Your friend came by while you were gone," Rufus said later as he slid into her car.

"Friend?" She checked her rearview mirror and pulled into traffic.

"That young policeman. Don't know his name. He said to tell you he's sorry, and he'll call you later." Rufus smiled. "Ahh, young love."

"Well, young foolishness, anyway. Not sure I'd call it love just yet."

"Seems as though he does, Jessie. That fella is quite smitten, I'd say."

She laughed. "Well, when you say it like that, it sounds pretty good. Smitten. I like that word."

At Home Depot, Rufus quickly found the right lockset, while Jessie browsed the Christmas decorations and chose a tiny artificial tree decked out in lights and ornaments for her table. They headed next through the crush of early holiday shoppers to Stop and Shop for groceries. Finally, laden with plenty of bags, they headed home. Good to his word, Rufus appeared at her door with his tools. Despite his seeming frailty, he worked effortlessly, replacing the old lockset with a new one, and handing Jessie the keys.

"Try it," he said and she did, marveling at the smoothness of the tumbler in this new lock. It was sturdy and tight and impenetrable.

"It's perfect," she declared.

Rufus nodded. "I'd keep that second key hidden somewhere. Don't give it away just yet. Let's see what's going on with that door of yours."

"I'd like to give it to you, Rufus. That way, if I lose my key, I'll know you have one." She dropped the key into his hand and kissed his cheek.

"I'm going to go sort my groceries. See ya later, Jessie." He slid the key into his pocket and headed back downstairs, his feet padding soundlessly on the stairs.

When Nick called later, Jessie considered hitting *decline*, but her Christmas tree, tiny lights ablaze, was in her direct line of sight, putting her in a forgiving kind of mood. She paused before hitting *accept*.

"Oh, Jessie, I'm so sorry. I can't believe I did that. I was drunk. I'd been celebrating. I drank too much…"

He continued to prattle on, but she'd stopped listening. She was locking and unlocking her door, jiggling the knob, and working to see if she could loosen the lock, but it wouldn't give. It was secure, just what she needed. "What?" she asked, sensing an awkward pause in the admittedly one-sided conversation.

"Just say you'll forgive me. Please." He drew out the syllables, taking longer to say the word than it would to write it out in cursive. "It'll never happen again. Yesterday was such a big deal for me. I'm a patrolman, but all that attention gets me noticed and might help me to move up." His words continued to pour out in a rush and she was sure she could hear a sniffle or two. "Please?" he whispered again.

She heaved a noisy sigh so that he'd know she meant business. "You have to promise you'll never do anything like that again. That includes drinking so much. Promise?"

"Yes, Jessie. Of course, I promise. I'll do anything."

She paused, the sincerity in his tone convincing her that he was at least trying, and she supposed that should be enough. But was it? A tiny seed of doubt sprouted in her brain. The silence between them grew until Nick spoke up.

"Can I stop by tonight after work?" he asked.

"No, midnight's too late. Call me later and we'll figure something out."

"I miss you, Jess," he said again just as she hung up.

She spent the afternoon helping Rufus to clear some of the clutter from his apartment. "You know, Mary and I moved here right after we married," he said wistfully. "I always thought we'd move on once we had kids, but kids never came and we never left, so here I am surrounded by more than fifty years of stuff. I know that a lot of it is junk, but a lot of it is precious, at least to me, so we have to be careful what we throw away. Agreed?"

Jessie nodded and sat on the floor, fishing through large boxes and holding up items one by one. "This?" she asked, holding up a cracked and dingy plaster knick-knack. It seemed to her to be just junk, but it might mean the world to him.

He wavered before agreeing she could toss it. Next, she held up an old, moth-eaten blanket. "Ahh," he said, fingering the edges. "Mary bought that for me our first year together. She said I needed more than her to keep me warm. She was like you, a little bit of a thing. I know it's worn and well past its time, but I think I'll hold onto it."

For the first time, Jessie began to understand why people held onto stuff. This stuff wasn't junk—it was the mementoes of a long life, of memories that might be erased without these reminders. She hoped that someday, she'd be sifting through mementoes of her own. They continued to work slowly.

He did agree to throw out all of his old phone books and bus uniforms, except for one faded work shirt, his name embroidered on the pocket. "I'll just keep it in the closet. Just one. For those days when I want to remember." He sorted through an old photo album, pointing out Mary and describing the moments the photos depicted, the corners of his eyes filling up at the yellowed prints taped into the fraying pages. "We aren't getting much done, are we, Jessie?" he asked with an impish grin.

"How about I start to go through those old newspapers? There are piles of them, and they're a fire hazard. I should have tackled them first." She motioned to one of the too-numerous-to-count piles of old papers.

Wrinkling his brow, Rufus looked longingly at the piles of old newsprint. "Well…" he began to shake his head. "I don't know."

"Rufus, you can't possibly want those. They've got to go."

"I understand that, Jessie. I really do. It's just that I saved some of those for the stories I found. I know I should have kept them in separate piles but I didn't, and now I'm not ready to part with the pictures and stories, and sometimes obituaries, of my old friends. Just let me go through them."

A warm flush rose to Jessie's cheeks. "I'm sorry, Rufus. I didn't mean to take over. I just want you to be safe here and to have room to move around."

"I understand, Jessie, and you can help, but I'd like to go through the newspapers first before I get rid of them."

Jessie squatted by a pile of papers, a quiet sigh slipping from her lips. "What are we looking for?"

"Well now, that's the thing. Any story that mentions me. I was hailed as a hero driver once for snatching a small boy out of the road."

"Wow. That's impressive. You should have had that story framed."

His shoulders slumped. "I guess, but I can do it now, if we can find it."

"When was it? If you remember the date, it will be easier to find."

"That's just it. It was about eighteen, no—maybe it was twenty—years ago. My memory's not what it used to be."

She sat cross-legged and started going through old newspapers, page by page, obituary by obituary. She read headlines from

President Reagan's visit to Boston and the Eire Pub in January of 1983. "Hey, isn't that the pub over on Adams Street?" she asked, holding the paper out to him.

Rufus nodded, a gleam in his eye. "That's a keeper," he said, his hands smoothing the crinkling pages. "You weren't even born yet, but what a day that was. The president coming to Boston and having a beer with the regular working folks at the pub."

"Were you there?"

"No. Although that was a pub I frequented in my day, I was at work the day he came. Still, it was pretty exciting for the city, and it's pretty nice to remember it now." He folded the paper neatly and placed it behind him. "That's exactly the kind of paper I want to save. Thanks, Jessie."

She continued to pore through the piles, none of which was organized in any rational way. Old news was piled on top of new, so she wasn't surprised to find the most recent headlines staring her in the face. Rob Hart, one story noted, had had plans to run for Congress, and the writer mused about his future now that tragedy had struck him. On her second read, she remembered what Nick had mentioned the night of the shooting. "A wunderkind," he'd said, describing Hart. No one had said that since, and she'd forgotten all about it. And though the mayor was disenchanted with him for luring away donors, would a guy considering a run for Congress really arrange to have his own wife shot? It didn't seem likely, despite her own theories. Maybe she'd run this by Sam. "Can I keep this one?" she asked.

Rufus nodded. "Help yourself, but be careful. In fifty years, you'll be like me." His eyes bright, he chuckled at his own joke.

When dusk was settling over the city, Jessie stood and stretched the kinks out of her back and knees. "Rufus, I'm going to put this pile in the recycle bin, and this pile I'll take upstairs and go through later, if that's alright."

"It's fine with me. Things are looking better already. Thanks, Jessie."

She filled a recycle bin, and climbed the stairs, clutching a stack of old papers, to her own apartment where she brewed a cup of tea and turned on the news. Jose Ramos was still the lead story, his family shedding noisy tears and shouting expletives for the camera—even the guilty could manage to muster that kind of support. She clicked off the news, plugged in her little tree, and streamed some Christmas music. Her mood was the best it had been in days, and when a knock sounded on her door, she rose quickly, assuming it was Rufus. She pulled the door open, her smile quickly fading.

"What are you doing here?" she asked icily.

Nick pulled a bouquet of roses from behind his back. "Trying to make it up to you," he said meekly.

Jessie exhaled noisily. "Aren't you working?" She opened the door wider and he passed her the flowers.

"I am. I'm on my break. I just wanted to apologize in person. I don't deserve for you to forgive me, but I hope you will. I care about you, Jessie. I'd do just about anything for you." Tiny pools of tears welled at the corners of his blue eyes, making the color all the richer and his words somehow more believable.

She leaned into him, the familiar fresh scent of him as comforting as a hug. He wrapped her in his arms and kissed the top of her head. "I just want to make you happy, Jessie. That's all."

"I know you do. Let's just start again."

"Tonight?" he asked, a gleam in his eye.

She shook her head as she carried the flowers to the kitchen and pulled down a vase. "Not tonight. Let's take a day or two off and go out later this week."

He watched as she arranged the flowers and placed them by her little tree. "It looks good in here, but why all those newspapers?"

"I'm helping my downstairs neighbor to clear away his stuff."

"By keeping it up here?" He tried to grin.

"No. I'm going to go through those and see if there any stories that he'll want to keep."

"Sounds complicated. You're a good woman, Jessie." He brushed his lips quickly against hers. "I won't stay. I'll call you tomorrow?"

"Okay. Have a good night. Be safe." She swung the door closed and slid the new deadbolt into place with a final click. She listened as Nick's footsteps bounded down the stairs, the front door slamming shut behind him.

CHAPTER TWENTY-EIGHT

Monday morning dawned too early for Jessie. It was two weeks after the shooting, a week after Ann Hart's funeral, and just three days since she'd identified Bert in the morgue. She wanted to get moving early so she could stop into the morgue and speak with Roger, to see if there was anything new on Bert's death. But the gods conspired against her. Her scrubs were hopelessly wrinkled and would require a good going-over with an iron before she could put them on. The iron took longer than she'd expected to heat up, and she ran it quickly over the fabric, but not quickly enough. She burned a sleeve and finally gave up, pulling everything on and heading out.

At the hospital, she parked in the garage, cut through the ambulance bay, and darted across the street to the ME's office. As soon as she pulled open the heavy entry door, she was hit by the now familiar smells of formaldehyde and old blood. She wrinkled her nose and pressed the reception bell, and once she gave her name, she was buzzed in. She found her way along a poorly lit corridor and up the stairs to the autopsy suite—and ready to hold her breath against any pungent odors, she pushed open the door and stepped inside.

"Hey, Jessie," Tony called from his seat at a metal desk. "You found your own way back here, huh?"

"I did. Is Roger around?" she asked, her eyes scanning the room which was mercifully free of bodies awaiting autopsy. "We're like the ER," Tony had once said. "Feast or famine, no in-between in this business."

"Roger?" she asked again.

"No time for me, huh?" The silver in his deep black eyes shimmered in the dim light. He was an outrageous flirt but never pushed it, and maybe that was why everyone loved him.

She laughed. "Not today, Tony, not today."

"He's upstairs in his office. Can you find it on your own?"

She nodded, pulled open the door and stepped back into the corridor, making her way to the stairs and the third floor, the acrid scent following her. Roger's door was open, the cinnamon scent wafting at the edge, the desk light glowing. She knocked softly, and he looked up.

"Jessie. Come in." He stood and held a chair out for her. "I'm glad you came. I have a question for you."

"I only have a few minutes. I'm on duty soon. I just stopped by to see if there's anything new on Bert's death."

"Actually, it's Ann Hart I wanted to ask you about. I've been going over her toxicology results. You sent a tox screen from the ER, right?"

"As part of her full trauma panel, yes. Why?"

He leaned forward, his elbows resting on the desk, looking a bit like an absent-minded professor, but she knew better. Roger was anything but. "Her tox screen revealed a lorazepam level of two hundred."

Jessie's mouth dropped open. Lorazepam was a widely used sedative, but that level was high, too high. "Two hundred? How? We drew those labs as soon as she arrived, and we never gave her lorazepam. Her Glasgow Coma Scale was three. She was barely alive and deeply comatose. She didn't require sedation. You're sure of that result?"

He smiled and sat back, tenting his hands in front of his face. "And that, my friend, is why I need you in this office to help me sort through some of this information. The ICU notes opined that the level was secondary to meds given in the ER, though that wasn't documented."

"Jesus, why didn't they just call us, or ask me when I was there?" She sighed and sank deeper into the chair. "Why am I asking that? They were busy, too, and from the moment she was shot, it was only a matter of time until she died."

"That's true, but I was curious enough to double-check. The lab, as they often do in big cases, still had her ER blood tubes. I requested them and sent them to an outside lab for retesting. They confirm that, when she arrived at the ER, her lorazepam level was two hundred."

He paused, as if wanting that information to sink in and allow Jessie to mull it over.

"Was she taking lorazepam?"

He shook his head. "Contraindicated in pregnancy, but I called her obstetrician and primary care physician anyway, just to check. Both said no."

"So, she had an OB? She definitely knew she was pregnant then, and was planning on keeping this baby. This whole thing gets more suspicious by the day." She picked at her fingernails, a nervous habit she'd only recently adopted. "You probably don't have Rob Hart's medical information, but I wonder if he was on lorazepam?"

"Good question. I wondered that myself. Detective Dallas is coming by today. I'll see if he can look into that."

"Tell him I said he has his motive."

"Don't be so sure. One thing I've learned in this office is that things are never as clear-cut as they might seem."

"I suppose you're right. I do have a tendency to jump to conclusions." She glanced at her watch. "Damn, I gotta go. I can't be late. My manager is about as unforgiving as they come." She stood quickly, almost toppling the chair in her haste. "Sorry," she said, steadying the chair. "I almost forgot, I wanted to ask if there was anything new on Bert?"

"I've listed his manner of death as homicide, but no labs back yet."

"Sad," she said. "But I'm glad you're working on this."

"Ahh, another reason to come and work with me. Most people are desperate to know exactly what happened to their loved ones. I don't know what drives people to do what they do, to hurt or kill people they love, but…" He shrugged his shoulders. "For me, the body is the crime scene. Even in death, people leave clues to tell me what happened, and if I follow their trail, I can help the police figure it all out. You can help me with that, and you can make a difference here. I wish you'd give it some thought."

Jessie smiled. "Be careful what you wish you for, Roger."

She raced across the street, gulping in the fresh, cold air as she went, clearing her airways and her mind of the morgue's lingering miasma. She raced through the ambulance bay doors, shrugged off her jacket and backpack and fished through her locker for her stethoscope and white coat. She made it to report with one minute to spare.

"Hey," Donna said wistfully, "you okay?"

"Me?" Jessie looked around, certain Donna was speaking to someone else.

"Yes, you. You don't have any lipstick on. What's up?"

Her hand flew to her face and she laughed. "I was running late. I had to iron my damn scrubs," she said, smoothing the front as she spoke. "I didn't even realize I'd forgotten my lipstick. I'll be right back." At her locker, she pulled out her lipstick and applied a fresh swipe of color to her lips before fluffing her curls with her fingers. When she returned, report had just begun.

"Trauma One has a gunshot wound to the belly, we're just waiting on the OR. Trauma Two has an OD—he's waking up—you can move him out anytime. Trauma Three is clear, thank God." Donna continued on, reciting patients' differential diagnoses, workups in progress, and the number of patients waiting for beds upstairs or discharges home. "The wait to be seen is only an hour, so at least the non-acute side is moving." She handed Jessie her clipboard. "You're in charge again. Sorry."

"No problem. Where's Sheila? I thought she'd be back from her vacation and tormenting us today."

Donna chuckled. "Then this is your lucky day. She never showed up. We figured she'd planned a longer vacation and Administration forgot to let us know. Enjoy your freedom. It won't last."

Jessie made quick rounds before taking the patient in Trauma One. She monitored vital signs and IV fluids, ran a hemoglobin to check for blood loss, and when the patient—a twenty-two-year-old man, a store clerk who was shot for the grand sum of thirty-eight dollars, cried out in pain, she drew up the medicine and injected it into his IV, watching as the medicine took effect and the patient's grimace faded away. "You'll be okay," she whispered as the door banged open and transport arrived. "OR's ready," he said, moving quickly to help hook the young man's lines to the portable monitors.

"Housekeeping to Trauma One," Jessie said into the intercom before heading out to see how the rest of the floor was doing. The Triage and waiting areas were starting to fill up. It had been too much to hope for a quiet night, but you just never knew in this business. It was just as Tony had described—deathly quiet one minute and total chaos the next. And that was what she liked best about the ER. It was a metaphor for life; unpredictable, unexpected, both deadly boring and wildly exciting, and you could have all of that in one shift.

"Jessie," the overhead speaker announced. "You have a visitor at the main desk."

That was not the type of unexpected she preferred. It was probably Nick to apologize again. She shook her head. His apology tour was getting old. At the desk, she saw an enormous vase filled with red roses, a small man barely visible behind them. "Jessie Novak?" he asked.

"Yes," she answered, knowing he'd never see her nod of affirmation.

"Sign here," he said, his fingers wiggling the piece of paper in his hand. She signed the paper, and he placed the vase on the desk. "Have a good night," he called as she read the attached note.

Thank you for your kindness, R.

R, Jessie wondered for only a moment who that might be, but of course it was Rufus; it just had to be. *What a sweet guy*, she thought, carrying the vase back to the staff lounge. She set it down on the counter and headed back to the acute side, running smack into Sam Dallas. "Jeez, this is like Grand Central tonight."

"Got a minute?" he asked, his gray eyes flashing, his forehead creased with worry.

She led him back into the lounge and closed the door behind them. "I don't have much time. We're busy tonight."

"This won't take long. I've just spoken with Roger."

"So, you know about the sedative?"

"Ativan?"

"Also called lorazepam. Ann Hart had a level that would have made her drowsy at the very least. She wasn't on that drug, but we were wondering if her husband was."

"Already on that. Nothing in his hospital records, but you probably already know that. I have a call out to his regular physician. Hope to speak to him tomorrow. I'm here because I've spoken to…"

"Rob Hart. Finally!"

"No, I'm still trying to reach him. I spoke to that young man who caught your eye, the one who was crying at the funeral. You were right. He and Ann were an item. They were in love, he says, and she was planning to leave her husband. As far as this guy—Frank Davis—knew, she hadn't told her husband about the pregnancy and her plans. Yet. An examination of her phone, by the way, supports that. There's nothing in there that connects her to this Frank except in casual, friendly texts, maybe a few more calls than normal, but nothing that Rob Hart would notice."

A satisfied smile slipped across her lips, but she swallowed the urge to say *I told you so*. "How did Frank feel about her waiting to tell Rob? Was he angry? Capable of hurting her, even if it was an accident and she was the one who was shot?"

"He has an alibi, lives with two roommates. They spent the evening watching Monday-night football and went to bed. Poor bastard woke up to the news."

"So, doesn't that bring you back to Hart? Couldn't his wife have told him about the pregnancy and this—what was his name—Frank, maybe he just didn't know?" She stood to pace slowly around the room, and turned back to Sam.

"She'd told her parents about the pregnancy and her plans to leave Hart," he said. "They'd never liked him, so it was welcome news to them. They didn't think she'd told Hart yet."

"Can't you force Hart to speak with you?"

"I've left messages. I've gone to his house. He's nowhere to be found right now. There isn't much else I can do. I have to step carefully, and remember, there's not one shred of physical evidence. This is all circumstantial and hypothetical, and even if I find he was on lorazepam or whatever you call it—the sedative—I can't prove he gave it to her. He'll say he didn't know she took it."

"What can we do?"

"*We* can't do anything. I'm still working this. I'm just discussing…"

"Jessie Novak line two," the intercom squawked out the message.

Jessie held up a finger to Sam and picked up the phone, pressing the blinking light. "Yes?" she asked. It was the OR calling to tell her that the young man she'd just sent up had died right after they opened him. "A liver injury. Sorry, Jessie, we tried. There was just nothing we could do. Thought you'd want to know. Tony's on his way over to get him."

"Thanks," she said, her shoulders sagging as she slipped the receiver back into the base. "What a night."

Sam edged closer and pressed his hand gently into her shoulder. "You okay?"

The door opened wide, and Nick stood there, his jaw dropping. "What the…"

CHAPTER TWENTY-NINE

"Hey, Nick." Jessie stood up. "Thanks, Sam. You'll notify the family?"

"I will. I'll take care of it." He squeezed by Nick, who remained at the door. They exchanged scowls and Nick slammed the door behind Sam.

"Hey, don't slam doors around here."

"What the hell was that?" Nick asked, his jaw clenched tight.

"There was a shooting tonight. Sam's the detective on it. That's all."

"Seems like he's the detective on everything these days, huh?"

"Listen, I'm sorry I told you what he said about your being a cowboy. Just forget it, okay?"

He grunted. "Geez, I'm sorry. I'm doing it again—making assumptions, aren't I?" He leaned in to kiss her, his eyes landing on the flowers. "Wow. Who got those?"

"I did," she said, "and before you assume anything, they're from my neighbor, that sweet old guy downstairs from me."

"Yeah?" He leaned in to peek at the card and Jessie rolled her eyes. He just couldn't help himself.

"R?" he asked, tapping the card. He seemed rattled, nervous about the flowers.

"Rufus. I just told you."

"Ahh, Rufus. Sorry, I know I'm being a total jerk. I'm afraid of losing you, Jessie. I'm just a little jealous, I guess." He pulled her into his embrace, his eyes shining, his breath hot on her neck. "Can I come over after work?"

She wriggled free, kissing his cheek as she stepped back. "I'll let you know how the night goes."

"Fair enough," he said, running his finger along her lips. "I'll see you soon."

He turned and left and she stood there, not sure if she should feel happy or sad. It felt good to be so important to someone, and she wanted to feel that way, too, but she just wasn't there yet. She'd just have to try to be more open. She was doing what she always did when a good guy came along—she was pushing him away. And that, she knew from experience, was a big damn mistake.

"Jessie Novak, line three," the overhead intercom buzzed.

"Dear God, what now?" She picked up the phone and pressed line three. "Jessie Novak." She nudged a chair out with her foot and sank into it.

"It's me," Sam whispered.

Jessie laughed. "You don't have to whisper. No one is listening."

"I didn't want to piss off your boyfriend again, but I wanted to tell you that you can see the texts that Bert sent to you. Thought you might want to see them for yourself."

"Yes! I wanted to ask about the video that showed the Harts walking to their car, too. How did she look? Was she staggering? Because that sedative likely would have made her unsteady on her feet."

"We'll have another look. When we first got it, we were looking for anyone following them. To tell you the truth, we didn't pay much attention to how they walked. Might be something there."

"Any news on the sedative? Have you heard from Hart's physician?"

"Nothing yet. I'll check again tomorrow, and you can come in then before work. I'll be at headquarters. You'll be safe. Believe me."

She laughed. He could obviously tell that she still didn't entirely trust him. And she trusted him a little bit more for that.

When Nick called later, she passed on going out. "I don't want to keep staying up late drinking. Let's do something later in the

week. I'm off Friday. We could go to Quincy Market, see the
Christmas tree and lights. What do you say?"

"You got a deal. Sweet dreams, Jessie."

"You too, Nick."

Just as she was getting out of her car to head up to her apartment, she froze. A shadow flickered just over her shoulder, and
she turned in time to see an image darting away, or maybe it was
only her imagination, her mind playing tricks on her once again.
She turned again, her eyes scanning the street, but with that
goddamn streetlight still out, there was nothing to see beyond
a few cars driving by. She sprinted to her front door, flowers in
hand, pulling it shut behind her, a heavy sigh slipping from her
lips. Upstairs, she was relieved to find her own door was locked
tight. She let herself in, slid the deadbolt into place, and peeked
through her blinds to be sure nothing was there. The street was
blessedly empty. She pulled a Diet Coke from her fridge, a glass
from her cabinet, and once she'd washed up and pulled on a
nightgown, she settled in front of the television, the soft glow of
it the only light in the room.

The next morning, Jessie woke to the final whisper of snow that
had blanketed the city overnight. Everything was transformed as
if by magic; the harsh grayness of the street had been replaced by
a pure white canvas, with only a few daring drivers making their
way slowly along the road. The houses and trees were bathed in
Winter white, the only sound the sure, steady vibration of shovels
and snowplows clearing the way. There was something reassuring
and safe about snow—she knew there were fewer emergencies,
assaults, and probably even murders when it snowed this heavily.
She needed this—the security a snow covering offered.

She sipped her coffee by the window and watched as a man across the street dug his car out from under the drift that had buried it. He pulled onto K Street, left his car idling there, and hurried back, pulling out a beach chair and beat-up old cooler to claim his spot. In Southie, the rule was you shovel it, you own it, and you saved it by filling it with old chairs or whatever you could find. Anyone who dared to move your things and take your spot, did so at their own peril, and more than one errant parker had returned to find his tires slashed. The city was trying to break that old practice by outlawing space-saving, but the residents of Southie resisted and the tradition continued.

On the best of days, parking here was at a premium and in these long, snowy Winter months, it was an impossible game of hide-and-seek. It wasn't worth it to Jessie to shovel her own car out, drive to work and then drive home after midnight and waste her time in a futile search for an empty spot. She poured another cup of coffee. No way she could go for a run. Maybe she'd knock on Rufus's door and thank him for the flowers. Between his and Nick's flowers, and her little Christmas tree, her place was looking pretty festive.

She sank down onto the floor to have a look through Rufus's old newspapers. Trying to sort through them was an impossible task, so instead, she scanned dates and discarded the most recent, whittling her pile to a manageable twenty or so papers. She picked up the first in that pile just as her phone rang.

"Morning," Sam said.

"Hey, good morning. Have you seen the snow?"

"I have. Do you need help shoveling out?"

"I'm not shoveling out. I live in Southie. My car can stay put till Spring."

He laughed. "Ahh, that's right. You need a place with a garage."

"Yeah, me and everyone else."

"Are you coming in?"

"Coming in?"

"To look at Bert's text and the Hart video?"

She rubbed her neck. "I'd forgotten. Damn, I'd like to, but I'll be taking an Uber to work. Can't afford one to headquarters, too."

"I'll pick you up then, if you're okay with that?"

"Give me half an hour. I'll wait for you downstairs."

Jessie showered and dressed and grabbed a pair of scrubs and clogs. It was an hour later that she finally saw Sam maneuvering the old police-issue Crown Vic along K Street. It skidded to a stop in front of her house, and she pulled on her gloves and ran out, almost sliding into the side of his car. "Whew," she said as he reached over and opened the door. "I didn't realize how icy it was." She settled in her seat and shivered. "No heat?"

"It takes a while. By the time we get where we're going, it'll come on."

She pulled her coat a little tighter, and sank into the seat searching for whatever warmth that might bring. Sam navigated the backstreets, past Boston City Hospital and onto a long boulevard, lined with weeds, overgrown shrubs and chain-link fences. Threadbare tents and trash, discarded by the homeless who'd claimed that stretch of road for themselves, dotted the landscape until it all gave way to manicured hedges, and newly renovated office and university buildings. Just as the heater clicked to life and began to spit out a wave of welcome warm air, Sam turned onto Tremont Street and into a spot in front of headquarters, a four-story gray cement building with a glass-windowed front that looked more like a public health lab than police headquarters. The cluster of police cruisers and the large blue Boston Police sign gave it away.

Jessie followed him through the main entrance and up the stairs, through a narrow hallway surrounded on either side by look-alike cubicles, to a large room with four desks clustered close, and just beyond that to a cramped office that held one desk, two telephones, one computer, one printer and the tangle of wires that held it all together.

Sam pulled out a straight-backed wooden chair. "Have a seat," he said. "Let me just get my stuff together."

Jessie plunked down onto the chair, squirming to find a comfortable spot. "Do you have suspects sit in these chairs?" she asked. "Torture them so they'll confess sooner?"

"Very funny. You'll be happy to know we don't waste taxpayer money on comfort here. We waste it on plenty of other shit, but not on comfort." He pulled a notebook from his top drawer before rooting around in the other drawers, pulling them in and out and rifling through the papers there. Hands on his hips, his eyes scanned the room. "Be right back," he said.

Jessie stood up, rubbing her lower back and stretching her neck this way and that. She glanced at the door before taking a peek at the items on his desk—a cell phone, probably his; a file folder of papers labeled "Hart"; another file labeled with Bert's name, a third with the sad notation of "unknown white female". There was also an assortment of old coffee cups, candy wrappers, three pens, a spray of paperwork covering his keypad, and off to the side a pile of newspapers. Jessie picked up the top one—the story was Bert's, the headline with Hart's alleged last words before going to the OR. She slapped it back down angrily, releasing a flurry of dust specks into the air. Approaching footsteps forced her back to her chair.

"Forensics still has it. They're checking with IT—looking for emails or anything else that he might have deleted."

"Has what?" Jessie asked.

"Bert's phone," he said, sinking into the padded chair behind the desk and swiveling it a half-turn. "I haven't downloaded the texts and calls yet. If I had, I could show them to you, see if there's anything that jogs your memory of Bert." A vein in his forehead pulsed.

"That's alright. It's not like it's an emergency."

"I know. I'm just tired. Sometimes this stuff just gets to you, you know? I expect everything to run like clockwork. I don't know why, since it never does."

Jessie smiled. "I feel your pain. It's the same in the ER, especially lately. But could we have a look at those surveillance videos of the Harts, maybe see how Ann Hart looked that night?"

"Good idea." Sam swung back and booted up his computer, his fingers flying across the keys. Jessie rose and stood behind him, watching as he clicked on a folder labeled Hart and ran his cursor along the files before clicking on *surveillance*. The file uploaded a series of thumbprint images. Sam chose one and pressed play on the first one, the grainy image filling the screen. She leaned in closer, her eyes intent on the images before her.

"Oh hell," he said. "Look at that."

CHAPTER THIRTY

A hazy shot of Warrenton Street flickered into view. Mondays after midnight were quiet in the theater district and especially so on this narrow street. No live theater meant fewer pedestrians and still fewer cars. The street was empty; a piece of trash skittered soundlessly along the sidewalk until the Harts stepped into the camera's lens. The image flickered as the couple moved slowly, almost teetering, along the street.

"Can you stop there?" Jessie asked, pointing to the screen. Sam froze the video. "See," she said, her eyes riveted to the screen. "There. See how tightly he's holding her, almost as if he's propping her up."

Sam hit *re-wind* and played it again. "She's definitely unsteady. Right there. We just assumed they'd been drinking, perfect targets for a robber." He pointed to the screen. The next tape, probably less than three seconds, showed more of the same. Ann Hart, leaning close, too close, to Rob. "Damn it."

Jessie straightened. "Well, that seems to show she'd taken, or was given, a sedative. Her alcohol level was zero. No one walks like that unless they're drunk or sedated, and a lorazepam level of two hundred is pretty high for someone who's never taken it."

"I agree. Did you ever hear the nine-one-one call the night of the shooting?"

"I heard something on the news. I don't remember if it was the actual call, or someone reading the transcript. Do you have the audio?"

"I do," he said, his fingertips navigating to another file and opening another tab. "This is it. Pull up your chair, and just listen."

She dragged a chair across the cracked linoleum and sat next to Sam, who'd nudged over so she'd be nearer to the screen. He fiddled with the volume button until it was at maximum level. He hit *play* and sat back. Jessie, her elbows on her knees, leaned in and tilted her head towards the speaker as it crackled and came to life.

"Nine-one-one. What's your emergency?"

Silence, no voices, no shouts, nothing. Just quiet. Jessie checked her watch.

"Nine-one- one. What's your emergency?" the dispatcher repeated, an unmistakable hint of tension in her voice.

"I... I need help. I don't know where I am."

"We'll get help to you right away, sir, but first, I need you to help us."

There was a pause, for minutes it seemed, though it was only eight seconds.

"Are you there?"

"Help me," the caller cried again.

"Where are you, sir? What's your emergency?"

"I... I've been shot. My wife, too. I think she's dying. We were robbed. He had a gun." The caller's tone was slow and steady, not the hurried, almost hysterical voice you'd expect. *But you never knew in this business*, Jessie thought. At least that's what you're taught to think. No judgements—just the facts.

"Can you tell me where you are?"

"I don't know. We've been shot. Both of us."

"Is the person who shot you still there?"

"No, no. I don't think so."

"What's your location?" This time there was a crispness to her voice, a practiced, almost calming response.

"I... I don't know. Just come. Please." The caller's words were punctuated by rapid breathing, but the cadence of his voice was somehow calm, calmer than it seemed—at least to Jessie—than it should have been.

"We will. We're here to help. What's your name?" This time her voice was low and soothing.

"Umm… my name's Rob."

"Rob, can you tell me what happened, where you are?"

"We were out… celebrating… and I don't know. A man came up behind us. Just get here. Please. There's so much blood."

Jessie angled her head to hear better. Rob Hart sounded composed, almost as though he'd rehearsed those words and was repeating them from memory.

"Rob, I need your location. I can send help as soon as you help me."

"We're in an alley. The one behind the theater on Warrenton Street, I think. I'm not sure. A man just robbed us and then he shot us. Both of us…"

"We have a hit on your location now. Help is on the way, but stay with me. Where is the bleeding?"

"My side. He shot me in the side." He let out a short whimper.

"And your wife?" There was an urgency to the dispatcher's voice.

"Her head," he answered in a strong, impatient voice, no trace of a whimper or whine. "I don't think she's breathing."

"Rob, I have units on the way. Can you check your wife for a pulse?"

No answer. Just silence. Maybe he was doing that, checking for a pulse. The tension was palpable.

"Rob? Are you there? I'll stay on the line with you. The ambulance will be there in just a minute or two."

There was only silence, as though a mute button had been hit. But to Jessie, the silence was sinister, and practiced. He'd told her he'd said goodbye to his wife there in that alley. He knew that she wouldn't survive. Why wasn't he frantically screaming for help for her? *Why was he so calm?*

Suddenly, in the distance came the familiar drone of approaching sirens. "Rob? I can hear the sirens now. Are you strong enough to get to the street so they'll see you?"

There was a click. The call had ended.

*

Jessie shook her head. "Can you play it again, Sam?"

He chuckled. "I bet you waited your whole life to say that."

"Can't help myself. Will you re-wind? And really listen this time."

"What am I listening for?"

"Just listen. Really listen." She pulled her chair closer still to the table, angling her head just so as she nudged Sam's chair with her foot. She raised a brow, her way of reminding him to pay attention.

Sam guided the mouse, dragging the start arrow back to the beginning. "Here you go," he said, pressing *play* once more. "What..."

Jessie put a finger to her lips to shush him.

He rested his chin in one hand and closed his eyes just as the tape began.

"Nine-one-one. What's your emergency?" the dispatcher's voice began. Jessie looked at her watch, timing the pause—ten seconds—a lifetime in a real emergency. There were more pauses, the next one eight seconds; the final, sinister pause before he'd hung up was fourteen seconds of silence until the sirens sounded. Fourteen long seconds of Rob Hart just sitting there next to his dying wife. Jessie shook her head angrily. That was bad enough, but it was the background noise that had grabbed her attention—it was the unmistakable echo of footsteps in that alley, filling that ten-second silence at the start of the call, the footfalls louder and more insistent at first before fading into the night as the seconds passed.

Sam hit stop and restarted the audio. He did it again and then again, the footsteps seeming to grow louder each time they listened. "We got that," he finally said, leaning back in his chair. "We think it's the shooter."

"Hate to one-up you, but there's two things wrong with that. First, do you remember in the ER when Hart said he waited to call nine-one-one? He wasn't sure how long he'd waited but he said it was enough for him to be sure the shooter was long gone."

Sam let out a low whistle. "I remember that, but we decided he was probably still in shock, not clear about the time. Was it minutes, or maybe seconds? He couldn't tell for sure." He paused, a wrinkle sprouting on his forehead. "But we haven't ruled him out. Not yet. And there's not much I can tell you about that part of our investigation."

She smiled to herself. So, they were looking into Hart. *About time.* "What about the shoes? That sound is more like a thud than the hard click of dress shoes. Maybe those rubber-soled work boots, or running shoes? But whatever the shoes, someone else was in that alley when he called nine-one-one. I'm not a detective, but I'm sure of it." She sat back. She'd gone too far… again. She'd be lucky if he didn't kick her out, but instead, he simply shook his head.

"CSU is already…"

"CSU?"

"Crime Scene Unit—I'll ask them if they've got a make on those shoes yet, and see what they've come up with."

"They can actually get a make on the shoes?"

He nodded. "Amplify what you just heard. You'd be amazed at what they can do with audio evaluation—they can use filters, work with the volume and tone of the recording, improve the clarity, and from there, they can enhance the sound and maybe get enough to name the type of shoe—hard-soled or rubber, and the type of footfall—heavy-footed, probably a man, light-footed more likely a female. There are people who actually specialize in this, the sound quality and clarification of audio evidence."

Jessie whistled. "Pretty damn impressive." She pushed her chair back just as a soft chime sounded on Sam's desktop computer.

Sam bent to his keyboard once again. "Ahh," he said with a sigh. "Gotta love these guys. Want to see some of Bert's texts to you?"

CHAPTER THIRTY-ONE

"Yes," she said, wondering if they knew about Bert's voice messages too. She hadn't told Sam about those, and she still wasn't sure she should. The first pulses of a headache began to drum behind her eyes and her mouth felt dry. Her morning caffeine was wearing off; she needed a refill. "Got any water, or coffee?"

"I do. The choices are lousy coffee from our coffee-maker, or bottled water. Me, I'd choose the water."

"Can I get one of each? I feel like living dangerously."

Sam left the office once again and Jessie checked her own phone. There were no calls, but there was a text from Nick. *Thinking of you*, he wrote, adding that stupid, meaningless, smiley sunglass emoji again. She was just shaking her head in puzzlement when Sam walked back in.

"Everything okay?" he asked.

"Yeah, just making sure the ER isn't looking for me." She stuffed the phone back into her pocket.

Sam placed a bottle of water and a plastic coffee cup in front of her. He sank back into his chair and set his own cup down before reaching into his pocket for a handful of sugar packets and little creamer containers. He took his time opening the sugar and the cream and mixing it all into his cup. When he finally took a sip, he sighed with pleasure.

"Sugar, Jessie?" He held up a packet.

"Not for me. Strong and black is how I take it."

He curled his lips in distaste. "To each his own, I guess. Let's get back to Bert."

"I unblocked Bert. Is there a way for me to access his texts?"

Sam shook his head. "No, once you block him his texts go to some black hole in the universe. Only place to see them is on his phone." His fingers raced along the keyboard once again, bringing up screenshots of Bert's texts, and there were plenty. "We'll start with his texts to you. They come up by name, just like on your phone. This is the first."

I need to speak with you. Please call me at this number. It's IMPORTANT! Bert

Jessie felt her stomach drop. "That was the Sunday—just nine days ago, the day before the funeral. That's when I blocked him."

Sam scrolled to the next text. "This was sent just two hours after the first."

Call me. PLEASE! IMPORTANT!

Five minutes later:

Jessie—I tried calling you, left a voicemail. Please call. Hope you get this. Please be careful. Rob Hart is not to be trusted. I'm not sure the police are either. I'll call tomorrow.

The next day, the day of the funeral, Bert sent only two texts.

Please call! I'm calling you! Please pick up!

There followed in his outgoing recent calls list a flurry of calls to Jessie. The last time he'd tried was the Tuesday morning.

"Check your phone, Jessie. See if he left you messages."

"I have already. I have four messages," she answered before she had time to think. She could have kicked herself, but it was too late now.

Sam's lips curled into a frown. "Why didn't you say something?"

"Because of what he said. I'm still not sure…"

"Jessie, you can't withhold evidence. Don't make me get a warrant for your damn phone."

She heaved a sigh. "When you hear what he says, you'll understand my reluctance. Just listen." She pulled her phone from her pocket.

"If you don't mind, will you put that on speakerphone?" he asked, his tone suddenly formal as though he didn't trust her now either.

She did as he asked and placed her phone on the desk. "You take it from here," she said.

Sam slid the phone closer and scrolled to Bert's first call, last Sunday, just an hour after his first text. And she had to listen all over again.

"Jessie, please call me back. This is important. I have to speak with you. Please." There was a pause and then a click.

"He sounded shaky, as though he was afraid," Jessie said, her own voice cracking,

The next message, left on Monday morning, the day of the funeral, was quicker, a total of four seconds: "Jessie, call me. It's important." This time his voice was firm, not a quiver at all.

Later that day, he left another message: "I'm leaving for London tomorrow, but before I go, I have to warn you about someone. I might have my biggest story ever, but I'm not sure I can ever use it. Just don't trust anyone. Call me as soon as you can."

His final message was Tuesday morning. "Call me, Jessie. Please. I think the police might be involved in the Hart shooting." His voice dropped to a near whisper, and Sam and Jessie both moved closer to hear it. "There's more, but I need to speak with you. Be careful. Don't trust the police on this. Just call me."

Her chest tightened at the last message. He'd called more than a dozen times, but had left only the four messages, the last one just three days before he was found dead. Jessie gripped the edge of her seat, her knuckles going white. She wanted to speak but she couldn't find the words.

"Look," she finally said, turning to Sam, a glint of anger in her eyes. "I haven't listened since I first heard them. His message seems pretty clear, though. Are the police involved in this? Are you protecting someone? What the hell is going on?"

Sam reached for her hand but she pulled away. "Don't," she hissed.

"Listen, I know you're upset, but I can assure you, the police are not involved except as investigators. There's no grand conspiracy here. We're trying to solve this crime." His voice grew sharper with each word.

"Really?" she barked. "I've been telling you to look at Rob Hart, and you've been blowing me off. Now, Bert's dead."

"We did not kill Bert, and we're not in cahoots with Hart. This is the first time I'm hearing his messages. *You* blocked him. Remember?"

Jessie closed her eyes. She had blocked him. Sam was right. She blew out a long, slow breath. "Did Roger have a time of death for Bert?"

"Tuesday," Sam answered. "Sometime Tuesday."

This time his voice was so soft, Jessie could barely hear him. She felt numb, and sad and angry. At herself.

Sam was typing at the keyboard. "Looks like Bert was calling the hospital. This number—recognize it?" he asked, pointing to the screen.

Jessie tugged at her hair, wrapping a strand around her fingers. "That's an ICU extension. He must have been calling Rob."

"And Rob was apparently calling him—twelve calls in total. The last one on Tuesday morning from Rob to Bert."

A chill ran through her. "Hart was discharged Tuesday," she whispered. "You don't think…"

CHAPTER THIRTY-TWO

Sam jerked back in his chair, his mouth curled in a grimace. "That Hart killed him? No," he said firmly. "There's no evidence to suggest that."

"But he was killed the day Hart was discharged."

"True, but we don't even have a reliable time of death. He might have been killed before Hart was even discharged. I just don't know where you come up with these things."

She shrugged. "I admit I've thought about it more than I should have. I feel as though I have a life before and a life after the shooting. I'm obsessed with this." She knew that it was more than her resemblance to Ann that had somehow taken hold of her. It had turned into something bigger—a search for justice for Ann Hart. Maybe it was because Ann's family had been so devastated, so broken, and Jessie was a nurse who needed to fix everything. Even this. But no way would she say that out loud and risk Sam's likely smirk. "It's as though I'm seeking revenge for Ann Hart."

"Not very healthy," he said, "but maybe you should think about working with the ME."

"Sam, it's not a stretch to think this is connected to Hart. They knew each other. Bert's message said I shouldn't trust the police or Hart. I think there's a pretty obvious connection there. You can't possibly discount that."

"I'm not discounting anything, and neither am I going to share the whole investigation with you. I'm not sure I should have shared what I have," he shouted, a bead of sweat trickling along his forehead.

A knock on the door interrupted them. A man in a starched white shirt and loosened tie poked his head in. "Everything okay, Sarge?" he asked, his eyebrows raised, his gaze fixed on Jessie.

"Yeah, we're fine," Sam said. "I'll catch up with you later."

The man nodded and pulled the door shut behind him. Jessie and Sam sat in stony silence. Jessie crossed her arms and Sam banged away at his computer. "I guess I'll get going," she said finally, standing and reaching for her coat.

Sam slumped in his seat. "I'm sorry, Jessie. I didn't mean to snap like that. But you have to let me investigate this. I'm still the detective."

"I know you are. I didn't mean to insinuate that you were screwing this up, though I admit that thought has occurred to me. Bert certainly thought the police were involved with Hart, and he should know. He was speaking to Hart. You heard his messages too. There's a connection there. I'd bet my life on it."

"Please don't. And I'd like to remind you to be careful. You're a material witness, and if anyone thinks Bert told you something… Well, just be careful." He sipped his coffee.

"I have another question."

"Shoot."

"Where did Bert live? If he fought back, and it looked like he did, wouldn't someone have heard it—a commotion, I mean?"

"He lived in a basement apartment over on Hemenway Street. That's a pretty noisy street, and a basement apartment almost guarantees no one will hear anything. Now, before you ask—yes, we did canvass the area, and no one heard anything or saw anything suspicious. Satisfied?" There was a certain smugness in his voice.

Jessie sighed. "Was anything taken? A robbery gone bad, maybe?"

"Nothing was taken, but he didn't have much to take, not even a television. His bags were packed, his passport and tickets tucked inside. He had an interview scheduled with the *Daily Mirror*, a British tabloid. He was leaving for a job, just as he said."

"So—and you have to humor me a minute longer—if it wasn't a robbery, and it seems it wasn't, why was he killed?"

"That's what we're trying to establish."

She sank back into the chair.

"Maybe it was someone he knew. A friend who had a grudge." He balanced one foot on the edge of his desk.

"I don't think he had any close friends. He was a creepy little guy." And she paused. She didn't want to lose sight of that fact, despite feeling sorry for the way he'd died. No one deserved that. "I know that sounds terrible to say about someone who's died, especially the way he did, but it's true."

Sam nodded. "Anything else?"

"Yeah—Rob Hart asked one of the ICU nurses for my phone number the day he was discharged. She told me not to be surprised if he came to the ER looking for me." She slipped her arms into her jacket.

He used his foot to push away from the desk, the chair rolling back and slamming into the wall. He sat rigidly, his back as straight as a ruler. "Tell me she didn't give it to him."

"She didn't. She just wanted to warn me."

"I'll add to that. Be careful."

She nodded and checked her watch. "I gotta go. If I show up early, I can probably get some overtime."

"Hold on. I'll take you." He stood and reached for his own jacket.

She shook her head. "No. If someone is keeping an eye on me, it's better if I don't arrive to work in a police car. I'll get an Uber, but thanks."

"You're sure?" he asked, a trace of worry in his voice.

But who was he worried about? Himself, maybe? She nodded. "You'll keep me posted?"

"As long as you do the same."

The silver flecks in his eyes shimmered. She couldn't help herself, and she smiled. "I will."

She decided to wait outside on Tremont Street, where a bitter wind was swirling the snow dizzily around. Her breath plumed out in frosty puffs. She pulled her coat tighter and when a loud screech filled the air, she jumped and turned. It was only a seagull swooping through the air searching for food. She was about to head back inside to wait when a lone car swerved its way down the street and stopped. "Jessie?" the driver yelled to be heard above the wind. She checked his plate number and car make with the one provided by Uber, and satisfied that he was the driver, she slid into the backseat, waves of comforting heat surrounding her.

In the ER, she peeled off her coat and went in search of Donna. "Thought I'd come early, see if you need help?"

"I do. You know how it goes—the first real snowfall means lots of staff sick calls."

"Great. Do I need to check with Sheila?"

"You'll be happy to hear she's not back yet."

"God, managers have it easy, don't they?"

"Seems like it," Donna said as she headed down the hall. "Just help out whoever's busy, though it's been quiet so far."

Jessie headed out to Triage to see how things looked, but aside from Eddie, who sat huddled in a corner, and a few stragglers waiting to be seen, the area was quiet. Jessie sat down next to Eddie. "How are you, my friend? Had lunch yet?"

Eyes suddenly alert, Eddie straightened up. "A turkey sandwich. Got anything else?"

"I'll make a run to the cafeteria. What do you want?"

"I won't turn down a hot meal, Jessie."

She returned with a roast beef dinner and sat next to him, watching as he inhaled the food. "Where do you stay on these cold Winter nights?"

"Here and there," he said, running a slice of bread through the gravy. "I can usually find a warm spot."

His hands were chapped, the skin dark, the joints swollen. "Where are your gloves?"

"Don't have any."

"Jeez, you need gloves. I'll get some and bring them in later this week."

"Thanks, Jessie," he said, his gaze falling back to his meal.

The first snow of the season kept the ER quiet, just as she'd expected, and when Nick arrived, stamping his feet to release the snow and slush that stuck to his shoes, Jessie smiled. "Hey," she said. "I need a ride home. Any chance you—"

Before she could finish, he pulled her close. "You don't have to ask. You know I will." He planted a kiss on her cheek just as his radio crackled to life. "Shit," he said. "You'd think the snow would keep things quiet."

That night, he was the old Nick, reliable, sweet and wholesome. "I'm going to take a shower," Jessie said. "Interested?"

He grinned impishly. "What do you think?"

In the shower, he pushed himself tight against her, his hardness pressing against her belly, the warm rush of water as intense as the feel of him. She let herself surrender to him, to his touch, soft and yet insistent, and when release came, the thrill of it racing through her, she moaned with a pleasure she hadn't known before. They sank to the tile floor, arms wrapped around one another, and stayed there, until the water washed away the last trace of their lovemaking, the pure memory of it burning into Jessie's brain. Nick reached up and turned the water off, a sudden chill filling the small space. He stood and grabbed a towel, wrapping it around Jessie before carrying her to bed. And her seeds of doubt frittered away. He was a good man. She was suddenly sure of that, and when he whispered that he'd keep her warm, she kissed him deeply, her tongue lingering on his lips before she sat up and drew the towel out so that he could share it.

"Ohh, Jess," he moaned, snuggling next to her. "I'm so lucky to have found you."

"I feel the same, Nick," she said. "I really do."

They spent the night with arms and legs tangled together. She couldn't remember the last time she'd felt this kind of contentment. She drifted into sleep, secure in his arms and his promises.

CHAPTER THIRTY-THREE

The days flew. The snow melted with a heavy rain, and there were no news updates on Hart or Bert or even Ramos. It was almost three weeks since the Hart shooting, and for the first time since that night, Jessie felt safe from the drama swirling around Bert's death.

Just as he'd promised, Sam called later that week. "Just checking in," he said, and she could hear the smile in his voice.

"Any word on anything?"

"Turns out you were right about Hart. Seems he had a girlfriend."

"I knew it," she almost shouted. "Is she involved? Tell me everything."

"Nothing I can share just yet, Jessie. Sorry. And keep that under your hat."

Jessie's mind was racing. "I bet she has his phone and wallet. I'm sure of it. Remember I said early on that he had an accomplice?"

"I do. I can't confirm anything."

"You're going to leave me hanging?" She paused. "Poor choice of words, but you have to tell me."

"I can't. Shouldn't have told you that much. It's still a very active investigation."

"Well, that's good to know. Are the charges against Ramos going to be dropped?"

"No changes there. Holding him on the other murder charge. No final decision yet on his involvement with the Hart case. It's up to the DA, and she's not saying much." He exhaled noisily. "Back to you. No messages from Hart? Nothing unusual?"

"No. Things are pretty good. For now," she added quickly. She didn't want to jinx herself. As soon as you started to settle in and believe things were good—wham! They'd blow right up. The lock on her door was still sturdy and no one seemed to be watching her, at least she hoped no one was. She hadn't had that spooked feeling in days. And things with Nick were good. So, actually, things were better than pretty good, but why say it out loud and tempt the fates?

"Okay then," Sam said. "Keep in touch." The soft click on the other end told her he'd hung up, probably to keep her from asking more questions. A girlfriend, after all, threw a wrench into everything, and confirmed what Jessie had thought all along. Someone had helped Rob Hart, and a girlfriend seemed a likely suspect. She shook her head and checked her watch. She'd have time to stop at Target for gloves and a hat for Eddie if she left now.

At work, she passed through the waiting room and handed Eddie the Winter gear she'd picked up. He pulled the woolen cap tight over his head, slid the scarf around his neck and slipped his hands into the gloves, all the while a broad smile draping his lips, still chapped from the cold. "Hey, Jessie," he called after her. "Thank you!"

"No thanks needed," she said over her shoulder. "Just stay warm."

She found Donna to get report, but instead Donna motioned her into a storeroom. "I have to tell you something," she whispered.

"Am I in trouble again?" she asked, running through a mental checklist of the last week, but aside from the usual arguments with security when they wanted to throw Eddie and some others out into the cold, she couldn't come up with anything. She braced herself for bad news.

"No, no. Why would you think that? It's not that at all."

"Why wouldn't I? But if it's not that, then why are we hiding in here and whispering?"

"Because it hasn't been announced yet." There was a giddiness in her voice.

"What hasn't been?" Jessie couldn't help but smile in turn. "Just say it."

"I'm the new acting nurse manager."

"You are? Where's Sheila?"

Donna shrugged. "Who knows? Administration said they're not sure when, or if, she's coming back. You know how close-mouthed they are. They didn't say anything else. We heard through the grapevine that she's a no-call, no-show, a fact that would have gotten any of us fired, so who knows? Maybe they did fire her, and they don't want to say it. Whatever it was, she's gone, and for the time being, I'm your new boss."

Jessie pulled her into a hug. "Congratulations! Things feel better here already." And they were: Donna was a straightforward, no-bullshit nurse, respected by everyone—a *just do your job* kind of nurse.

"So, because the day charge position is open now, I have a question for you."

"Don't even ask. I'm not interested in working days. Too many bosses."

"True, but I'm one of the bosses now, so at least say you'll think about it."

"I will say it. It's a lie, but I'll say it."

"I had to ask, and I wish you'd said yes. But since it seems you're not interested in being the day charge nurse, I have another offer for you. You know the ME put in a request to have you work part-time for him as a forensics nurse?"

"He'd asked. I didn't know he'd made the request." She felt a warm flush of pride. At least he thought her opinions were worthwhile.

"He had to go through the mayor's office, the police and the DA first. Pretty impressive, Jessie. They all signed off. So, the only question is—do you want to do it? You'll do part-time here, part-time there, depending on needs. You're still in the union, your pay will stay the same including overtime. What do you say?"

"Are you kidding? Yes! Hell, yes!" She felt validated, light as air; her theories would carry weight now, no matter what Sam or anyone else thought. She hugged Donna. "Thank you. I know you had to agree to this, too. I'm so excited."

"Don't be too excited. You still have to finish out the December schedule. It ends after Christmas. You okay with that?"

"I'm okay with anything you say. You're already a great manager."

She called Nick to tell him, and she could almost see the frown on his face. "I don't know, Jessie. You'll be hanging around those detectives."

"I won't be *hanging around* with them. I'll be working with them. Sometimes. And I'll be with the ME as well. I'm excited about this, but you seem… I don't know, disappointed or something. Are you?"

"No, no. I'm happy for you. A little jealous, that's all. But we can celebrate tomorrow. We'll do dinner. How's the Top of the Hub sound?"

"Expensive, Nick. It sounds expensive."

"We have a lot to celebrate—your new job and my arrest of Ramos. I'd say we deserve this." This time, she could almost hear the smile in his voice.

"Ohh, Nick," she whispered. "This will be fun."

That evening, a bouquet of white roses arrived in the ER for Jessie. The card said simply "R", nothing else. Rufus, she thought, inhaling the fresh scent. He shouldn't be spending his money on her; she hadn't even thanked him for the earlier bouquet. She made a mental note to stop by in the morning to see him. She needed to get back to work going through his newspapers, too. A part of her just wanted to toss them out; there likely wasn't anything in any of them that mattered to him. But she'd promised him. She'd tackle that tomorrow too. Maybe she'd even get a manicure, clean up her raggedy nails.

Nothing could break her mood that night. Not the drug seekers who demanded pain medicines, not the seemingly endless line of people who needed primary care, not emergency care, and not even the gangbangers who pulled out guns ready to settle some score in the ambulance bay. That one was easy—a quick call to the nine-one-one dispatch center and the ER was inundated with cops, the idiot instigators hauled off to jail. All in all, it wasn't a bad night.

The next morning, she went for a run, and stopped for coffee and a muffin at Patrick's store. At home, she knocked on Rufus's door to thank him for the flowers.

"Good morning, Jessie," he said. "Want to come in?"

She hadn't really wanted to, there was so much to do today—hair, nails, maybe buy a new dress for tonight. Still, Rufus was her friend. "Yes," she answered. "Sorry, I only got the one coffee."

"No problem there, Jessie, I prefer a cup of tea."

She passed him the muffin. "Hope you like blueberry."

"Why thank you," he said, slipping his bony fingers into the bag and drawing out the muffin.

"None for you?"

"I'm all set." She wished she'd had more sense and thought to get an extra. "Anyway, I stopped by to thank you for the flowers. They're beautiful, I love them, but please—I don't want you to spend your money on me."

He scratched his head. "I'm not sure what you mean. I haven't sent any flowers, though now I wish I had. Must be that boyfriend of yours. Nice fella, that one."

Jessie nodded, trying to ignore the knot tightening in her belly. *If not Rufus, then who was R and who was sending the flowers?*

CHAPTER THIRTY-FOUR

Nick wore a dark suit, Jessie a tight black dress that hugged her in all the right places. She'd pulled her curls into a loose knot, swiped a swath of bright red color along her lips, draped pearls around her neck and a smile on her face. Her mirror confirmed that she looked pretty damn good for a last-minute fancy date, and when she opened her door at his knock, he whistled his approval.

He glanced towards the white roses Jessie had brought home from the ER, a small crease appearing in his forehead. "Flowers again?" he asked. "Who sent them?"

"Rufus," she lied, not sure what to say, the knot in her gut tightening a little bit more. She wasn't sure who'd sent them, though she was leaning towards Roger as the enigmatic *R*. Still, she didn't want to share the puzzle of the flowers with him right then. "Don't say anything to him. I already told him he spent too much, and I think he's feeling sensitive."

"No worries," Nick said, draping his arms around her. "As long as he knows you're my girl."

They parked in the Prudential Center garage and took the elevator to the fifty-second floor, stepping into the reception area where a crowd milled at the entrance. "Reservations?" the maître d', a smiling young woman in a cocktail dress, asked. Nick shook his head.

"No, didn't even think of it. Any chance we can get a table?"

The woman shook her head. "Sorry, I could seat you at ten if you want to wait."

Nick sighed, a long frown almost making the shimmery blue of his eyes wilt.

"The lounge is available," the woman said, seeming as though she wanted to please Nick. His eyes, his appearance, had that effect on women. Jessie smiled to herself. She wasn't jealous, just amused. She ushered them to the lounge, where they slid into comfy, upholstered seats with a view as grand as any in the city. She passed two menus to them. "You can order appetizers and small plates here. Enjoy your evening."

They feasted on shrimp, oysters and crab cakes as well as a bottle of champagne while the city's lights and snow-topped roofs glistened an arm's length away. When a jazz trio began to play, Jessie leaned into Nick. "This feels like heaven, Nick. Thank you." He kissed her then, his lips and tongue sweet with the taste of champagne. "Let's go," she whispered, taking his hand.

The rest of the night was a blur of lovemaking and laughter and joy. He was sensitive and gentle and kind—holding open doors, pulling out her chair, slipping her coat over her shoulders, sliding his hand into hers every chance he got. He was the Nick she'd been drawn to, the Nick she wanted, the one she needed in her life.

In the morning, he nudged her awake. "I have to go, Jessie. I'll call you later." She curled under the covers, thoughts of the night before swirling through her brain. It was almost noon when she finally woke, the midday sun filtering through her blinds.

She rose, showered, pulled on sweats, brewed some coffee and watched as sudden rain began to pelt against her windows. Damn. Too wet to run, she turned to Rufus's pile of old newspapers. At least she could get through those. She sank to the floor, clicked the television on and began to sift through the pile, flipping through the pages in search of a headline, or a story with Rufus's name. Six newspapers in, every word seemed to fade into the next. She took a coffee break and started again, this time focusing her eyes and her attention to the task at hand.

Her eyes scanned every page of every newspaper, the pages yellowed, the oldest issues brittle. The last newspaper in the pile was dated Saturday, May 14, 2005. The paper was thinner than most—less news on Saturdays, she supposed, all the better for her. She'd be done soon enough, the day ahead of her. Maybe even time for a late lunch with Nick.

Her fingers, stained with the black dye of newsprint, skimmed through the pages, her eyes searching the words. Then she saw the headlines and the photo and she froze, the paper fluttering from her hands. Her breath caught in her throat as though she'd been hit in the chest; her brain had somehow short circuited. *None of this was possible, none of this was true.* She picked up the paper, raking her eyes across the story once again.

Best Friends Forever Heading in Different Directions

Nick Dolan and Rob Hart, recent graduates of Charlestown High School, have been best friends since they sat across from one another in kindergarten. Now one is headed to Harvard and the other to the Army. Both say they want to make the world a better place, and they expect to be friends for a long time. Such different futures, but such good friends. "I want to be a cop," Nick said. "Keep people like Rob in line."

The photo below the story was small and grainy and faded, but it was impossible not to recognize Nick, his eyes shimmering even in black and white, and next to him, Rob Hart—his round, boyish face, his tight smile, his eyes closed against the flash.

She dropped the paper again and stood perfectly still. *This can't be*, she thought. *It's some kind of mistake.* A different Nick? "No," she said out loud. "That was him." He knew Rob. It was here in black and white. Why wouldn't he say something? She shook her head. "Damn it!" she shouted. She'd have to tell Sam. She couldn't keep this a secret. She reached for her phone and began to scroll through her contacts, before she stopped. Shoulders sagging, tears welling in the corners of her eyes, she sank onto her couch.

She couldn't make any sense of this. Nick had come to the ER that night. He'd been at the scene... or had he? He'd said something about the victim being someone important. She remembered that he'd said to have security lock the place down, and keep reporters out. He had to have known it was his friend. She ran her fingers through her hair. She felt as if her head was spinning.

She tried to remember the details of that night, but it was Rob Hart she remembered best, his coolness, his worry about himself instead of his wife. She tried to focus on Nick. He'd wanted to go for a drink at the private club the police ran after hours, but she'd turned him down. Maybe he didn't realize the victim was his old friend; but he should have learned that the next day at least. Why not say something? Why the secrecy? What the hell was going on? She let out a long, slow breath. She'd just ask him. That's what she'd do. She'd ask him first. She owed him that, and he owed her an explanation.

She gathered the papers into a pile. She'd get rid of them, all of them. She dropped the pile by her door and stopped. What was she thinking? She tore out the page that held the story, and placed it on her table. She'd drop the pile into the recycle bin, come back up and decide who to call first—Nick, or Sam. This whole thing was probably nothing. Nick was a good cop, a good man. He could explain this away. She was sure of it. She collected the pile and pulled open her door.

Nick was standing there, a lopsided grin on his face. "Hey, you," he said.

And Jessie's heart stopped.

CHAPTER THIRTY-FIVE

"Why so quiet?" he asked. "What's wrong? Not hungover, I hope. That champagne was great though, wasn't it?" He continued to prattle on and Jessie just stood there, her mouth hanging open. "What is it?" he asked again, leaning into her, the familiar scent of him, the touch of him, a salve to her fears. "Are you alright?" he asked, his eyes crinkling with worry.

She smiled. This was Nick, her Nick. This was okay. *Or was it?* "A little hungover, I guess," she said, her voice sounding uneasy, even to her.

"Come on then," he said, pushing her gently back into her apartment. "I'll get you some Motrin." He started for the kitchen, and she could see it—the article lying face up on the table. Suddenly, she wasn't ready for him to see it, for him to know what she knew. She needed time to think about it. That's all—she just needed time.

"Hey," she said. "Will you bring these downstairs first? To the recycle bin?" She didn't wait for an answer. She pushed the papers at him. "Please, I can't relax if there's clutter in here. I've finished going through these for Rufus."

"Alright," he said, taking the pile. "Lie down. I'll be right back."

She folded the news story and stuffed it in a kitchen drawer. By the time Nick returned, she was lying on the couch, one hand draped dramatically over her eyes. The truth was she wasn't feeling well. It wasn't the flu or a hangover, it was the fact that Nick knew Rob, and he'd never said a word. The very thought that he'd keep a secret like that made her stomach churn and her mind race.

"What can I get you, Jess?" Nick asked as he knelt by the couch and stroked her hair.

She couldn't speak; she couldn't risk tears or anger or both, so instead she shook her head and swallowed the hard lump in her throat. He got her a glass of water and set it down beside her. "You look as though you just want to sleep."

She nodded in the affirmative. He kissed her forehead. "I'll let myself out. Get some rest, babe. I'll check in on you later." He left, pulling the door shut behind him. A sharp click and the thud of footsteps on the stairs signaled that he was gone. Jessie pulled herself up, slid the deadbolt lock on her door, and retrieved the article from the drawer. She smoothed the page and read it again, and she wondered if it was possible to forget a best friend. The article had been written fifteen years ago, and she tried to remember the name of a friend from those years in her own life. She could only come up with one name—Tracy Something-or-other, and as for high school, her best friend had been Emma, the same friend who'd stolen her fiancé. Of course, she remembered Emma, though she hoped that someday that would just be a name, a person she couldn't recall. Ever.

Maybe that was the case with Nick. She shouldn't be so dramatic—she should have just asked him. She sighed heavily. She'd call him, and do what she should have done—ask him.

That evening, she had her opportunity. They'd decided on a quiet Saturday night. Nick would pick up pizza and beer and they'd stay in, and after her second slice of pizza and third beer, she was feeling ready. "Hey," she asked, an uneasy squeak in her voice. "Did you say you knew Rob Hart in high school?"

Nick's head snapped up. "What? What are you talking about? Rob Hart? *The* Rob Hart? No, I don't know him. Jesus, where'd you get that idea?"

"Actually, from an article in the *Globe*. You were best friends, it said. He was heading to Harvard and you to the Army."

He hesitated a beat too long. "What article? Do you have it?" he asked, his voice shaky, his face pinched. He wiped his hand across his brow.

"No," she said almost too quickly, not even sure why she'd decided to lie. "It was in that pile you put into the recycle bin. They've already been picked up today. It's gone."

"Ahh," he said, leaning back into the couch, the tension seeping from him like a layer of dust blown away. "I grew up here in Boston, over in Charlestown, and I think I heard that he did, too, so I might have run into him, but I didn't know him. At least, I don't remember him. Must have been someone else in the story."

Jessie seemed to absorb the tension that Nick had released; her neck felt stiff, and a thin thread of worry, or maybe it was fear, wove itself into her mind. When the beer was finished, they headed to bed, where he wrapped himself around her, falling asleep quickly. It took Jessie a bit longer, but finally, sleep brushed away the last bits of unease, and even Bert's warning that the police must be involved in the shooting that had taken over her mind, and now maybe her life, and she slipped into the sweet oblivion of sleep.

She woke early to the creak of her door as Nick pulled it open. "Morning, sweetie. I didn't want to wake you." He turned back and kissed her softly. "I'm working a double today. I have to get going. Can I get you anything before I go?" His eyes were shimmering pools of blue, the gentle eyes of the Nick she liked so much. She nudged his chin down and kissed him full on the lips, lingering there, wishing she knew him as well as she'd thought.

"Have a good day. I'm back to work today, too. See you later?"

He backed away, blowing her a kiss as he went. "You will, you absolutely will."

With that he was gone, leaving Jessie with a yellowing, old news page and too many questions. She did what she did best when she had to think. She went for a morning run, and tried to picture Tracy What's-her-last name and she couldn't, but Emma—who'd betrayed her only a few years before, came quickly to mind. Tracy was in her long-ago past and Emma was still fresh, so maybe it did make sense that Nick wouldn't remember Rob. They'd gone their separate ways and lived quite separate lives—Nick in Iraq and Rob in Harvard. By the end of her run, she felt better. Friendships and memories were fleeting things.

But maybe, just to be safe, she'd share the article with Sam.

CHAPTER THIRTY-SIX

By Monday, three weeks after the shooting, she was calm. The only one hiding anything was her. And if she wanted things to work out with Nick—and she did—she needed to be upfront with him. Maybe she'd ask him to come over after work.

Roger called her to ask her to stop by the morgue, a message she thought she'd never get used to. She arrived at his office just as he was finishing lunch, the last bits of tuna salad rimming his mouth. "Come in, come in," he said, motioning her in and running his finger over his lips to wipe away the last traces of food. When he swiped his finger along his white coat, she turned away. There was going to be a lot to get used to here.

"You wanted to see me?" she asked.

"I did, I did," he said. "Sit, sit."

She smiled. He was repeating himself to be sure she could hear him. Tony was right—if he wasn't discussing autopsies, he wasn't used to dealing with the living. "I got your message," she said as she sank into the chair by his desk.

"Thank you, thank you for coming by. I just wanted to confirm your position here. I'm so happy you'll be working with me, with the whole team here."

Jessie moved to the edge of her seat. "I'm pretty happy, too."

"I wanted to help get you a little settled." He swept the crumbs from his desk and pulled open a drawer. "Here's your ID, and your office key," he said, sliding both to her. "The key is for this office. You're welcome to come in here anytime. The ID is what you'll need to get into the building. Just swipe it across the sensor and you'll have access to the main entrance and any of the rooms here that are locked. Come on," he said, standing, wiping away still more crumbs from his lap. "I'll take you around. It's a different place when you know you'll be spending time here. You need to get used to it."

She followed him back down the stairs and into the autopsy suite, where two figures lay under the white plastic shrouds the hospital used to wrap the dead. A yellow toe tag hung loose from one shroud. "I'll get to these two later. Just wanted you to look around a bit."

She took a deep breath through her mouth and let her gaze drift slowly around the room. She wasn't sure if she was supposed to be looking for anything special. She'd never let herself get used to this place, and she never wanted to. This place held people who'd been loved and had lived lives that mattered. That was how she wanted to approach this—respectfully and humbly. Then she realized that Roger was speaking.

"So, you're on the books to start here two days after Christmas, just in time for New Year's Eve." He chuckled. "That can be hellish, but don't worry. I've arranged for you to spend your first two weeks with the Homicide Unit. Sam Dallas will be in touch. I think you've met him?"

She could only nod as her stomach churned. Nick was not going to like that. Not one bit. Roger guided her around, pointing out a locker room and a break room before introducing her to some of the technicians—Joe, Mark, DeShawn, and two others whose names she'd forgotten as soon as she stepped back into the fresh chill of Winter air.

She took a deep breath and dodged traffic as she headed across the street to the ER, and as though he'd known that his name had just came up, Sam Dallas texted her. *Please call!* he'd written, and she sighed. She'd ignored an eerily similar last text from Bert. She wouldn't ignore this one.

*

Once inside the ER, she returned his call. "Hey," he said. "Thanks for getting back to me. I need to see you. Can you come in?"

"I'm at work, so the answer is no."

"I have to speak with you, Jessie. It's important. Today." His voice was toneless, his words almost calculated, and she wondered if he was targeting her for something that wasn't good.

"Can't you just tell me on the phone?"

"I suppose I could, but I'd prefer to say this in person."

The hairs on the back of her neck stood up. Maybe he knew about Nick. "I... I can't leave."

"I'll come to you, then. You don't start until three, correct?"

"Right."

"I'll meet you outside by the ambulance bay in ten minutes."

"Okay," she whispered, swallowing the knot of fear in her throat.

She stood by the sliding glass doors of the ambulance bay waiting for Sam, and wondered what was so important that he had to tell her in person. As the minutes ticked by, the tinge of fear she'd felt was replaced by her old familiar fury at being inconvenienced. He just wanted to make a show of something or other. He couldn't solve two damn murders, so he'd decided to harass her. She turned on her heel and was about to step back inside the ER when a car horn broke through her thoughts. She turned to see his Crown Vic idling at the curb. By the time she pulled open the passenger door, her fury was at full force.

"What the hell is this all about? I have a job, Sam. I don't work for you."

His jaw dropped open. "Please get in, Jessie," he said softly. "I don't know what you're so pissed off about, but I have something important to tell you—to show you. We're gonna take a quick ride to my office."

She slid down in the seat, her anger simmering as she snapped the seatbelt into place, catching her finger in the lock. "Shit," she said, pulling her finger free and putting it into her mouth.

"Having one of those days, huh?" He had the nerve to smile.

Jessie didn't answer. She stared straight ahead and tried to remember why she was so angry. She hated disruptions. That was it. He was disrupting her day. He should have told her whatever it was he had to say on the phone. Instead, he'd forced her into this little joyride. By the time Sam parked and exited the car, Jessie had marinated in her aggravation enough to slam the car door shut with such force, she was almost certain it was hanging by its hinges. She stopped and turned back to look. The door-banging had released some of her anger, but luckily, the door remained firmly in place. Satisfied that she'd made her point, she smiled smugly to herself and followed Sam up the stairs to his office.

"Have a seat," he said, his tone official. She almost expected him to take out his badge and read her her rights. But aside from opening her mouth and expressing her opinion on the Ann Hart and Bert Gibbons murders, she'd done nothing wrong. Her only vaguely questionable action was to hold onto the *Globe* article about Nick and Rob Hart, and there was no way Sam knew about that. Or was there?

He sat behind his desk, banged away at the keys and looked up, his gaze catching hers. "I have something to tell you."

"So?" She crossed her arms across her chest.

Sam leaned back in his chair and inhaled deeply. "We've been looking very closely at Rob Hart, and we think it likely that he was involved in his wife's murder."

Jessie's back stiffened and she sat up straight. "About time, since I've been saying that all along. You had to drag me here to tell me I was right?"

"Sorry about that, but I will tell you—we still don't have the evidence we need. We haven't been able to locate Hart. He apparently called his office and told them he'd be taking some time off. We never had a chance to question him thoroughly before he left, and as you know, we weren't allowed to question him at any length when he was in the ICU. We did get a warrant to search his home, his financial records, and we finally have his phone records."

Jessie sat on the edge of her chair. "And?" She held her breath, wondering if he knew about Nick and Rob.

"There's plenty there, Jessie. Plenty. I'm telling you because you could be in danger. Real danger."

CHAPTER THIRTY-SEVEN

The air was suddenly still. Sam's voice seemed far away and the first stirrings of a headache pricked at her eyes. She wasn't sure what to say, so for probably the first time in her life, she kept her mouth shut and waited for him to continue.

He exhaled noisily. "Are you ready for this?"

She shrugged. "I don't have a clue what you're talking about, so just spill it."

"You've received two flower deliveries at work recently, right?"

She nodded.

"From an R?"

"Yes. How did you know?"

"Do you have any idea who R is?"

She scowled. "I thought it was my neighbor, Rufus, but it wasn't him, so the answer is no. I don't have a clue, but they were delivered to the ER, so I assumed it was a patient."

"It was Rob Hart. He's your secret admirer."

It was as though the breath had been knocked out of her. She hadn't expected that. Once she'd ruled out Rufus, she'd convinced herself it was Roger, and had somehow forgotten to ask him. But *Rob Hart?* "Why?" she asked, her voice barely audible.

"You said it yourself weeks ago. He seemed interested in you when he was in the ICU."

"How did you find out it was him?"

"The warrant for his financial records included his credit cards. He never canceled them, never applied for a new driver's license, never did any of the things people do even when they just lose a wallet. It's almost as though the wallet he says was taken was empty, or not taken at all. He's been using his credit cards. He used them to send you flowers."

Jessie sank further into the impossibly hard wood of her seat. "It's creepy, for sure, but it's not dangerous, is it? Am I in danger?" And then she remembered the eerie feeling that someone had been watching her, following her.

"We don't know where he is."

"There is something," she said, interrupting him. She told him about the shadowy figure outside her apartment, the troubles with her lock, and the frightening feeling that someone had been watching her. "But that started when Hart was still in the hospital. Actually, it started that night. I thought I was just spooked because of the shooting."

"Did you report it?"

She smirked. "Really? Report an unsettling feeling? The police would have laughed me off the phone."

"Maybe. Maybe not."

"No maybe about it. So, what does this mean for me?"

"It means you have to be careful. I think maybe you should stay somewhere else if you can, or we could keep an eye on you."

She shook her head. "Keep an eye on me? No, thanks."

"Well, then watch yourself. Any spooky feelings—just call me."

"I can just call Nick. He's in Southie now." As soon as she said it, she regretted it. She crossed her arms and waited for his snide answer.

"That's something else I wanted to discuss."

She rolled her eyes. "He's a nice guy, Sam. He really is."

"Not saying he isn't. But did you know he grew up in Charlestown? And he and Rob Hart were best friends in high school?"

"That doesn't mean anything. I can't even remember the names of my high school friends," she lied.

"You'd remember quick enough if one of them was injured in a tragic shooting that was covered in the national nightly news. I know I would. And Nick's a cop."

"So, he doesn't remember. So what?"

"How do you know he doesn't remember? Did you ask him?"

Her cheeks flushed red. "I did. They both grew up in Charlestown…" Her voice began to crack, her nerve too. Should she tell him about the newspaper article? Would she be in trouble for holding onto it? But it had only been a few days. What could they do to her? A bead of sweat trickled along her forehead.

"Jessie?" Sam had leaned forward across the desk, his forehead creased in worry.

"I have to tell you something." And as though he'd been waiting to hear those words, his expression softened and he nodded.

"Go ahead," he said.

"Well, first—do I need a lawyer?"

"Jesus, Jessie. Only if you're directly involved, but if you'd prefer to speak with a lawyer first, make your call." He pushed the desk phone towards her.

She ignored it. "It's just that I'm afraid for someone else. Not me."

"Just tell me."

"I was helping my neighbor clear out his old newspapers and I found a story about Nick and Rob Hart—"

Sam held up his hand. "We already have that. Anything else?"

A flood of relief washed through her. She wasn't withholding information after all. "No, just that when I asked Nick about it, he said he couldn't really remember Hart."

Sam heaved a long, drawn-out sigh. "Interesting, because according to Rob Hart's phone records, they were in touch the night of the shooting."

Jessie slumped in her chair, the blood draining from her head, and even though she was sitting, she thought she might faint. She held on tight to the chair's edge to steady herself. "That can't be," she said, so softly that Sam leaned closer, turning his head to hear.

"Why can't it be?"

"I don't know. I mean, Nick was in the ER that night. He arrived when the ambulance did. He was at the scene, wasn't he?"

Sam narrowed his gaze and shook his head. "Nick was assigned to West Roxbury. His shift had ended. He wasn't at the scene."

"I... I just assumed. He came with the ambulance and then later asked me to go to the police club for a drink."

"And did you?"

"No. I was exhausted. I wanted to just go home. That was the first night I felt as though someone was watching me... when I walked to my car. But it was just shadows from those reporter's camera lights. I have an active imagination." She folded her hands and dropped them to her lap.

"So now you're going to imagine this all away?"

"I don't know what you're asking or what you're saying. Is Nick involved? Is that what you're trying to say?" There was an edge to her voice.

"Don't shoot the messenger, Jessie. He might be. We're having a look at him and Rob Hart."

"You said you had Rob Hart's phone records. Was Nick calling him regularly?"

"No. Nick didn't call him at all. Hart called Nick the night of the shooting. Before he called nine-one-one. Peculiar, to say the least."

"So, you might be making something out of nothing. Do you even know if Nick answered?"

"I know they were on the phone for at least four minutes. That certainly implies a conversation."

She bit her lip to keep any tears at bay. *Never let them see you cry.* "So, where's Hart?"

"That's what we'd like to know. For now, he's gone, unreachable. We have no idea where he is, and if he has a new phone, we don't know about it. He's on a leave from work. But his girlfriend, by the way, is consulting a lawyer, and he's making arrangements to bring her in for questioning."

"Does she know where he is?"

"She says not. We'll see."

"Can't you put out a warrant for his arrest?"

"For what? We have our suspicions but no evidence, no gun, not his phone or his wallet. We have nothing, and the DA requires more. I'm hoping the girlfriend can provide us with the information we need, and I'm telling you all of this because you need to be careful. Around Nick, too."

She wanted to tell him that was all bullshit. Nick was a good guy, but they'd figure that out soon enough. "Anything on Bert?" she asked, eager to change the subject.

"Ahh," he said, punching at his keyboard. "We have some prints from inside Bert's apartment. His landlady said he had no visitors, seemed like a loner. We've eliminated the police at the scene, and now we're just putting them through the database, but right now—nothing."

"This will sound crazy, but since they knew each other, did you check Rob Hart's prints?"

"We don't have him on file. He's never committed a crime. And now he's gone."

She stood. "I hope you won't focus on Nick just because you can't come up with anyone else."

"That's not how we work, Jessie. I think you know that."

"Yeah," she huffed. "I'm ready, then. Will you bring me back?"

"Sure. One more thing, though. The footfalls—that sound that you noticed on the nine-one-one tape? Audio came up with a probable shoe match. Rubber-soled, and in testing it's the same sound a police shoe or construction boot makes."

"Could it still be Ramos?" she asked, knowing in her gut that he wasn't involved in this murder.

He shook his head. "We're keeping it quiet for now, hoping to flush out anyone who was involved, but his alibi is good. Ramos is a criminal and a murderer, but he wasn't there."

And the world stopped turning once more.

CHAPTER THIRTY-EIGHT

Sam was silent during the ten-minute drive to the ER, and Jessie was lost in her thoughts. It seemed at least an hour before he pulled into the ambulance bay and dropped her off. "Call me, Jessie. For anything, even an eerie feeling, and please—not a word to Nick."

She could only nod. She still hadn't processed what he'd said. It was just words strung together. She had to remember that. It was just words.

She took report early from Donna, who was still day charge in addition to her new duties. "It's quiet," Donna said. "With Christmas so close, we might be in the pre-holiday lull. People are busy, too busy to be sick or start trouble that might mean a trip to the ER. But I could be wrong. Anyway, have a quiet night."

But Jessie wished for a busy night, and a degree of chaos that would allow her to lose herself in the busyness, at least for that one night. Instead, the first few hours dragged. Even Eddie found somewhere else to be, but just as they decided to order Chinese takeout, the C-Med radio crackled to life. Jessie raced to answer it. A three-car accident on the expressway had resulted in four victims, and they'd all be coming here to Boston City. Jessie called for trauma teams to gather in the Trauma hallway and assigned roles and rooms. The patient with the least serious injuries would go to the acute side to be evaluated.

The victims were all kids—teenagers who'd been speeding and had crashed into the unyielding concrete barriers on the expressway. The two boys in the backseat had been thrown from the car, both landing on the opposite side of the highway. One of them had died en route to the ER, the other had serious head injuries and facial fractures, not to mention the chest trauma he'd suffered. "Trauma One," Jessie called, "and page Neurosurgery stat."

A frowning Tim Merrick appeared behind her. "It was too much to hope for a quiet night, huh?" And in the midst of the harried activity, she smiled. At least he was the same old Tim. He directed the next two patients to the trauma rooms. "Jess, will you keep an eye on everyone and keep me posted?"

She nodded. "Blood bank is prepping uncross-matched blood and CT and the OR are ready for us." This time, Tim smiled. "We make a damn good team, Jessie," he called over his shoulder as he swung open the door to Trauma One. She moved from one trauma room to another, starting IVs, hanging blood and antibiotics, and grabbing the ambu bag to breathe for one patient while the resident got ready to intubate.

She moved swiftly, checking the patients as Tim decided who'd be moved first to the OR and with which surgical team. It was a delicate balance, but she was relieved that Tim was in charge. For all of his quirks, he was the best in the business of trauma. She could hear him from the hallway barking orders, shouting at staff to move quicker. "Time," he shouted. "Time! Let's move." And the first trauma room door swung open, the patient barely visible on the stretcher among the tubes and monitors and portable machines, as he was propelled along by the staff racing him to the OR.

"Jessie, send Trauma Two up in thirty minutes. Ortho's taking the patient in Trauma Three now," Tim said. She nodded and turned and stepped into Trauma Two to help. She was drawing up antibiotics when Elena nudged her and pointed to the doorway. Out of the corner of her eye, she caught sight of Nick.

"I need to speak with you," he mouthed.

She finished drawing up the antibiotics she was about to mix in an IV bag. "I'm busy, Nick. This is a bad time." She shook her head angrily and turned back to her work.

"I'll come back later," he said, ducking out of the room. "It's important."

The next few hours were a blur; three of the patients were still in the OR and their parents gathered in the family room to wait for news. The parents of the fourth teen had been inconsolable and had required IV sedation. When Tony came to take him, Jessie asked him to wait. "Give us an hour or so, Tony. His family's still saying goodbye."

"Anything for you," he whispered. "Call me when you're ready."

Her shift flew, her worries forgotten and at eleven-thirty, as she got ready to leave, Nick arrived. "I have to speak to you, it's important," he said, his eyes bright, a sheen of sweat on his forehead despite the frigid night.

"Not here," she whispered. "And not at a bar, either."

"I'll come to your place, then."

"Okay, but fair warning—you can't stay tonight," she said almost too quickly. "I have an early morning." Lies were slipping easily from her lips these days.

"Okay. I'll see you there in ten minutes," he said as he turned to go.

She watched as he left, his head down, his hands shoved into his pockets, and she wanted to run after him, to tell him it would be alright. But she didn't know that for sure. So instead, she slid into her car and headed home.

She wasn't surprised to see Nick standing in front of her building, an uneasy smile on his face.

Once inside, he opened the bottle of wine he'd brought and poured them each a full glass. "I'm in trouble, Jessie," he blurted out. "I need your help."

She sank onto the couch and took a long swallow of her wine. "What is it?" she asked, though she was pretty sure she knew.

"Homicide has learned that I knew Rob Hart. They think I'm hiding something. I have to go in tomorrow to headquarters to be questioned." His words came out in a rush, his fingers tapping nervously on his knee.

"Nick," she said, moving closer, "you did know him. Just say that. You don't have anything to hide. Just be honest."

"You don't know how they twist things, Jessie. Internal Affairs, Homicide. If they put you in their sights, you're screwed."

"They're not out to get you. They're trying to solve that murder, and if you can help, if you know something, anything, you have to speak up."

"That's just it. I don't know anything. I haven't spoken to him in years—not since high school. He went to Harvard. I went to Iraq. I think I tried to call him when I came home, but I never heard back from him. It's been years."

"He hasn't been in touch at all?"

He hesitated and dropped his head. "Nick?" she asked.

He sighed. "He called me the night of the shooting. I didn't know it was him. The number wasn't one I knew, but I answered anyway. I wish the hell I hadn't."

"What happened?" Jessie asked, her brain ticking off the little she knew.

"Nothing. That's just it. Nothing happened. I couldn't really hear him. He said who it was. He sounded like he was in a hurry, the connection was lousy. I hung up. And I came to the ER to see you." He drained the last of his wine and refilled his glass.

She smiled in relief. "Just say that, Nick. Just tell them that." She leaned back and felt the tension ease from her neck.

"The thing is, I need you to back me up."

"I saw you there. Of course I can back you up. I thought you arrived with the ambulance, but I definitely saw you. You asked me to go out for a drink."

"Yes," he said, his eyes shining. "Exactly. Just tell them I was there to ask you that."

"I will."

"I have one favor to ask, though. Could you just say I was there before the ambulance arrived? I was, you know. I was there."

"I believe you, but I can't say that. Just trust that this will be okay." She nestled against his chest and he ran his fingers through her hair, the skin of her scalp tingling with the pleasure of it. She pulled him closer and kissed him before pushing him gently away. "Now, go home and get some sleep. Call me tomorrow."

"I don't know what I'd do without you, Jessie," he said.

CHAPTER THIRTY-NINE

Jessie slept in the next day, waking only at eleven when her phone began to buzz and ping relentlessly. She knew if she didn't answer, the noise would continue. She reached over and grabbed the device. "Hello," she said in her haziest morning voice.

"Oh, sorry, did I wake you?"

That question, she decided, didn't even deserve an answer. "Who is this?"

"Sam. Sorry to wake you. I thought you'd be up by now."

"Well, you thought wrong. What do you want?"

"Nick's here. He says you can confirm that he was at the ER the night of the shooting."

"I already answered that yesterday." But yesterday seemed like months, not just twenty-four hours ago. "He arrived when the ambulance did. He might have been there earlier, but I didn't see him, so I can't swear to that."

"I need an official statement, Jessie. You have to come in."

She sat up in bed, pushed her hair out of her eyes, and glared, though she knew he couldn't see it. "What time?"

"Whenever you can get here."

"Fine." She hoped he heard the *screw you* in her voice. She took her time in the shower and over coffee, and two hours later, she pulled on scrubs, grabbed her backpack and headed out, thinking that maybe Nick was right. Maybe they were going after him because there was no one else. By the time she'd been given the okay to go to Sam's office, she could feel the rush of heat on her cheeks. Her feet pounded on the stairs and more than one police officer turned to look. She didn't care. Not one bit.

She walked through the small area by Sam's office; only one detective was there, and he was on the phone, his voice a whisper. He didn't seem to notice as she pushed open Sam's door. "I'm here," she announced, standing rigidly. "And I have to be at work by three."

"Hello to you, too," he said, looking up. "Have a seat. I'll be right with you."

She sat stiffly, her back straight, her feet planted firmly on the floor. "Am I here to sign something?"

"We can actually film your statement."

"Why?" And it hit her suddenly. They wanted it on film to show Nick, to squeeze him. "Nick knows what I'm going to say. Why are you guys so focused on him?"

"We just need some answers."

"Is he still here?"

"He is. It's been a long day for him, and it's not over yet."

Before she could stop herself, she wondered if it was possible that Nick had been involved. She swallowed the lump in her throat.

"He has the union lawyer with him. We're not after him. We're after Hart. Nick just has to help us."

"You really think he knows something?"

"We do. Turns out, he was the officer on the scene at a fender-bender involving Rob Hart in West Roxbury a few months back. He wrote the report so it was favorable to his old friend. Not sure why he wouldn't just tell us that. He must have known we'd find it. He must have given Rob his number that night because Rob called him the night of the shooting, about fifteen, maybe twenty minutes before the nine-one-one call." He paused as if he wanted that to sink in.

Jessie fidgeted in her seat. She still trusted Nick, but that trust wasn't as iron-clad as it had seemed just an hour ago.

"We'll be asking Nick for his phone. And just so you know, if he refuses, we'll get a warrant."

She picked at her fingernails. "Just for the record, I don't think he'll refuse."

"Here's hoping. I can type up your statement, have you sign it, and if we need you on film, you can come back another time. Okay with you?"

She nodded.

"Can you tell me again about the night of the shooting?"

So Jessie started from the beginning, from the C-Med notification to Nick's appearing when the ambulance did, but she wanted to help Nick, to put a wrench in Sam's theory. "I can't say for sure when he arrived at the ER, only when I first saw him. Once the ER had quieted, and I was leaving for home, Nick was in the ambulance bay, said he'd been waiting for me and asked me to go for a drink. I was tired and I said no. And that's all I know."

Sam typed as she spoke and printed out her statement, passing it to her. "Sign there and there," he said. "And then you're free to go."

She scribbled her name and stood. "When will Nick be done?"

"I can't say. It's up to him."

"Is he in one of those rooms with two-way mirrors where you can watch?"

"No, we film it and have a live video feed into a television in a room down the hall. We can watch from there and pass in any questions that we might want asked."

"Any chance I can see it? See him?"

Sam's gaze flickered. "I assume you're kidding, but the answer is no." He held open the door and smiled.

And she wondered what the hell she had ever seen in him.

CHAPTER FORTY

Jessie went through the motions at work, never really noticing her patients or co-workers. She'd said once she could do her job with her eyes closed and tonight, she proved it. She triaged countless ambulance patients, started at least as many IVs, drew up meds, hooked up monitors and caught one old man just as he was about to fall from his stretcher, and she did it all without blinking an eye. She tried calling Nick more than once, but her calls went straight to voicemail. *Jesus*, she thought, *could they still be questioning him?*

At nine o'clock, Elena took her aside. "I think you should go home," she said. "You just don't look good." She rested her palm flat against Jessie's forehead. "I think you might have a fever. Go home. Take care of yourself. We'll be okay."

Jessie nodded. She was feverish, not with the flu, but with worry and anger, but she was glad to get out of there and get home, where she pulled off her scrubs, slid into a robe and curled up with the rest of the wine that Nick had brought just last night. She finished the bottle and lay there, the television flickering soundlessly, her head drumming with the beat of her own worrying thoughts. When her eyelids drooped with the onset of sleep, she pulled a blanket up and prayed that she'd find some peace.

It was a loud banging that woke her. She bolted upright, her eyes still heavy with sleep, her mind still foggy with some forgotten dream. The banging stopped. But for less than a minute, and then it started up again, more insistent this time. It was her door. Someone was trying to break it down, at least that was how it sounded. She reached for her phone ready to call for help when she heard it.

"Jessie, open up. Let me in!" It was Nick.

She looked at her watch. Twelve-fifteen. She pulled the door open. "I was about to call nine-one-one. Keep the goddamn noise down," she hissed. He walked in and collapsed onto the couch.

"I'm in big trouble," he said, his eyes bloodshot.

"Have you been drinking?"

"I had a few beers, that's all, but I'd like to get good and drunk." He spied the empty bottle of wine on the floor. "You've been drinking too, huh?"

She might have been wrong, but he seemed to smirk. "I had some wine, hoping it would help me to sleep. What's going on with you? What happened today?"

"They're trying to tangle me up with all this Hart stuff, that's why what you say is so important. I need you, Jessie. You *have* to say I was with you at the ER *before* the ambulance arrived."

"I can't say that. It's not true, and anyway—I gave my statement."

"When?" He sat upright, his arms folded across his chest.

"Earlier today. I went to headquarters. I said you were at the ER that night, but I couldn't say when you got there, and I can't. I saw you when the ambulance arrived. I'm sorry, Nick, I didn't see you before that."

He stood and began to pace. "You can change your statement. Tell them you were confused."

"I wasn't confused. How about you just tell them the truth?" She pulled the door open wide. "And how about you just leave?"

He slammed the door shut and slid the deadbolt into place. "You have to change your statement. Otherwise I might go to jail. Do you understand that? Do you want that?" His eyes were cold as ice, his voice raw. A ripple of fear ran through Jessie's veins. This wasn't her Nick. She didn't know who the hell he was.

"What's wrong with you?" she asked softly, hoping to appeal to his rational side.

But he seemed to have no rational side tonight. "You're going to change your statement, Jessie. Get a pen."

The whoosh of her pulse pounded in her ears. Her phone. She needed her phone. She had to call Sam or nine-one-one for help. She reached her hand for it. "My pen," she said, hoping to divert his attention, but he was too quick and he knocked the phone away. Her heart began to race.

"I can't change it, Nick. Even if I write something new, they'll know it's a lie. I can't do it. It will only make things worse for you."

"It won't. Just listen to me." His voice rose to a shout. "What don't you get? You *have* to do this for me."

Jessie backed away. If she could get to her bedroom, she could lock the door and maybe he'd come to his senses and leave. "But..."

He moved behind her and blocked her in. She tried to push him away but he stood firmly and she tripped and fell to her knees. "Nick," she said, suddenly certain that he meant her harm if she didn't do what he said, or maybe even if she did. There was no way out. She was trapped, and with nothing to lose, she did the only thing she could think of—she screamed, loud and long, and Nick reached down and grabbed her by the hair.

"Shut the fuck up," he shouted.

And she did. The quiet was deafening, and then she heard the soft knock at her door. "Jessie? It's Rufus. You okay?"

Nick put his finger over his lips to shush her, but she was beyond that. "Call nine-one-one," she shouted, just as Nick pulled her up to her feet. By the time she was standing, Rufus had unlocked the door and was standing there, his trusty metal baseball bat in hand.

"Get away from her," he said, his voice steely, his hand gripping the bat tightly, his knuckles white with the effort.

Nick laughed, and moved toward Rufus, and Jessie felt her fear melt away. She jumped onto his back, pulling his hair and scratching his face. He wrestled her away and they both fell to the floor, Nick on top, Jessie pinned beneath him. She struggled to free herself but he was in control. She could hear shuffling above them and the sudden whistle of the bat as it swung through the air and landed with a thud somewhere on Nick, who lay stunned and motionless. Rufus pulled him away and reached for Jessie as the piercing shrill of sirens filled the night.

"I called nine-one-one before I came up, Jessie. That'll be them now. You okay?"

She could only nod and watch as Nick rolled himself over and sat up, his eyes red with tears. "What the fuck is wrong with me?" He dropped his head into hands and began to cry, his tears mixing with snot, his shoulders heaving. She tried to feel sorry for him, but she couldn't.

*

It was only minutes later that the patrolmen arrived, cuffed him, and led him away. Sam appeared just as they were leaving. He shook his head sadly as the procession passed him. Jessie had folded herself into Rufus's arms and blinked away any hint of tears that threatened her composure. *Never let them see you cry* wove itself into her thoughts. Besides, it was anger she felt—at Nick, at herself. She could write a book on misjudging men.

"Jessie?" Sam said softly.

"Don't," she answered. "Just don't."

Rufus patted her hair and led her to the couch. "Sit," he said. "I'll get you a glass of water."

She wiped her sleeve over her face and folded her legs underneath her. Sam sat down beside her. "I'm sorry this happened," he said. "We told Nick we'd question him again tomorrow. He seemed okay. There was no way we could have predicted this."

She cleared her throat. "You don't have to make excuses. I'm not blaming you. But what happened today? You at least owe me that."

"You're right. I do." He leaned back and drew in a long breath. "He finally admitted that Hart had called him that night and asked him for help with something, but Nick says he couldn't understand what Hart wanted and he hung up and continued on to Boston City to see you."

"That's what he told me. Tonight, he said I had to change my statement, tell you that he was at the ER before the ambulance arrived." She shook her head. "He may have been, but as I told you, I didn't see him. I couldn't say that. He was unhinged when I refused. I was afraid and then—miracle of miracles—Rufus let himself in." Her eyes rested on him as he returned to the room. "He saved me. I owe you everything, Rufus." She stood and wrapped her arms around him.

"Now, now," he said, gently extricating himself from her embrace and pushing her back onto the couch. "Drink this and rest." He passed her the glass of water. "I think it's probably a bit of whiskey you should be drinking, but have this for now." He winked and turned to go. "I'll be right downstairs, Jessie, and I'll be holding onto these," he held up the key she'd given him and retrieved his bat from the floor. "You've put a spark back in an old man's life, that's for sure."

An uncomfortable silence descended on her small space once Rufus was gone. She could tell that Sam had questions, but she wanted him to get the hell out. She didn't want him here. She just wanted to be alone.

"Jessie?" he said, his eyes shimmering in the light. "You know, I have to ask you some questions, and they'll want you to go down to the station to press charges. They can hold him overnight, but they'll still need your statement."

"I'm not making any more statements. I have nothing to tell them. I'm not pressing charges either. You saw him. He's in enough trouble as it is, and he knows it. I won't add to his problems. Just tell me what he's done." She had no idea why she was so angry at

Sam. He hadn't done anything except being right about Nick all along. But she needed someone to blame and he was there. She paused to steady herself. "Tell me all of it."

"There's nothing to tell until he comes clean, or we get his phone records. The only thing I have right now is the transfer to Southie that he requested right after the shooting. He asked for an emergency transfer to be closer to his dad who was ill. If anyone had checked, they would have seen that his father died years ago." He cleared his throat. "My guess is that he did it to be closer to you, to keep an eye on you."

She closed her eyes. "Why?"

"I don't know for sure. I can guess. He wanted to make sure you weren't seeing anyone else."

She rolled her eyes. "That's not exactly a crime, is it?"

"No, but he had your work schedule in his wallet."

"My work…" She stopped, her jaw dropping open. "It was missing from my fridge. I thought I'd lost it. But why?"

"To keep tabs on you."

"I was transferred to the ICU for a week." She paused again, her brain on rewind remembering, or trying to. He'd called her from the ER one night, wondering where she was. "He took my schedule. He must have been breaking in here. More than once, my lock was loose, my door unlocked. I haven't had any trouble since I got a new lock." She dropped her head into her hands. "How could I have been so wrong?"

"You couldn't have known, Jessie, and you had no way of knowing he has a record of complaints in his file: drinking at work, assaulting a bystander who'd tried to film him, threatening a driver who'd cut him off. There's more, nothing too serious, and the complaints always seemed to disappear before Internal Affairs could make a case. I couldn't tell you until tonight. He was monitored for a time and he was fine. Seemed like he'd worked out his demons. Until this mess." He shook his head sadly.

Jessie finished the water and set the glass down. "That was why you said he was a rogue cop?"

"I did. Should have kept my mouth shut."

"Me too. I told him what you said."

A line creased his forehead. "That couldn't have helped."

"He won't get out tonight, will he?"

"No," Sam said. "He's in for the night. Tomorrow, he'll be back at headquarters for more questioning. After this, he might be more amenable to answering those questions." He stood, his jacket swinging open to reveal a gun and his gold shield hooked to his belt. "I'm going to head home, Jessie. I've got a patrol car out front to watch over you tonight."

In spite of herself, she smiled. He'd used that same phrase the night of the Hart shooting and it had given her then, and now, a feeling of safety that was hard to explain. It was exactly what she needed.

Especially tonight.

CHAPTER FORTY-ONE

Jessie slept fitfully and at the first trace of daylight seeping in through her blinds, she rose and checked her watch. Seven-thirty. She called the ER and asked for Donna.

"Hey, I heard you were sick. Do you need some time off?"

And for the first time, Jessie choked up. Donna's kindness spoke volumes. She was so different from Sheila, who would have advised her to get her ass to work. Thank God she was gone. "I'll need a few days."

"Take your time, Jessie, and let me know if you need anything."

Her next call was to Sam. "Sorry to call so early, but any news?"

"Nothing yet. I can let you know how things go later."

"Can I come in to see him?"

There was a silence that seemed to last forever. "I can't help with that. The best I can do is let you know how today goes."

Jessie went down to Rufus's and knocked on his door. He pulled it open and drew her into his arms. "You poor girl. What a night." He took her chin and looked into her eyes. "You'll be okay, Jessie, and I'm here to watch out for you."

She kissed his cheek and padded back upstairs, slid the lock into place and crawled back into bed and slept until Sam called. It was three o'clock. "We're just taking a quick break, Jessie, but I wanted to let you know Nick's talking. He feels terrible about last night, and asked if he could see you."

"What did you say?"

"I'm not in the room with him, I'm watching from a monitor down the hall, but he was told that it depends on the DA and whether he charges Nick or makes a deal. You're still considered a material witness, so no contact until his case is settled."

A bead of sweat ran along her forehead. "How long?" She should have been furious at Nick, but instead, she felt sorry for him. And for herself. Once more, true to form, she'd chosen the one person she should have stayed away from.

"Can't say. With any luck, we'll have an idea by the end of the week. He's got quite a story."

"Oh, Jesus, he didn't shoot Ann Hart, did he?"

"No, but he knows who did." She could hear muffled voices in the background as if he was covering the phone with his hand. "Listen, I've got to go. Do you need anything?"

"No," she answered. "You know I'm scheduled to start with you guys in two weeks, right?"

"Yeah, you're all set. They're making an orientation schedule for you."

"This stuff with Nick won't be a problem?"

"No, it'll all be over by then." He sighed and then added, "At least, I hope it will. I'll be in touch, Jessie." The click on his end let her know the call was over.

He didn't call back until Friday, three long days. She called in sick for each of them. The news about Nick was leaked to the press, and the *Herald* and *Globe* started running stories about the unnamed cop who'd helped Rob Hart cover up Boston's infamous murder. Each day, the headlines were more salacious. "Hart-less Hart" seemed the favorite nickname, but there was no satisfaction for Jessie in having been right. She'd been wrong about too much else. And Rob Hart was still out there somewhere, though maybe not for long.

"The DA's just announced a warrant for Hart's arrest for the murder of his wife," Sam said, satisfaction in his voice. "And we've got a deal with the DA for Nick. Details will be released tonight, but he'll be pleading guilty to accessory after the fact, obstruction of justice and interfering with an investigation. Because he cooperated, even handed over his phone without a warrant, he likely won't get much jail time, but that's up to the DA. That's probably it for him."

Jessie sighed. "So, it's over?"

"Not until we find Hart, but for Nick, it is."

"It's hard to believe he was involved."

"Some of Nick's interview tapes will be released later with the announcements, which means they're in the public domain now. Want to see them?"

"Hell, yes!"

"I'll call you tomorrow. If anyone asks, it's part of your orientation."

Jessie called Donna and filled her in. "I just wanted you to know. It'll be on the news tonight, so if it's okay, I'd like to take a few more days, and come back to work on Monday." It occurred to her that Monday would be four weeks since the Hart shooting—four weeks since the world changed.

"Take your time, and I'll see you on Monday."

Jessie slept well that night, and might have slept through the day but for Sam's call. "It's snowing again. I can pick you up," he said. And though she didn't want to rely on him for anything, she accepted, huffing out a curt yes, and then she could have kicked herself for being such an unrelenting bitch. But she'd always done that—chosen the wrong guy, and when things didn't turn out the way she hoped she'd treated the good guys like crap. On the plus side, at least it meant she was back to normal.

By the time Sam pulled up in front, the snow had turned to sleet, the streets slick with a fresh coating of ice, and the car slid all the way to headquarters. Aside from hello, Jessie hadn't said a word to him. She wasn't sure what she should say. Sorry was probably appropriate, maybe even thank you, but she just wasn't ready yet to say either.

He led her to the room where the live feed of Nick's interview had played. She slid onto one of those barely padded folding chairs. She leaned her elbows on the table, clearing a path through the old coffee cups, crinkled-up pages of notes and a cup filled with pens.

"Can I get you anything?" he asked. "Before we start—coffee, water?"

She shook her head. "But I have a question. Have you spoken to Hart's girlfriend, the woman he was having an affair with?"

"We have. She's cooperating. She knew that Rob was married, but he'd told her they were separated and his wife had been having an affair. He told her in no uncertain terms that he'd be single again soon. She thought he meant divorce. When the shooting happened, she was too afraid to come forward." Sam shrugged out of his suit jacket and placed it on the back of the chair. "He'd called her twice from the hospital, asking her to keep quiet about their relationship. Prince that he is, he told her that it was to protect her from public scrutiny. He also asked her to get him a couple of those burner phones from Walmart. As far as she knew, he wasn't a suspect, and the public, present company excluded, still saw him as the grieving husband, so she bought the phones and met him at the hospital when he was discharged. She gave him three hundred dollars in cash, and dropped him off near the Boston Common. Interesting, huh?"

"That's, like, a few blocks from City Hall, right?"

Sam nodded.

"Has she heard from him? Does she know where he is?"

"She says she hasn't heard a word from him, but we're keeping her and her phone under surveillance. If he gets in touch with her, we'll know about it."

"Did Nick know her, the girlfriend?"

"No. They both deny that, and there's no evidence to suggest they even knew of one another. Rob was a secretive man."

Jessie exhaled slowly and slumped down in her chair. "Okay. I guess I'm ready. Can you play it, Sam?"

She watched as he fiddled with buttons on a computer and suddenly the screen filled with a video image looking down on an almost identical room—metal table, folding metal chairs, empty until a scowling Nick, in rumpled clothes and uncombed hair, was walked in, a detective on his heels, another man—his lawyer, probably—following.

"I'm going to fast-forward through this. These are just the introductions, explanations, Miranda reading. You don't need to see any of that right now. In the future, you'll need to be familiar with that, but not right now." The video raced forward until Sam hit pause. "You ready?" he asked.

"Ready? I don't know, but I need to see this, so go ahead." She folded her arms tight across her chest and focused her eyes on the screen. When the video started to stream again, she saw that Nick had been sitting much the same way as she was, arms folded, angry and defiant. She uncrossed her arms and pulled at her hair, twirling her finger around a tendril of curls until it was hopelessly tangled.

The video began again, this time with the squeak of chairs as the detective, his tie loose, his long sleeves folded up, pushed his chair back, and nodded. "So, tell me again what happened. *Exactly* as it happened, this time."

Nick leaned forward, resting his hands on the table. "I told you. I left the station and was headed to Boston City to see a nurse there."

"Yeah, I heard that. Try again, and start with the call from Rob Hart. You knew him, correct?"

Nick nodded and seemed to stiffen. "Me and about five hundred other kids in Charlestown. I don't know him now."

The detective picked up a folder and seemed to be reading. "You were the officer who responded to the scene of a minor accident in West Roxbury last year, correct?" He didn't wait for an answer. He just rushed ahead. "Your report on that date supported Hart's claim that he was cut off by another driver and he couldn't help but rear-end the other driver. Sound familiar?"

Nick nodded.

"So, we've established that you saw him within the last year. We don't have his phone, but we have the records from that phone." He waved a paper in the air. "We know that he called you the night of the shooting, a full eleven minutes before he called nine-one-one."

Nick looked away and slumped in his seat, sighing heavily. He didn't move for what seemed like minutes, and then he swiped a hand across both eyes and sat a little straighter. "How much do you know?"

"How about you tell me what you know."

The door opened and another detective walked in and whispered to the other who stood. They both walked out, leaving Nick to squirm in his seat. His lawyer reached a hand to his shoulder. Nick shrugged it off, stood, stretched and walked to the door, leaning against it, listening before sitting back down. The lawyer whispered something to Nick, who shook his head angrily.

"What's going on?" Jessie asked.

"They're making him uncomfortable. You can bet they walked back here to watch him, see if anyone here had any thoughts or questions. It's uncomfortable for the person being questioned. He likely wondered if they already knew everything. His lawyer was trying to advise him, but Nick didn't seem to want to hear it."

Jessie turned back to the video and watched as both detectives returned to the room. One sat on the edge of the desk, the other on the chair. The one who'd just arrived leaned close to Nick. "Just come clean, Nick. We might be able to help you."

"How can you help me?" Nick asked, clasping his hands over his head and leaning back in his chair as though he was the one in charge. His lawyer frowned.

"Tell us what you know. Was Rob Hart involved in his wife's murder?" The detective put his hand out in a stop motion. "Before you answer, consider that right now, you're an accessory, before or after is the question. Protect yourself, Nick. Think of that before you speak."

Nick's swagger faded away. His head down, he slouched in his seat, his eyes seemingly focused on his feet. He leaned forward and held his head in his hands for what seemed an eternity before he cleared his throat and raised his head.

"He did call me that night. I could hardly understand him. He was shouting, or maybe crying. He said he needed me, that I had to meet him right away, that he was in trouble. I was aggravated. He'd never called me before, never answered my calls when I came back from Iraq, and then he calls me late at night, said I had to help him. He said he was in an alley off Warrenton Street. I wasn't far. I was off duty and on my way to see Jessie at the City ER. I'd been meaning to do that for a while, so I said I'd stop, but only for a minute." He paused, took a sip of water and ran his fingers through his hair, one tuft sticking up.

His lawyer tried to intervene. "My client..." he began, but Nick stopped him.

"Go on," one detective urged Nick. "How did you know where to find him?"

"He told me exactly where he was, and when I pulled up, I could see him motioning to me from the edge of the alley. I was in uniform, and I still had my gun, but it wasn't my district, so I hurried over hoping I wouldn't be seen. He shoved a gun, a wallet and his phone into my hands. I remember I asked him what the fuck was going on. He said he couldn't tell me anything, just to get rid of them and get out of there. He said he'd fill me in later. I said I'd call it in, and he pushed me away and said to get the hell out. And that's when I caught the scent of flowers. Weird, you know? He's giving me a gun and other stuff, and I could smell flowers. I remember hoping that scent wouldn't cling to me. Then he turned, and I thought I saw blood on his jacket, and I tried to follow him. I pulled at him and he sneered at me, told me to get out fast and get rid of what he'd given me, so I jogged to my car.

"I didn't know what to do, so I just sat there for a minute trying to sort it all out. But as soon as I started my car, I heard the call over the radio about a double shooting in that alley, so I knew someone else was there, too. I thought it was a drug deal gone wrong. He wouldn't have been the first hotshot to get involved in that kind of trouble. I didn't want any part of whatever he'd done, so I stepped on the gas and got the hell out of there." He sank into his chair, seeming exhausted.

"I was never so scared in my whole life."

CHAPTER FORTY-TWO

Jessie sank into her own chair, exhausted from listening and remembering the flowery scent that had clung to Nick that night. "Can we stop for a minute?" she asked. Sam paused the video, the tick of the clock the only sound in the room.

"Can I get you anything?"

"Water?" she asked softly.

When Sam returned, she nodded. "Go ahead, it's okay. Might as well get it over with."

She rested her gaze on the screen.

"Just so you know, these interviews were done over a few days. This video is spliced together. These are the relevant highlights. We've edited out his complaints about the force, the unfairness of life and how he's been screwed." He raised a skeptical brow.

Jessie nodded. "Okay, I get it. Can we just watch?"

Sam pressed a button and the video continued.

"I could hear the sirens as I drove away," Nick said. "I knew, I just knew this whole stinking mess would fall on me. Rob Hart was a big fucking deal, a big shot, and he knew it. I knew that alley would be swarming with cops and media. The goddamn gun, his wallet—which was empty, by the way—and his phone were on the seat next to me." Nick's gaze rested on the camera that was recording him, and he twisted in his seat as if trying to get out of the camera's range. "I had to figure out what to do, but first I had to get rid of his stuff. I turned around and drove to the Mass. Ave. bridge and threw everything over. There were no cameras there, and I made sure no one saw me. After that, I headed to the ER. I needed to see what was going on. I got there just as the ambulances pulled in."

The detective who'd been perched on the edge of the desk stood, rubbing his back. "That's all? You'll swear to this?" he asked.

"Yes, that's all," Nick said. "I don't know if you can find anything now, but check the Charles River by Mass. Ave."

"What happened then?"

"I tried to find out what happened. By then I knew his wife had been shot, so it was no drug deal. I didn't know what to do. I'd thrown the gun away. Who could I tell? I knew he'd say it was me. I had to protect myself. I was a damn fool to answer his call and even stupider to meet him that night. I had to figure out how to save myself, and I had to do it fast. I knew that Jessie would know what was happening, so I waited around to see if she'd go to the club with me for a drink, but she wasn't interested. I followed her to her car, thought I'd ask again, but she seemed spooked. She never saw me, so I just gave up and went home. I decided the best thing to do was to lay low and keep my mouth shut."

Jessie remembered that night, that feeling that someone was watching her. It had been Nick. Her cheeks flushed red with anger, or maybe it was embarrassment. She couldn't be sure. She turned to Sam. "Can I watch this alone?"

"No, but we can stop if you need to," Sam said.

She shook her head, and sat stiffly watching as Nick picked lint off his pants and looked into the camera again. "Are you going to use this against me?" he asked.

"As long as you're telling the truth, this might help you. Let's go on."

Nick smoothed his hair and started again. "Rob called me the next morning, said he'd told the police a Hispanic male was the shooter. He said he needed help in finding someone who would fit that bill. I still thought it was just a shooting, that his wife would be okay. I told him to tell the police everything. They'd find the shooter. He said he couldn't do that. He reminded me that we were from Charlestown, that we had our own secrets, and that meant sticking together no matter what. He knew that would get me." He sat forward, elbows resting on his knees. "He knew I had to help him."

The detective in the chair leaned back, folding his arms and crossing his knee over his leg, and then he smirked. "Really?" he asked, the sarcasm in his voice unmistakable.

"You just don't understand that kind of loyalty. It means something to be a *Townie*, to have grown up there. That loyalty to one another—whatever happens—is fed into you as soon as you're born. If you're from Charlestown, you're as good as family to everyone else, and Rob knew he had me as soon as he mentioned that. He knew I couldn't turn away. We'd been best friends once, and that meant relying on each other, no matter what." He exhaled noisily, his hands balled into tight fists in his lap. His torment was etched into his every movement. Jessie wanted to turn away, stop the video, but she had to see this for herself.

The second detective, who was perched on the edge of the desk, leaned close to Nick, so close that he could probably count the eyelashes over Nick's once bright blue eyes. "So, you want us to believe that, because you're from Charlestown, you're bound in some kind of blood oath to cover for one another? Bullshit! I'm from Charlestown. I never heard that one."

"I… well, you must be from a different part."

The detective slammed his hand down on the desk. "Try again, and tell me the truth this time, not some bullshit you're hoping I'll believe. What did he have on you?"

A bead of sweat ran along Nick's forehead and he reached to swipe it away, his hand trembling. He turned to his lawyer and whispered something. The lawyer nodded. "I'd like to speak to my client in private." He looked straight at the camera. "In another room. Without Big Brother watching and listening."

The detective on the desk stood and walked to the door, opening it wide. "Be my guest. The room right there is surveillance-free. Nick can have a look to confirm that for himself."

Nick and his lawyer shuffled out, and the tape fast-forwarded to their return. "I want assurance that any past illegal activities will not be used against my client."

One of the detectives raised a questioning brow. "As long as the statute has passed, that's fine. Unless Nick has been involved in another murder."

"I wasn't even involved in this one," Nick said with a sigh as he dropped into his seat.

"Okay, then tell us everything. Start from what Hart has on you."

Nick sat forward. "We were about fifteen, maybe sixteen, and Rob and I were both being raised by single moms. My parents were divorced, his dad had died."

"Hey, how about you just cut to the chase. We don't need a sympathy lead-in."

Nick huffed out a sigh and crossed his arms over his chest. "We robbed three or four variety stores. We wore ski masks, pretended we had guns, and went to those stores late at night. We never robbed a store in Charlestown. We stuck to Chelsea and Revere, maybe Everett once."

"Noble of you to help keep your own neighborhood safe," a detective mumbled.

"Listen, I know it was stupid. I knew it then but Rob convinced me we'd get away with it, and we did. No one ever asked us why we suddenly had money. It had been easy. Too easy. Once he got into Harvard, after his mother died, he swore me to secrecy. He said if I ever said anything, he'd deny it, and say I was the one robbing stores. He said no one would believe me anyway. I knew he was right, so when he called me that night and told me I had to help, his meaning was clear. I had no choice."

"Okay, so we know you threw the gun into the Charles River by the Mass. Ave. bridge. When did you see him again?"

Nick seemed suddenly animated. "He called me from the hospital just hours later. Said to find a Spanish speaker with something specific that he could tell the police. I had just read a bulletin on Ramos—a Salvadoran member of MS-13 with two distinctive tattoos. Ramos was already wanted for murder, so I described his tattoos—the one on his face and the one on his hand, and Rob just repeated that to the detectives on the case. I knew the police would land pretty quick on Ramos, and you guys did." Nick smiled, a strange, self-satisfied smile. "I was damn surprised when I spotted Ramos and pulled him over. I have to tell you—I knew I'd be seen as a hero. Forget the Hart shooting. Ramos was a murderous thug."

"Like your friend Hart, you mean?" the detective said.

"So, why arrest Ramos that day if you knew he wasn't involved?"

Nick's smile faded as quickly as it had appeared. "Any way you look at it, I helped get a murderer off the street."

"And gave another one time to escape."

"I didn't know he was going to disappear. Check my phone. He hasn't called me since he was discharged."

"What about Bert Gibbons, the reporter? Do you know anything about him?"

A visible shiver went through Nick. "The reporter who bothered Jessie?" he asked, his voice shaky. "I never met him, but Rob did. He said that guy snuck into his room in the ICU, but that he'd been helping him plant stories that would put him in a good light, so he was useful for a while."

"Did you know that Hart told Bert the police were involved in his wife's murder?"

Nick's eyes opened wide; his hands gripped the chair. "Rob told me he was going to do that. I thought it was an empty threat, but he said it would guarantee I'd have to keep my mouth shut."

"You never went to Bert's apartment?"

"Hell, no! I don't even know where he lived."

"That's easy enough to find out, isn't it?"

"I guess, but I wasn't worried about Bert. Not a bit. I had no reason to bother with him. I was worried about Rob, and that detective who seemed to be talking to Jessie all the time. When I slipped into Jessie's apartment, or watched from the street, I was looking for him, too, for any hint that he was sharing information about Hart with her, but that was a dead end, a waste of time. I decided that if I just kept quiet, it would all go away."

"Do you think Rob had anything to do with Bert's death?"

"He killed his wife. I think he's capable of anything. But why? What did he have to gain?"

The detective shrugged. "Maybe he was afraid he told Bert too much."

Nick was silent.

"So, back to Ann Hart. Why did he shoot her? Why not just get a divorce?"

"His wife was pregnant by another guy. He said she was planning to leave him, to humiliate him, to stick the knife all the way in. Rob was a guy who always got what he wanted and Ann was taking that away. He was not a guy you screwed. I'd always known that. Ann didn't know it until it was too late."

The detective raised a brow and looked at the camera as if asking *what the hell?* Finally, hands on his hips, he turned back to Nick. "Did you know that Hart was having an affair?"

"No, but I'm not surprised."

"Has he been in touch again?"

"Not since he left the hospital. He used to call from his room, said it couldn't be traced. He talked about Jessie, said she was his nurse in the ICU, and I blew up. I told him to stay the hell away from her. That's why he sent her flowers. They were really for me—to let me know he was watching me. And her. I was trapped, and he knew it."

"Where is he now?"

"I don't have any idea."

"Has he called you?"

"You have my phone. Just check. No calls since he left the hospital."

"And you have no idea where he is?"

Nick shook his head. "Rob's a guy with stardust sprinkled all over his life—Harvard, the mayor's office, a bright future. He'll land on his feet somewhere, and the rest of us will be left to pick up the pieces. He's probably hiding in plain sight. You know what he always said? *Follow the stardust.* So, that's my advice to you. Follow the stardust and you'll find him."

The video stopped, Nick and the detectives frozen in that final moment. *Stardust*, Jessie thought, *follow the fucking stardust.* What a crock of shit. And she wondered if Nick had really cared about her, or if she was only a convenient source of information. It didn't really matter. It was over. Out of the corner of her eye she caught Sam watching her. She turned and gave him a wary glance. "Where is Nick now?"

"Confined to his mother's house with a GPS ankle monitor and a court order to stay away from you. The DA will decide what kind of deal he'll get."

"And you have no idea where Hart is?"

"We're working on it."

"Anything on Bert's murder?"

"We have some prints from his apartment, nothing workable on surveillance tapes, so we'll see if we can get a match on the prints. My guess is they belong to Rob Hart. We have a search warrant for his apartment. We'll try to pick up his prints and his DNA there. Bert had someone's skin under his fingernails. I think we'll get a match."

Jessie slid down in her seat. She hadn't realized her heart had been racing until it slowed, the tightness in her chest easing. Her gaze was drawn to the window and the street beyond. Everything was white. She stood and walked to the window, rested her hands on the sill, and let the quiet, clean image of the falling snow surround her. Sam was still speaking behind her, but his words were lost somewhere in the peaceful swirl of snow until finally, he cleared his throat. Twice. Jessie turned reluctantly and shifted her gaze to Sam.

"We're going to keep you under surveillance."

"Why? Nick won't bother me now."

"Rob Hart is still out there. He might. We're trying to trace him through the burner phones, trying to get a hit on them, see where he is, but until then…"

Jessie nodded and turned back to the window, placing her hand flat against the pane—the cold seeping into her skin as the snow spun and swirled, the world outside a blanket of pure white. She leaned her forehead against the glass and closed her eyes, wishing she could lose herself and her racing thoughts in the whirling lacy flecks. A lone tear coursed along her face, and she wiped it away before Sam could see.

She had no idea how she'd gotten into this mess.

CHAPTER FORTY-THREE

That night, she slept fitfully, waiting for news from Sam. The next day she puttered about, and when it seemed the wait would never end, she closed her eyes and curled up on her couch. A soft rapping on her door startled Jessie from her nap. Her eyes flew open, the room was dark but the world that filtered in through her blinds was that stark, clean white of fresh snow. She rubbed the sleep from her eyes.

"Jessie, are you in there?" the familiar and welcome voice of Rufus asked.

"Yes," she said, pulling open the door. Rufus stood holding a bouquet of white roses and a warm smile.

"These came for you," he said, holding them out.

Jessie took the flowers, aware that her hands were trembling. "Come in," she said as she pulled out the card.

"You're quite the popular girl these days." He watched as Jessie read the card, a wide smile draping her lips. "A new suitor?" he asked.

"Better," she said. "The final chapter on an old story."

"Ahh, now that's cryptic. Well, I'll be going. Let me know if you need anything."

Jessie closed the door behind him and read the card aloud. *"We're making a big announcement at The Parkman House on Beacon Hill. Thought you'd like to be there. See you there at 7 p.m. Sam."* The Parkman House—the grand old mansion bequeathed to the city over a century before. It was used now for receptions, announcements, fundraisers. She glanced at her watch. It was six-thirty. He probably should have just called, but that didn't matter now. At least he wanted her there. *They must have Hart*, she thought giddily.

She tried to call Sam but it went to voicemail. She called a ride service, hurriedly pulled on jeans, a heavy sweater, her leather jacket and boots and grabbed her bag, arriving to the street just as the car pulled up. She slid onto the backseat. "The Parkman House on Beacon Hill," she said to the driver.

"Fancy digs. Is the city having a party there tonight?"

"Kind of," Jessie said as she sank into her seat, her gaze on the falling snow and the backdrop of twinkling Christmas lights along the street.

"Hey," the driver said as they pulled away. "Did you call another car service?"

"No, just yours," she answered. "Why?"

"Some guy jumped out of his car waving his arms and shouting. I can't see him now. He probably slipped on the ice and fell."

Damn, he must be her surveillance. Sam must have forgotten to tell him about The Parkman House, or maybe she was supposed to go with him. Too late now. She'd apologize later. Though the plows were out, the snow was falling quickly, the roads as slick as ice. Jessie checked her watch. Five to seven. Damn—she hoped Sam would wait for her. The driver eased onto the expressway and headed downtown where the streets were empty of people but alive with sparkling holiday lights draped over trees and in windows, the scene framed by the softly falling snow.

It was after seven when he pulled onto Beacon Street, the grand old brownstones on one side, the glittering lights of the Boston Common on the other. "This is it," the driver announced, pulling up in front of an elegant four-story brick home.

Jessie craned her neck, but couldn't see any cameramen, or police for that matter. "You're sure this is it?"

"Thirty-three Beacon," he answered. "Maybe you're early. Want me to wait?"

Jessie hesitated, that all too familiar bubble of fear blooming in her gut. She forced it back down. She couldn't be afraid of everything. "No, he probably got the time wrong. They must be inside."

"Looks kinda dark, though. I don't see any lights on, do you?"

"No," she answered, her hand on the door handle. A car trying to get by honked its horn.

"Tell you what, I'll just make a circle. If you're outside in five minutes, I'll pick you up and drop you off at that Cheers bar or somewhere warm to wait. Okay?"

"Thank you," Jessie said, her fear evaporating. "If no one's here, or they're late arriving, I'll take you up on it."

The car beeped again. "Goddamn Boston drivers," he said.

A light went on in the first-floor window as she stepped from the car. "Thanks anyway. Looks like they're here." She waved as he drove off and then turned for the entrance, wishing she'd thought to dress a little more formally. Jeans and boots might not be the best attire for The Parkman House, even if she was here only for an announcement. She lifted the knocker and before she could let it drop, the door swung open, revealing a grand staircase and an empty hallway. *Where was everyone?*

"Sam?" she called, suddenly nervous. An arm appeared and pulled her in before slamming the door behind her. She spun around, her eyes resting on Rob Hart, a beard hiding his features, a crooked smile plastered on his face.

"Good to see you, Jessie. Did you like the flowers? I thought they were a nice touch. I bought flowers for Ann that last night, too."

Her heart pounding, she swallowed the hard lump of fear in her throat and took a step back toward the door.

"Why so quiet?" he asked, turning the lock.

"What do you want?" she asked softly.

He smiled. "I thought that would be obvious. You were so good to me in the hospital. I thought maybe you'd help me out."

"Help you?" She wanted to tell him to piss off, but she knew she had to buy time. That policeman who'd been assigned to her would surely be calling Sam, and then the car service, to find out where she went. That thought soothed her, gave her a tiny bit of courage, and right then, that was enough.

"Let's talk," he said. "Back there." He pointed to the long hallway as he turned off the overhead light. "Don't want anyone to notice the lights on and call the police, do we?"

A shiver ran up her spine. "I can't see," she said.

"Your eyes will adjust. We can turn on the lights back here in the office."

She hesitated and turned towards the door, wondering if she could get it unlocked and open before he grabbed her. But as though he could read her mind, he spoke up.

"Jessie, just give me a minute," he said, scowling. "I'm not going to hurt you."

She wondered if he'd said the same thing to Ann. She had no choice but to follow him along the hall. He turned into what appeared to be an office and switched on a small desk lamp, the light so dim, she could just make out a sturdy polished desk and several chairs in the room's center.

"Have a seat." He motioned to the chair furthest from the door, cutting off any chance of escape.

She sat on the edge of the chair, her back rigid, her feet tapping the floor. She wanted to be ready to run.

"I'm sorry we didn't get to know each other when I was in the hospital. You must have noticed that I liked you."

She stayed perfectly still and perfectly quiet. For once in her life, she'd keep her damn mouth shut. She looked around, trying to get her bearings and gauge the layout. There were windows to her right, and to her left an open doorway that led back to the front of the house.

"Well, since you're not going to speak, I will," Rob said. "Have you spoken to Nick about me?"

"About you? Why?"

"You must know by now that we were best friends a long time ago. I loved him like a brother, but he's turned on me. I know that he's lying to the police about me, about Ann, about the night she was shot. I know he's trying to convince people that it was me who shot her. Am I right?"

Jessie crossed her arms. "I don't know what you're talking about." The only way out of this mess, she decided, was to lie. And she was pretty good at that.

"I know that you're seeing him, I know that he's been questioned by the police, and I know that you're working with the detectives."

"How do you know that?"

"I have a lot of free time on my hands these days. This beard, a baseball cap, a pair of sunglasses, and I can go anywhere, and keep an eye on you and Nick. Most days though, I can sit right here and follow the investigation." He pointed to the computer. "Amazing how much information a city employee has access to. Not to mention easy access to this grand old place." He swept his arm around the room. "It's a shame the city doesn't use it much. I've been right here all the time. And no one ever noticed. Genius, huh?"

The room seemed suddenly airless. Jessie tried to slow her breathing.

Rob Hart sighed noisily. "I wish you'd say something."

Jessie shook her head. "I don't know what you want with me. I'm a nurse, for Christ's sake."

"Ahh, Jessie, you're so much more. Tell," he said, leaning towards her. "What did Nick say? Did he blame me for the shooting?"

He placed a hand on her thigh and she pushed it away, her fear fading, her anger growing. "I saw you in the ER," she said. "And the ICU. I was the one who first said that you were the shooter. Nick was covering for you. It sounds as though he always has. He's no boy scout, but he's no murderer either. What reason could he possibly have for shooting your wife? You, on the other hand, had plenty of reasons. Your wife was pregnant. She…" Jessie stopped herself when she saw the flash of anger in Hart's eyes.

"So, you know then that she betrayed me."

"So just get a divorce!" Jessie shouted, and immediately wished she could take it back. He was already angry enough. She couldn't afford to antagonize him anymore.

"You think it would have been that easy? She humiliated me. How could I just divorce her?" He seemed to sink into the chair, exhausted from remembering. "She had to pay. I mean, think about it. She told me that night she was leaving me to be with her baby daddy." He shook his head. "How sordid is that? She cried when she told me, said I had made her miserable and she just wanted to start afresh." He shook his head angrily. "Can you believe that? She was sleeping around, but *I* was the one who'd made *her* miserable. Un-fucking-believable."

Jessie was frozen, unable to speak, riveted to his words, and the callous way he spoke them.

"I bought her flowers and slipped her some Ativan to soften the end. I'm not heartless. She was. I'm not." He swiped his hand across his forehead. "I thought of the flowers at the last minute. I knew the cops wouldn't suspect a man who'd just given his wife flowers."

"And she was still crying?" Jessie asked.

"She was. She was relieved that she'd told me, and when I said I'd divorce her, she believed me. I never intended to just let her go. She was always a fool. But not me, which is why I shot myself. Although I was afraid I'd overdone that, that I might actually have a serious injury. Lucky for me, I didn't and lucky for me, that surgeon said I reminded him of a soldier he'd lost in Afghanistan.

Everyone was rooting for me, protecting me. It was all so perfect."
He paused and looked Jessie square in the eye. "Until it wasn't."

The room felt cold as ice. Jessie pulled her jacket close. Out
of the corner of her eye, she caught a flash of movement in the
hallway. It was Sam. It had to be. She had to keep Rob's attention
diverted, get him talking again. "I'm sorry," she said. "You're right.
It must have been very hard for you."

His head bobbed up. "I knew you'd get it. I knew you'd
understand..."

A uniformed policeman, his gun unholstered and trained on
Hart, moved into position at the doorway. Jessie tried to keep her
eyes focused on Hart as he spoke. "Go on," she encouraged him.
"What about Bert?"

Rob chuckled. "What about him?"

"He's dead."

"I know. He'd been helping me with stories and he was happy to
do it. At first. But I asked him to write one story too many. I wanted
a piece about my run for Congress, and my plans to put Ann's death
and the shooting behind me, and he balked. Said I'd been using him.
He wasn't as stupid as he looked, and when he told me he'd found
my connection to Nick, well, what could I do? He said he never
saw an ounce of grief from me, that he had no real proof, but the
stories I'd asked him to plant were evidence enough for the police
to suspect me. He was about to spill his guts, tell the police and
the world that I was involved. He said with that story, his future
would be set. No need to work for a tabloid in London, since he'd
be the most sought-after reporter in the U.S." Rob smirked. "Can
you believe it? Bert? The most sought-after reporter? I confronted
him and he lied to my face. He actually swore that he'd keep his
mouth shut, but I knew he wouldn't. What could I do?" He shook
his head in mock sadness. "It was him or me. Easy choice."

"So, why am I here?"

"You're going to tell the police that Nick shot Ann, not me. You can say that Nick was the father of her bastard baby. That's believable." He continued to speak, the sound of his voice muffling the footfalls of the police as they moved into place. Gathering her courage, Jessie stood and made for the doorway. Rob grabbed her arm, forcing her back.

"You bitch," he said. "Just like Ann. Just like Bert. Even like stupid Nick."

A ripple of fear ran through her veins and she struggled to pull herself free.

"Let go of her," Sam said, his voice firm.

Rob's head jerked back in surprise and he yanked Jessie in front of him, one arm tightly wrapped around her neck in a hold while the other darted out quickly and grabbed a pair of scissors from the desk. He held them tight against her neck, the sharp tip pricking her skin.

"Drop the weapon and let her go. You won't get out of here," Sam said, nodding toward the group of uniformed officers that filled the hallway.

Jessie could feel Rob's arm tighten around her neck. A trickle of sweat—or was it blood? —oozed around her neck. She watched as Sam stiffened but never took his eyes off of Rob.

"You have guns. I have her," Rob said smugly. The wetness from her neck reached his hand and he loosened his grip for just a second. But that second was all Jessie needed to jam her elbow into his gut and pull away, darting to the safety of the doorway and Sam's open arms. He wrapped himself around her, and she felt herself sink into the safety he offered. She listened as the officers swarmed around Hart, shouting for him to get down. She heaved a sigh when she heard the click of handcuffs and the shuffle of feet as they pulled Hart upright. Someone read him his rights and he began to whimper and then to shout that he wanted a lawyer.

"You can't use anything I said!" he shouted as the officers marched him to the front door and guided him into the backseat of the waiting patrol car.

Sam loosened his grip and lifted her chin. "Are you okay?" he asked as he pulled a handkerchief from his pocket and dabbed the blood from Jessie's neck. "Let's get you to the ER. We can get that wound looked at and have you checked over." Beads of sweat pooled around his forehead.

She caught his hand in hers and took hold of the handkerchief, swiping it across her neck and having a quick look. "I'm okay. From the looks of this," she said, pointing to the drops of blood on his handkerchief, "this is a scratch. I don't need the ER for a scratch."

"Are you sure?" he asked, his eyes locked onto hers. "You've been through a lot these last few weeks, and tonight, well…"

She couldn't help herself, and she smiled and rested her palm softly against his face. "Thank you," she whispered as she kissed his cheek. Everything else seemed far away—Nick, Rob Hart, Bert—all of it. It was just herself and Sam and this moment. He leaned towards her, his eyes shimmering, and Jessie knew she had to break this spell. The timing was wrong. All wrong. For both of them. "So, does this mean you didn't send the flowers?" she asked with a sly smile.

He laughed shakily. "Not really my style." The silver in his eyes glittered in the glow of the hallway lights. He tucked a strand of hair behind her ear. "Are you really okay?" he asked softly.

And Jessie could only nod, her relief suddenly palpable.

CHAPTER FORTY-FOUR

The next morning, Rob Hart was back as the main story on the news. Unfortunately, Jessie was too. The DA and Detective Sergeant Sam Dallas said that much of the credit for Hart's arrest and capture was due to an ER nurse who believed from the start that Hart was responsible for his wife's death. Hart, they said, was already trying to negotiate a plea deal to avoid a trial.

At headquarters, Jessie was allowed to view Hart's interrogation along with the detectives, and she marveled at his ability to deflect the blame onto his wife, Nick, and finally onto the hospital for not saving Ann Hart's life. "This would only be an assault charge if those doctors were better."

Jessie stood up. "I can't watch anymore," she said angrily as she left the room. Sam followed her out.

"Don't take what he says personally."

"I won't. I just can't listen to his lies."

"I hear you, but before you go, there's something else you should probably know," he said. "It's a missing person report."

She shrugged. This couldn't possibly matter to her, but she kept her eyes fixed on his.

"It's your nurse manager. She's been reported as missing."

Jessie struggled to remember—was it yesterday, or the day before that she'd last spoken to Donna? She shook her head. "I just spoke to her. She's not missing."

"When did you speak with her?"

"I think yesterday. Anyway, you can call the ER. Donna's fine."

"That's not the name we have," he said, his eyes shifting to the paper in his hand. "It's a Sheila Logan."

Jessie, who felt as though she'd heard too much today and seen too much these last weeks, felt a kind of numbness settle over her. She hadn't much cared for poor Bert, but Sheila? Well, she'd actively disliked her. "We heard she wasn't coming back. Who said she was missing?"

"Her family in Ohio. She was supposed to be there for Thanksgiving. When she didn't arrive, they assumed the ER was busy and she couldn't get away."

"Thanksgiving was almost three weeks ago, a lifetime. Why did they wait to report her missing? Christmas is in ten days."

. Sam shrugged. "They said she wasn't a great communicator, so they weren't worried. At first. But they've been trying to reach her, without luck. They finally called her landlord who went into the apartment and found everything in order, but no Sheila. Her car was still in the garage. They called the ER and learned she hadn't been to work either. She lived in Natick, so they reported her missing there. The police there called us because she worked in Boston."

"Interesting, but why does that make her missing?"

"Why wouldn't it?"

"I don't know. We were happy to learn she was gone. Sheila was a lousy manager, all show, no substance, and disliked by everyone. Including me."

"Did you realize you were just talking about her in the past tense?"

"Why wouldn't I? She *was* our manager. Past tense. Now you're telling me she's disappeared. That doesn't change the fact that she's gone from the ER."

"Can I give you some advice?" He gave her a wry smile.

"You will, whether I want it or not, so go ahead."

"When you're questioned, and you will be, use the present tense. Don't raise any red flags."

"This is ridiculous. She was a pompous ass, and she's likely off somewhere on some sun-splashed beach. I'm not holding my breath hoping she'll show up. If she's really missing, she probably staged it."

Sam put his head in his hands. "Please, don't say any of that. You can say you didn't like her. That's fine, but keep any statements you make short and to the point."

She smiled. "I thought you were going to say short and sweet."

Despite himself, he grinned. "Just a little advice. I hope you'll take it."

By Monday, four weeks after the Hart shooting, detectives from Natick descended on the ER and questioned the staff to see if anyone knew where Sheila might be, or if there'd been any indication that she'd been under undue stress. "This ER," one detective said when he took Jessie aside, "seems like a pretty stressful place to work. Did it seem especially hard on her?"

Jessie couldn't help herself. She raised a brow and smiled. "She didn't actually work with us. She mostly stayed away from the ER, only showed up to give us grief about one thing or another."

The detective, who'd never offered his name, leaned forward. "So, is it fair to say you didn't like her?"

"It is fair to say that," she answered, a smugness in her voice that she hadn't intended, and when she saw the suspicious glint in his eyes, she cursed herself. *Red flags*, Sam had warned her, and once again, she'd failed to keep her damn mouth shut. But not liking someone was no crime. "Are we finished?" Jessie said, opening the door. "The ER's busy and I *do* work here." She wanted to throw in that she was about to start with the ME's office and Homicide, but decided now was the time to stop.

The detective stood, smoothing his pants as he did. "Well, okay. Let us know if she returns, or if any of you hear from her."

Jessie nodded and went back to the welcome chaos of the ER.

She worked the day shift the following day, and that evening, for the first time since Nick and Bert, Hart's arrest, and even the news of Sheila, she had hours to herself and she found she didn't much like it. When she heard a knock on her door, she raced to answer it, pulling it open before asking who was there. Her mouth dropped open, a tentative smile on her lips.

His eyes sparkling in the hall light, Sam raised a bottle of Scotch and a pack of Marlboro Lights in the air and smiled. "Thought you might need these after the month you've had."

And she opened her door wide and let him in.

A LETTER FROM ROBERTA

Dear reader,

I want to say a huge thank you for choosing to read *Dead Girl Walking*. If you did enjoy it, and want to keep up to date with all my latest releases, just sign up at the following link. Your email address will never be shared and you can unsubscribe at any time.

www.bookouture.com/roberta-gately

As an ER nurse, I've always been interested in forensics and crime investigation, and thoroughly enjoyed researching and writing every aspect of this story. I hope you loved reading *Dead Girl Walking* as much as I enjoyed writing it. And if you did, I would be so grateful if you could spare the time to write a review. It makes such a difference helping new readers to discover one of my books for the first time.

I'd also love to hear your thoughts about Jessie Novak, so please get in touch on my Facebook page or Twitter or through my website.

I hope that you'll follow Jessie Novak in Book 2, due in May of 2021. Thank you for your support!

Roberta Gately

RobertaGatelyAuthor

RobertaGately

robertagately.com

ACKNOWLEDGMENTS

I am enormously grateful to Cynthia Manson and Judy Hanson, my incredible agents and even better friends, for their extraordinary guidance, their cherished friendship and their unshakable faith in my ability to craft a story. I am more grateful than a simple "thank you" can ever convey.

To Maisie Lawrence, my brilliant editor at Bookouture—your edits and your encouragement have inspired me every step of the way, and have helped this story to come alive. To the wonderful team at Bookouture, including Kim Nash, Noelle Holten, Lauren Finger, and so many others who have helped along the way, thank you. I am enormously grateful to be a part of the extraordinary Bookouture family.

A special thank you to my good friend Kate Conway, who gave me an insider's view of South Boston and helped me to carve out the perfect niche for Jessie Novak. And many thanks to Detective Sergeant James P. Wyse (BPD Ret.) for his technical guidance and tips into homicide investigations, and for his lifetime of service at the Boston Police Department.

To my family and friends, who've always believed in me, my gratitude is endless.

Made in the USA
Las Vegas, NV
30 May 2021